THE DEVIL'S ODDS

This Large Print Book carries the
Seal of Approval of N.A.V.H.

THE DEVIL'S ODDS

MILTON T. BURTON

THORNDIKE PRESS
A part of Gale, Cengage Learning

GALE
CENGAGE Learning·

Detroit • New York • San Francisco • New Haven, Conn • Waterville, Maine • London

GALE
CENGAGE Learning®

LIBRARY OF CONGRESS CATALOGING-IN-PUBLICATION DATA

Burton, Milton T.
    The devil's odds / by Milton T. Burton.
        pages ; cm. — (Thorndike Press large print mystery)
        ISBN 978-1-4104-4899-6 (hardcover) — ISBN 1-4104-4899-1 (hardcover)
    1. Texas Rangers—Fiction. 2. Witnesses—Protection—Fiction. 3.
Murder—Fiction. 4. Gambling—Texas—Galveston—Fiction. 5.
Mafia—Louisiana—New Orleans—Fiction. 6. Large type books. I. Title.
PS3602.U77D48 2012b
813'.6—dc22   2012011399

Published in 2012 by arrangement with St.Martin's Press, LLC.

Printed in the United States of America
1 2 3 4 5 6 7 16 15 14 13 12

Fondly dedicated to the memory of David Thompson (1972–2010). He was a bookman, a lover of good mysteries, and a true friend.

ACKNOWLEDGMENTS

Many thanks are in order: once again to Stanley Haskins and Nancy Thomas-Haskins for their endless favors and faith in the project, and especially to Nancy for her careful proofreading and many valuable suggestions; to Terry C., The Hud, The Rabbi, Steve Black, Captain Jack Dean, Jim Graham, George and Sallie Wier, Connie Vaughan, Alice Alexander, Lise Horton, Patty Howe, and to all the fine folks on my Southern Noir crime forum, to Bill Montgomery and Margie Crisp, Seth and Arlene Montgomery, Gus Ramirez, and to Joan Hallmark of KLTV here in Tyler. All of these folks have kept the faith and have, through their unstinting encouragement, bolstered my sometimes fragile confidence enough that I could keep plodding onward.

A special thank-you to my old friend from high school Carol Kerr DiGangi for giving me my first computer and refusing to get off my back until I gave writing a shot. And to Dorothy Davis, the first person outside the industry to read one of my manuscripts. These two ladies' early enthusiasm meant more to me than I could ever convey.

And lastly to Kat Brzozowski, Thomas Dunne, and Ron Goldfarb, who are respectively my editor, my publisher, and my agent. They, too, have kept the faith.

AUTHOR'S NOTE

Anyone wishing to know more about that unique ecological and cultural area of Southeast Texas that is the Big Thicket can do no better than Dr. Francis Abernethy's *Tales from the Big Thicket*. Ab, who was for three decades secretary of the Texas Folklore Society, has studied the Thicket for years and has known many of its natives.

Those who would like a more thorough treatment of the golden age of Galveston and the Maceo gambling syndicate are directed to Gary Cartwright's excellent *Galveston*. To my mind it is far and away the best history ever written of this romantic island.

Readers interested in learning more about the South Texas political machine in the 1940s are advised to get a copy of *Boss Rule in South Texas* by Evan Anders.

Readers should also note that both Sam Maceo and George Parr were real people

who were very much as I have described
them.

He who wagers his life
must play by the Devil's odds.
— ancient Spanish proverb

CHAPTER ONE

It was a little after six in the evening when I spotted the girl I was supposed to meet. It was December 10, 1942, and she was sitting alone in the Longhorn Barroom of the Weilbach hotel in San Gabriel, Texas. She was installed at a table in the far corner of the room, dressed in a navy blue suit with one of those sailor's collars that were popular that year. Petite and small boned, she had dark auburn hair, china blue eyes, and a splash of rust-colored freckles dotted across a delicately sculptured nose. I also noted that she was blessed with everything a woman's supposed to have to make her interesting to a man. What intrigued me most about her, though, was the pinched, worried look that swept across her face each time somebody entered the bar. When I got closer to her table where I could see her better, I put her age as late twenties. "Hi," I said.

She looked up at me with an expression that was half frightened, half plaintive, like that of a person who needs help badly but is afraid to ask for it. Or afraid of whom she has to ask.

"Waiting for somebody?" I asked.

"Ahhh . . . yes," she answered, quickly looking back toward the door.

"Mind if I sit down?"

She glanced nervously toward the doorway once again and shuddered. "I guess not. I'm not even supposed to be in here without an escort. The only reason the bartender let me stay was because I told him that I was waiting for a gentleman to join me."

"I understand," I said with a nod. The Weilbach was prim and proper about that sort of thing, at least on the surface. Fourteen stories of gargoyle-trimmed sandstone built in the high Victorian style of the previous century, its floors were Spanish tile, its furniture heavy mahogany and walnut, the sofas and chairs covered in leather and tufted velvet. San Gabriel itself is a West Texas city of about seventy thousand that lies on the Devil's River halfway between Waco and El Paso, Waco being a town on the Brazos well known in Texas for hard religion and easy morals.

"The gentleman has joined you," I said.

14

"You're Madeline Kimbell, aren't you?"

"How did you know that?" she gasped, her eyes growing even bigger and more frightened.

"I'm the man you're supposed to meet. Didn't Jim Rutherford tell you what I'd look like?"

She shook her head, her wide blue eyes still wary.

"But he did say that a man named Virgil Tucker would find you here in the hotel bar about six-thirty, didn't he?"

"Yeah. You're Tucker?"

I nodded. "Yeah. Do you need to see my identification?"

"I guess not," she replied with a nervous shake of her head. I sat down and smiled and tried to look as inoffensive as possible while she gave me a close examination.

I hoped what she saw was reassuring to her. I was in my midthirties and slim, with wavy, coal black hair that was going gray at the temples. My manners were impeccable, and I was decently dressed in a suit of dark blue pinstriped wool and held a cream-colored western hat in my left hand. The only thing about me that might have been alarming to her were my eyes, which were hard and gray and looked out at the world from behind thick-lensed glasses with thin

15

gold wire rims. The previous year a woman I was dating told me they made me look just like Lucky Luciano, the big-wheel New York gangster who was in all the papers a few years back. She hadn't meant it as a compliment.

"But how did you know who I am?" the girl finally asked.

"Do you see any other pretty redheads in this room?" I asked.

She gave me a nervous smile and shrugged. "I guess not. How do you know Jim?"

"He's an old family friend. He served practically his whole border patrol career in Matador County, where I come from."

She nodded, her eyes still a little wary.

"What are you drinking?" I asked.

She held up the half-empty bottle of Pabst Blue Ribbon and wrinkled her nose in distaste. "I don't really like beer all that much, but . . ."

In those days, bars in Texas couldn't serve mixed drinks. They were limited by law to beer. If you wanted to drink something more potent you had to bring your own bottle and buy what was called a "setup," which was a glass of ice and some soda or some other kind of mixer. This quaint practice was known as brown bagging, and was the norm of the day. For some unfathomable reason it was considered bad manners to take your bottle out of the sack. I'd brought my own, a fifth of James E. Pepper. The waiter appeared beside our table, and I asked the girl if she liked bourbon.

"You bet I do."

I ordered two glasses of ice. When they came I poured a couple of ounces of whiskey into each glass. She picked hers up with a shaking hand and drained it in two long pulls, then put the glass down and looked across the table at me as though she was trying to make up her mind about something. At last she said, "A couple of guys are after me. That's why I'm so nervous."

"Who's after you?"

"My ex-boyfriend, Nolan. And a buddy of his. I'm scared to death. Jim didn't tell you?"

I shook my head. "We didn't have much time when he called. I was in a hurry. He just said you were in trouble and asked me to help you."

She gave me a hesitant nod, but she didn't look like she was nodding inside. Instead, she appeared ready to jump out a window and run screeching down the street at the least provocation. I'm naturally calm, which should have reassured her but obviously didn't. Maybe it was the Luciano thing.

17

"Maybe we ought to forget all about this," she muttered as she glanced nervously toward the door once again. "I probably shouldn't have listened to Jim and gotten you mixed up in this business in the first place."

I studied her closely for a few seconds before I spoke. "Is that what you really want to do?" I asked.

She buried her face in her hands for a moment, then looked up at me with eyes that were on the verge of tears. "No," she replied, shaking her head. "I'm just afraid somebody will get hurt."

"I wouldn't worry about that if I were you," I said as reassuringly as I could.

"Mister, you don't know Nolan and his friends."

I gave her a serene smile. "You leave Nolan to me. I'm pretty good at dealing with the Nolans of this world. That's why Jim sent you to me in the first place, so try to settle down."

"Do you live here in San Gabriel?" she asked.

I shook my head. "No, I've just been in and out for a couple of weeks working on a case. I've got a room upstairs."

"You do?" she blurted. "Can we go there? Now?"

18

I regarded her speculatively for a few moments while she seemed to shrink inside her own skin. "Sure, why not?" I finally said with a shrug.

I stood and held her coat for her. As she slipped into it, our faces were only a few inches apart. Her eyes widened and she muttered something under her breath and choked off a burst of manic laughter.

"What?" I asked.

"Nothing. I'll be okay as soon as we get somewhere that's not public."

"Come on, then," I said, and took her elbow.

When I paid our tab, I got a small bucket of ice from the bartender, and we headed toward the elevator.

Once we were safely in my room, I carefully locked the door and began mixing each of us another drink. I didn't really need one, but I wanted the girl to calm down as much as possible. If that meant getting her a little drunk, fine. She'd already removed her overcoat, and when I handed her the drink, she took a quick, nervous sip.

"Thanks," she muttered. Then she put the glass on the nightstand, threw her suit coat aside, and began unbuttoning her blouse with trembling hands. "Can we hurry up

19

and get this over with?" she asked.

"What?" I asked, puzzled.

"You know . . . ," she said and gave me a little shrug.

I tilted my head a bit to one side and stared at her for a few seconds, then smiled in amusement. "Silly, silly, silly," I said and took her hands and gently pulled them away from the buttons. Her breasts were full and milky and above her bra they were sprinkled with freckles like her nose. I began to re-button the blouse from the bottom up. "You've been reading too many cheap novels," I said. "There are still a few gentle-men left in the world."

Her eyes widened. "You're not going to make me —"

"Do you do this with every man you meet?" I asked with a soft laugh.

"Of course not! I just thought it was what I was going to have to do to get you to help me."

"I'm already helping you. And as far as getting it over with quickly, is it so difficult for you to believe that there's been a woman or two in my life who've liked me well enough that they weren't in such a hurry?"

Her eyes were big and round and full of surprise. She said nothing as I retrieved her drink from the bedside stand and handed it

20

to her. "Sit down and let's talk," I said.

She took the glass and curled up in the middle of the bed. I took the armchair at its side and pulled a pack of Chesterfield Kings from my inside coat pocket. "Want one?" I asked.

"Oh God, yes. And how."

I held my Zippo for her, then placed the ashtray on the bed so we could both reach it.

"Are you part Mexican?" she blurted out before she could stop herself. "I know it's awfully rude to ask something like that, but you look like —"

"I don't mind. My great-grandmother was a Mexican girl from San Antonio named Rosa Veramendi. She was said to be one of the great beauties of her day."

"The Veramendi Palace!" she exclaimed. "I read about them in Texas history. The Veramendis were the leading citizens of the town back then."

I nodded. "That was her family."

"You look sorta like those pictures of the Aztecs that used to be in schoolbooks. That's why I asked."

"I've been told that before," I replied with a shrug. "The Veramendis came up from Mexico City in the seventeen hundreds, so we very well may have some Aztec blood.

But we need to talk about more important things. I want to know all about your boyfriend, Nolan. Why's he chasing you?"

"Ex-boyfriend," she corrected firmly. "He's a deputy sheriff down in Jefferson County."

"He works for Milam Walsh?"

"Yes. You've heard of Walsh?"

"Sure," I said. Milam Walsh was one of a new breed of Texas sheriffs. Born in Port Arthur, he'd gone to France with the American Expeditionary Force in World War One, gotten a taste of Continental life and liked it. Once back home he worked his way through college, earning a degree in government and business administration. Then he turned his attention to politics and was soon hired as the city manager in the small, recently incorporated town of Kemah in Galveston County, a job and a time and a place that taught him a number of important lessons about how the world really works. After a few prosperous years he returned home to Beaumont to run for sheriff with the backing of several prominent local families and the financial support of the Maceo brothers of Galveston Island, two energetic Sicilians who controlled all the gambling on the upper Texas coast. Now in his midforties, Walsh was a smooth, sophisticated man enjoying the pinnacle of his career unburdened by either scruples or conscience.

"I met him once," I told her. "A friend of mine in the attorney general's office in Austin says he's probably raking in ten thousand a month in bribes from the rackets. He's got a yacht and a big house in the best part of town. Two fine cars. How many other county sheriffs you know that live like that?"

"None," she replied. "And Nolan's his chief deputy. They're real tight."

"Tell me about Nolan."

"He's thirty-two, and he grew up in Beaumont. He was a great athlete. Played for one of Detroit's minor league teams for a couple of years, but he got hurt and never made the majors."

"He's already a chief deputy at just thirty-two?" I asked. "He must be an energetic lad. So why's he chasing you?"

She shrugged. "He wants me to come back home and marry him. We'd been seeing one another for about a year when I broke it off. But the big jerk won't let me go."

"Who's this buddy of his you mentioned?"

"An old guy named Heck McAdoo. He's a county constable down home."

"I see." I nodded and studied her face

intently until she dropped her eyes to look down at the bed. "But there's a little more to this business than just a persistent boy-friend, isn't there?" I asked.

"I hope to God I can trust you," she said in a voice that was a near whisper.

"Call me Virgil, please. And it doesn't seem that you have much other choice but to trust me."

"No, I guess not," she agreed. "It's just that I'm so damned scared. Why did you want to get involved in a mess like this anyway?"

I shrugged. "Let's just say that I owe Jim Rutherford, and I couldn't very well turn him down when he called and asked me to help you."

"What are you doing here in San Ga-briel?"

"Chasing a ring of cattle thieves. Beef prices are rising fast with the war on, and rustling has become popular again."

"Cow thieves?"

"Yeah. I'm a detective for the Texas Cattle Raisers Association. Before that I was a deputy U.S. Marshal for four years, but now I've got a Special Texas Ranger commis-sion. The governor issues them to stock detectives so we can make arrests."

"Then you're a cop?"

24

"Technically, yes. But enough about me. Get your mind back on your problem and tell me your story. I'm entitled to know what you're dragging me into."

She drained her glass and took a deep breath. "I saw a murder."

"Really? Where?"

"Behind a nightclub over in Port Arthur."

"What happened?"

"Last Friday night one of my girlfriends and I decided to go to this place called the Snake Eyes Club. You know, snake eyes like in craps?"

"Sure," I said impatiently. "Go on."

"Anyway, the parking lot in front was full, so we pulled around back. My friend had to jump out and run in to use the bathroom even before we found a parking place. I'd just got parked and stepped out of my car when I noticed a man climbing out of a big Cadillac a few cars over. As soon as his feet hit the pavement two guys came up behind him. One of them slipped this noose thing over his head and started choking him while the other one tripped him and got him down on the ground." She looked at me with stricken eyes. "They just killed him, that's all. Just choked him to death."

"They saw you?"

She gave me a nod. "I sorta screamed."

25

"Then what?"

"I jumped back in my car and took off. They tried to stop me, and I almost ran over one of them. Then I hid out a couple of days at my parents' house, but when I went by my apartment to get some clothes my landlord told me two guys had come by looking for me. That's when I went to Jim Rutherford. He called you and put me on a bus out here. He said it would be safer if I left my car at my place. That way people would still think I was in town."

"Who knew you were coming to San Gabriel?"

"Just Jim and my folks. And my girlfriend Alma."

Her girlfriend Alma. I shook my head, annoyed but not surprised. "What's her full name?" I asked.

"Copeland. Alma Copeland."

"Had you ever seen the killers before?"

She nodded. "Yeah. They work for a hood named Marty Salisbury. Ever heard of him?"

"No. What are their names?"

"One them is a guy called Johnny Arno. I don't know the other one's name, but I've seen both around Salisbury's place several times. They're always together, and people say they're queer for each other. Anyway, the talk is that Salisbury was sent up here by somebody in New Orleans to take over all the gambling in Jefferson and Galveston counties."

"I see," I said. "And just who did they kill?"

"A lawyer named Henry DeMour. He was on the Beaumont City Council."

"Oh my God!" I blurted out, almost dropping my drink.

"You know him?"

"Not personally, but I've heard of him. Hell, everybody has. He was one of the top attorneys in Southeast Texas. His family settled in Beaumont way back before the Civil War and got rich in the import/export business."

"Really?"

"They're old money, Gulf aristocracy. And I'll tell you something else. If this Salisbury guy had a man like Henry DeMour killed, then Salisbury is either a very heavy hitter or a complete fool. How in the world did you get mixed up with people like these in the first place? You seem like a decent girl. They're hardly the kind of friends I'd expect you to have."

She shrugged. "Nolan and I used to go to Salisbury's place a lot. He came to Beaumont about a year ago from New Orleans and opened up a fancy supper club called

The Grotto in the old part of town."

"It has gambling too, I suppose."

"Yeah, in back. Blackjack, and a couple of craps tables and a roulette wheel. The place books good acts. Louis Armstrong was there a few weeks ago, and Harry James and His Orchestra are coming next month."

"So it's becoming the in place in Jefferson County, huh?" I asked.

"Yeah, but I'm surprised you haven't heard about DeMour being dead. The story was in all the papers. Didn't Jim mention it when he called?"

I shook my head. "Like I told you, he and I didn't get to talk long. I had to move fast or miss an arrest."

"Say, could I have another drink?" she asked.

"Sure," I said and got up to splash more whiskey in her glass. "Where did you hear this rumor about Salisbury taking over the gambling?" I asked.

"It's more than just a rumor," she replied. "Nolan told me about it himself, and he gets around enough that he should know."

I grinned at her. "Tell me something . . . what do you do when you aren't running around with gangsters and crooked cops?"

"I'm a schoolteacher," she said sadly. "Can you believe it? Or at least I was up until a few days ago. Second grade. I guess I'm fired now since I just ran off without telling anybody."

"How did you meet Nolan?"

"A friend introduced us at a dance last year. I thought at first he was a nice guy, but now I think he's sort of a hood himself."

"Well, he works for Milam Walsh," I said bluntly as I handed her the drink. "That should have told you something."

"I didn't really know that much about Walsh at the time. Besides, Nolan can be real smooth and convincing when he wants to be. But he's mean, and when he got mean with me and I left him —"

"Mean? How?"

"We got into an argument, and he slapped me around. That's when I broke it off. Anyhow, he said that he could square it with Salisbury if we got married. Otherwise, Salisbury was going to have me killed. But I think I'd rather be dead than married to Nolan."

"How did he think he was going to square it with Salisbury?"

She shrugged. "I guess he had the idea that he could put enough pressure on the guy. Maybe close him down or something if he didn't cooperate. I mean, Nolan is a cop and —"

"Not much of one, I wouldn't think. Not from what you've told me. Have you ever met this Salisbury character?"

"Yeah," she said with a nod.

"What's he like?"

"He's about thirty, smooth, a real sharp dresser. Quiet, doesn't say much."

"Okay. So now we know what your problem is, what do you want me to do about it?"

"Jim thought maybe I could hide out at your ranch. Do you have a ranch?"

I nodded. "My family does. Then what?"

"Jim said you'd know what to do."

"I'm flattered that he has such confidence in me," I said with a rueful laugh. "But you really ought to go to the state authorities. The Rangers, maybe."

She shook her head, but before I could say anything more there was a loud knock at the door. I motioned for her to be silent, then rose soundlessly from my chair. By the time I was on my feet a second knock rang out, this one even louder than the first. I frowned and gritted my teeth. It was a cop's knock — a knock with a persistent, demanding quality to it that said its maker was used to giving orders and having things his own way, and I found it sublimely irksome.

Quickly I pulled a long, lead-loaded billy

30

club from under the bed, then stepped over to the door. Staying carefully to one side, I reached down and turned the knob. Just as I'd expected, the instant the door was opened a heavy body crashed into it and slammed it to one side, its useless safety chain ripped loose from its moorings.

The intruders had counted on surprise and they got it. The first man was moving fast and it was a simple matter for me to stick out my foot and trip him. He fell, crashing face-first into the coffee table, shattering it to pieces. A fraction of a second later his companion tripped over his feet and they were both down in a tangle of arms and legs. Swinging the club hard and fast, I hit the second man three times, once where his neck joined his right shoulder and twice more in the lower ribs. Then I pushed him roughly to the side with my foot. Tossing the club to the floor behind me, I stepped back and deftly slipped my Colt .38 Super auto from my shoulder holster. The big man on bottom rolled over and managed to get himself into a sitting position. I saw a thick shock of blond hair and an expression that was in transition from surprise to rage. "Hi, Nolan!" I said cheerfully and kicked him as hard as I could squarely in his handsome, bovine face.

CHAPTER TWO

Two minutes later the door was once more firmly locked, and both men were disarmed and facedown on the floor, their hands secured behind them with their own handcuffs. I pulled out their wallets and quickly rifled through them both.

"Well, well," I said. "We have here one Nolan M. Dunning. You must be the famous Nolan the young lady has been telling me about. And this other gentleman seems to be one Mr. Hector McAdoo. Hi, Heck. What the heck you doing out here, Heck? San Gabriel's a long ways outside of your territory, isn't it?"

"You better let us go, mister," Nolan said. "We're the law and you're already in enough trouble." His words were lisped. His lips were broken, one front tooth was missing, and blood dripped copiously from his mouth.

I grabbed his thick blond hair and pulled

his head up to where I could look him in the eyes. "Nolan, if you speak again without being spoken to, I may decide to kick out the rest of your teeth."

"You can't do this, you asshole!" he raged, his voice nearly shouting. "I'm a cop."

"And you're a thick-headed son of a bitch," I muttered. I whipped a large bandanna handkerchief from my pocket and stuffed it into his mouth. Then I pulled off his belt and strapped the gag in place. I grabbed the little finger of his left hand and folded it neatly back until it almost touched his wrist. The bone broke with an audible *pop* and Nolan's eyes nearly bulged from their sockets as he screamed a silent scream against the handkerchief.

I waited a few moments until he settled down and recovered his breath, then asked, "My young friend, have you got any more doubts about who's running this show?"

He shook his head, his eyes wild and full of pain and fear.

"Good. Now I'm going to pull this gag out and you're going to tell me what I want to know or I'll stuff it back in and start with the other hand."

"Mister, you're crazy," McAdoo said.

"Nahhh . . ." I replied cheerfully. "Just playful." I jerked the gag from Nolan's bat-

33

tered mouth. "Now talk," I ordered.

The man coughed and groaned. "About what?" he finally asked.

"Why did you force your way into my room?"

"We've got an arrest warrant on her —"

"What!" Madeline shrieked from the bed.

I motioned for her to be quiet. "What kind of warrant?" I asked.

"Bad checks."

"I never wrote a bad check in my —" the girl began.

"Hush, dammit!" I growled. "I'll get this straightened out. Where's the warrant?"

"It's in my coat pocket," McAdoo said.

I squatted down and felt around in the man's pockets until I found a long manila envelope. I ripped it open and scanned the warrant, then shook my head. "A seven-dollar hot check," I said with disgust. "This is nothing but a damned misdemeanor, even if it's not bogus. You're trying to tell me that you came halfway across the state to serve a misdemeanor check warrant? And who's this Judge Smith?"

Nolan was getting his manhood back, and it was overriding his common sense. "The warrant's legal," he said. "It's legal and you're going to be in real trouble if you don't turn us loose."

I stared at him thoughtfully for a moment, then got to my feet. "I believe I told you to mind your manners, Nolan." I kicked him once again in the mouth, then quickly knelt down and stuffed the handkerchief back between his broken teeth. "That little outburst is going to cost you another finger."

"Leave him alone, mister," the older man pleaded. "For God's sake, please leave him alone and I'll tell you what you want to know."

"Sure. Just as soon as I break me another finger. I'm going to make a believer out of this prick."

Nolan whined desperately through the gag, shaking his head back and forth, his eyes wild with fear.

"No?" I asked. "You got religion now? You sure about that?"

Nolan nodded vigorously.

"Okay," I said. "But one more peep out of you and you're going to be one very un-happy young man." I turned to McAdoo. "Talk, old fellow. What are you two doing up here?"

"It's Nolan. He wants her back."

"How did you get involved?"

"He's a friend of mine, and he asked me to come with him."

I squatted down and locked eyes with

McAdoo. "That's real loyalty on your part," I said. "I don't think I've got any friends who'd help me kidnap somebody. Who do you work for?"

"I'm an elected official. A county constable."

"Ahhhh . . . I see. And just what part of Jefferson County is your precinct in?"

"The southwest."

I smiled. "Why am I not surprised? Down close to Galveston. Some of the Maceo joints are in your jurisdiction, aren't they?"

"So what?"

"So they've been supplementing your income, that's what. How long have you been in office?"

"Twenty years."

"Well, you must be keeping somebody happy or else you wouldn't have stayed there that long."

I rose to my feet and stood contemplating the two men. My guess was that despite Nolan's position as Walsh's chief deputy, he and McAdoo were both bottom feeders. Neither seemed smart enough to be anything else. I also figured that if the girl really had seen something that could connect Salisbury to DeMour's death, then Nolan's notion that he could "square things" if she came home and married him was a pipe dream. I also realized that if they knew anything beyond what they'd told me so far, it would take more time than I was willing to spend and more violence than I was willing to commit to get it out of them. And even then I couldn't be certain I had the whole truth. At the moment I needed time more than I needed information — time to take the girl and leave and put several hundred miles between us and San Gabriel.

I looked over to where she sat in the center of the bed, her glass still in her hand. Her wide blue eyes were riveted on Nolan, who lay bleeding on the floor, and a faint hint of a smile played at the corners of her mouth. I shook my head and rolled my eyes. When she raised her face to look at me, I gave her a tight grin and reached for the phone. Two years earlier the Weilbach had put telephones in all the rooms, but they didn't have dialers. The system worked through the hotel switchboard and there was an operator on duty all night.

"What are you doing?" the girl asked as I jiggled the button to get the operator.

"I'm calling the law. A friend of mine named Ollie Marne is a detective with the sheriff's department here in town."

"No," she said, her voice pleading. "Please, no cops —"

"Don't worry," I told her with a grin. "This guy is different."

Twenty minutes after I picked up the phone, Ollie Marne knocked on my door. Behind him loomed a huge, cretinous-looking uniformed deputy who stood at least six and a half feet tall and must have weighed three hundred pounds.

Marne was a pudgy man of medium height with a round head and a wide, bland face whose only point of interest was a pair of bright little eyes that were never still. His attire was as undistinguished as his appearance; that night he wore a floppy, shapeless gray suit, a broad-brimmed plainsman's hat, and a pair of scuffed boots. Now in his late thirties, Ollie had been with the San Gabriel sheriff's department most of his adult life, a job that gave him an outlet for his considerable entrepreneurial talents, one example of which was the extensive network of reliable informants he'd built up that stretched from the Brazos River to the New Mexico border. Over the years he'd become known as the man to see if you were a lawman who needed information in West Texas.

Finally it dawned on Ollie that he was both putting his sources at considerable risk and gaining nothing for himself. At that point he hatched the idea of wholesaling his snitches out to other cops. From then on, if you wanted information about the criminal underworld in such far-flung cities as San Gabriel, Lubbock, Big Spring, or El Paso, you went to see Ollie Marne, and Ollie quoted you a price. Then in a couple of days you had what you needed. His fees were reasonable and his customers always found his information reliable. It was a system that worked to the satisfaction of all. How much of the money actually percolated down to the informants was anybody's guess and nobody's worry since the snitches were hardly in a position to complain.

I moved aside to let the two men enter.

"Jesus, Virgil!" Marne exclaimed as soon as he saw Dunning and McAdoo lying handcuffed on the floor. "What in hell's been going on here?"

"Unlawful intruders," I said casually. "I had to subdue them."

"Subdue my ass," he said and pointed to Nolan. "This poor bastard looks more like he's been butchered than subdued."

"It's just busted lips, Ollie. Busted lips always bleed a lot."

Marne squatted down and peered at the man's face. "Are you sure he's even got any lips left?"

"Don't worry about it."

Marne shook his head and laughed a harsh little laugh. "Oh, I won't, Virg. Never fear. But what in hell do you want *me* to do with them?"

"Lock 'em up for a while so I can get out of town."

Marne rubbed his chin thoughtfully for a few seconds before answering. "Yeah, I guess I can do that," he said at last. "Do you want to go ahead and charge them with unlawful entry?"

I shook my head. "They're cops, and it might cause more trouble than it's worth."

"Damn! Cops?"

"That's right," I said. "They've got a warrant on this young lady here, but it's probably bogus. The blond one is her ex-boyfriend, and he won't take no for an answer. A real caveman. He came up here to drag her back home and make her marry him."

Marne examined Madeline closely for the first time and liked what he saw. His eager little eyes lingered on the swell of her breasts. "Where they come from?" he asked.

"Beaumont. The boyfriend works for Milam Walsh. In fact, he's Walsh's chief deputy."

Ollie Marne turned and stared at me in

wonder for several seconds before he spoke. "Is that the whole story?" he asked.

"No."

"Virgil, do I really want to know what this mess is all about?"

I shrugged. "It's your call, Ollie. I'm willing to tell you, but I sure as hell wouldn't want to hear it if I were in your shoes. I think I'd just let it pass."

"Right," he agreed firmly, his head bobbing up and down like a fishing cork. "But I got to cover my butt. How about if I tell the sheriff that you're going to come in tomorrow afternoon and sign the complaint? Then when you don't ever show up, we can just turn 'em loose."

"Sounds fine to me. But try to keep them until late tomorrow evening if you can."

"Sure. Let me see that warrant for a minute."

I retrieved the warrant and handed it over. He quickly scanned the paper and then glared down at the two men on the floor. "And they really pushed their way in here on the strength of this bullshit?" he asked in disgust.

"That's right," I replied.

"Damn," he muttered, shaking his head. "What a pair of nitwits. Let me keep this warrant and show it to the sheriff. It may piss him off enough that he'll keep them jugged an extra day on his own." He motioned to the big deputy. "Get 'em up," he said.

"You might want to be careful with the blond guy's hand," I said. "He's got a broken finger."

"Oh yeah? How did that happen?"

"Beats me. It must have got busted in the tussle."

Marne shook his head and laughed. "In the tussle, huh? You're a card, Virg."

After the giant man hauled the two intruders to their feet and pushed them out into the hall, I shook hands with Marne in the doorway. "Thanks, Ollie," I said. "I'll owe you one after this."

"Any time," he replied, looking once more at the bed where Madeline still sat, wide-eyed and waiting. "Have fun," he whispered.

"I don't think it's that kind of deal, Ollie."

He smiled a knowing smile, and the last thing I heard as he swung the door shut was his hard, skeptical little laugh echoing down the hallway. By the time I had the door secured once again, Madeline was out of bed and busy with the whiskey and ice.

"I need another drink," she said. "How about you?"

"Sure."

She splashed bourbon into both glasses, then handed me mine and swung back onto the bed. "What now?" she asked.

"We go to the ranch."

"When?"

"Tonight. In a little while. But that won't solve your problem for good. I hope you realize that this business isn't over."

She nodded sadly. "What happens after we get there?" she asked.

"I intend to make a few phone calls, and you need to think about talking to somebody on the state level."

"You sure were rough with Nolan," she said, changing the subject.

I shrugged. "So what? You didn't really mind seeing him get a taste of his own medicine, did you?"

"I guess not," she said.

"Guess not, hell. You enjoyed it, and you know it. Am I right?"

"You shouldn't say things like that, you know," she said, her voice husky. "It's rude."

I stared impassively down at her and sipped my drink without replying. Our eyes stayed locked until finally she dropped her gaze and asked, "Are we leaving now or . . ." She let the word hang in the air a few seconds. ". . . later?" Her voice was a bare whisper.

"I suppose that's up to you."

She watched me as I drained my drink. She quickly finished hers, and we put our glasses on the nightstand at the same time. I continued to gaze at her silently while her hand crept up to her throat and slowly unfastened the top button of her blouse. She said nothing, but she raised her eyebrows minutely, and there was an unspoken question in her expression.

"Go ahead if that's what you want," I said softly. "But if you do, I'm not going to button it back for you this time."

She nodded faintly and began to undo the buttons, and this time her hands didn't tremble a bit.

CHAPTER THREE

World War II was three months into its fourth year. Back in the spring the Battle of Midway had turned the tide in the Pacific, though few realized it at the time except the Japanese high command. According to the newspapers, the Germans and the Russians were locked in a titanic struggle around a city called Stalingrad in southwestern Russia that commentators were saying would determine the outcome of the war in Europe. Men in uniform were everywhere on the streets, and it seemed like half the homes you passed had service stars in their windows. Gasoline rationing was in effect, but as a detective for a powerful organization, I had an unlimited ration card. We stopped and I filled the tank before we left San Gabriel a little after eleven that evening. My car was a 1940 Ford convertible, dark blue with gray upholstery. It was a fast, agile machine, and I'm a fast driver by habit.

Even so, the trip took six hours. The girl slept fitfully most of the way to San Antonio. She finally awoke when I had to stop at a little all-night café for a coffee and doughnuts. I suffer from low blood sugar, and I'd skipped supper.

"Which way from here?" she asked as soon as we were back in the car.

"Straight southwest."

"And that's where your ranch is?"

I nodded in the darkness. "In Matador County, right down on the Rio Grande."

"Is it a big place?"

I shook my head. "Just medium-sized for this part of the country. Sixty-seven thousand acres. It's been in my family for almost two hundred years."

"Really?"

"Yeah. It was originally a land grant from the king of Spain to the Veramendis. My great-grandfather Isaiah Tucker got it as his wife's dowry. Her name was Rosa, and he named the ranch after her. She was tall and slim and gorgeous, but she was facing spinsterhood because she'd scared off all her suitors."

"How?"

I looked at her and grinned. "Her father was a man of the world, and he'd educated her and encouraged her to read widely. As a

46

consequence, she was very opinionated and outspoken, which was considered unbecoming in a young Mexican girl of that era. My grandfather was their only son. Their only surviving child, actually. Their other two kids were both girls, and they died of typhoid when they were little."

"Aww . . . that's terrible," she said.

I shrugged. "The Texas frontier was a rough place."

"What happened to Rosa?"

"Isaiah died in 1905, but she lived until 1925. She was past ninety when she passed away."

"That long?" she asked with surprise. "Why, you must have known her."

"Sure I knew her."

"What was she like?"

"Still as outspoken as she was when she was a girl. Loved fun, loved family gatherings, loved to read. Kept up with world affairs. She was a grand old lady."

"That's a wonderful story," she said. "Who runs the place now?"

"My aunt Carmen. She's my dad's sister."

"And your parents are dead?"

"Yeah, and Carmen's husband died the same year as my dad. He owned almost twenty thousand acres adjoining La Rosa. When he and Carmen married, the families merged the operations."

"Do you have any brothers or sisters?"

I shook my head. "Just one cousin. She's Aunt Carmen's daughter."

"Where's she?"

I sighed in resignation. "I may as well tell you the story because you don't want to make the mistake of mentioning her to my aunt. She went off to the University of Texas and married a hotshot Dallas surgeon right after she graduated. The truth is that she's ashamed of her Mexican blood and ashamed of her family. She only comes home when she has to. Aunt Carmen is thoroughly disgusted with her. She's got two kids that we barely know."

"But your ancestors were pioneers. She should be proud of them. And the Veramendis were aristocrats."

"None of that makes any difference to her. She's a blue-eyed blonde, and when she hears the word 'Mexican' she thinks greaser. She's also a social-climbing half-wit."

"Don't be too hard on her," Madeline said. "Maybe she'll grow up some day and —"

"The hell with her," I said firmly. "I don't care if she does or not."

We didn't speak for several minutes. Finally she asked, "Does your aunt manage the ranch all alone?"

"At the present, yes."

"But why don't you move back home and help her?"

I gave her a rueful grin in the darkness of the car. "I get enough of that from her, so I don't need to hear it from you too."

CHAPTER FOUR

We fell silent once again. An hour later the sky in the east was growing gray with light when we turned off the highway through an unpretentious gateway onto a graveled road. "This is it," I announced. "La Rosa."

"How far does it go?"

"It's roughly eight by thirteen miles. Our property extends right on down to the Rio Grande."

She gazed out the window into a landscape that was flat, relieved only by occasional low hills, and covered with chest-high undergrowth.

"What's that?" she asked.

"What?"

"All that stuff growing out there."

I laughed. "Blackthorn. Mesquite, desert yaupon, cactus. This part of Texas is called the Brush Country. Anything out there that doesn't stick you will bite you or sting you."

"How can cattle live on that?"

"There's grass. You just don't see it. But it does take an average of twelve to fourteen acres to graze a beef cow in this part of the state, and that's in a year with good rainfall."

The road opened into a large clearing in the brush. There on a low knoll sat the main house, surrounded by a pair of tall palm trees and a half dozen live oaks. A hundred yards or so behind it loomed a large barn, and off in the distance could be seen several smaller dwellings made of concrete blocks.

I pulled around behind the house. Light shown through the kitchen windows, yellowish light that I knew came from kerosene lamps. I smiled to myself. Two years earlier, at great expense, electricity had been run out to the ranch from town, but Tía Carmen still preferred the soft, gentle glow of kerosene in the morning.

I honked the horn, and by the time we'd climbed from the car my aunt had opened the back door and stood framed in the doorway. She was a small woman with short, iron gray hair and dark, hard eyes. Stepping aside so we could enter, she ushered us into the big kitchen.

Nothing had changed in the months of my absence. It was all just as it had been my whole life — the great round oak table, the twelve-burner butane stove, the gas refrigerator. Here, surrounded by the familiar odors of burning kerosene and frying bacon and fresh coffee, I felt a weight lift from my shoulders, just as it always did when I entered this room.

My aunt raised her eyebrows inquiringly.

"This is Madeline Kimbell, Tía Carmen," I said. "She's in a spot of trouble."

My aunt stared at the girl for a few moments, her face stern and implacable. Then her expression softened and she held out her hand. "Welcome to La Rosa, dear."

Madeline shook her hand with hesitation. "I hope this isn't an imposition," she said diffidently.

"Not at all," Aunt Carmen replied. "Sit down and have some breakfast."

My aunt put three coffee cups on the table, then filled them from the great enamel percolator that had been bubbling at the back of the stove. A few seconds later she set three places, then pulled a pan of biscuits from the oven. A plateful of homemade sausage from the stove followed, and we began to eat, buttering the biscuits from a bowl of fresh-churned butter that already sat in the center of the table.

"Where are you from, young lady?" Tía Carmen asked.

"Beaumont."

"And how did you manage to meet this malingering nephew of mine?"

I interjected, "Jim Rutherford called me a few days ago and asked me to help her."

My aunt smiled. As I'd told Madeline, Rutherford was a retired border patrolman who had been a friend of our family for many years. Indeed, after Tía Carmen was widowed, there had been some chance that she and Rutherford would marry. Unfortunately, geography defeated them; Rutherford was committed to a daughter in Beaumont, and La Rosa was my aunt's life. Still, I knew she held considerable affection for the man, which was precisely why I'd told her about Rutherford's request. It could only put a strange situation in a better light.

"So you're acquainted with Jim?" Carmen asked.

Madeline nodded. "He and my dad grew up together."

"How is he?"

"Fine," Madeline said. "Except that he has bad days on account of his arthritis."

We fell silent and ate. After a few minutes Aunt Carmen noticed that Madeline's cup was untouched. "You don't drink coffee?" she asked.

"Oh, yes, ma'am. It's just that I'm afraid it will keep me awake. I'd hoped you would let me sleep a little while, if you don't mind."

"She's been on the run for several days," I said. "She's pretty worn out."

"I dozed in the car coming down here," Madeline said. "But I'm so nervous I'm afraid I'll have trouble getting to sleep even if I don't drink any coffee."

Aunt Carmen picked up the girl's cup. "I've got the remedy for that." Going to the cabinet she emptied the cup into the sink, then filled it about a third full from a bottle of bourbon that sat on the countertop. Then she reached into the cabinet and pulled out a small pill bottle. She shook out a pill into her hand. "Take this," she told the girl as she returned to the table. "And drink this whiskey."

"What is it?"

"Half a sleeping pill. I get insomnia sometimes. Go ahead, take it and drink the whiskey. You'll be out like a light in twenty minutes."

Madeline dutifully swallowed the pill and drained the cup. Aunt Carmen went to the hall door and called out in Spanish. A few seconds later a tall, stone-faced Mexican woman of late middle age entered the kitchen. Seeing me, she broke into a radiant smile. *"Buenos días, Señor Virgil."*

I got to my feet and hugged her warmly. *"Buenos días, Helena,"* I said. "How are you?"

"Bien, bien. You have come home to stay, I hope?" she asked in heavily accented English.

"Maybe . . . ," I replied noncommittally.

Aunt Carmen gave Helena instructions. "Go with her, dear. She'll show you your room. The bathroom is at the end of the hall. Take a hot bath and then get into bed."

"I hate to be such a bother —" Madeline began.

"Nonsense. Go now, and get some rest. I'll wake you up around noon so you won't have trouble sleeping tonight."

As the pair left the room I got up and poured myself another cup of coffee, then came back and took my place at the table. My aunt stood staring coldly at me for a few moments, saying nothing. "What?" I finally asked.

She didn't answer. Instead, she slapped me hard. Twice. I made no move to stop her. I gave her a lopsided grin and said, "If you're going to do that again, let me take my glasses off. They're expensive."

"Bah!" she said with disgust. "What foolishness . . ."

I sighed and shook my head. "I'll take her

55

somewhere else, if you want."

"I'm not talking about your friend. Besides, when have we ever refused hospitality to a decent person in need? Eh?"

"Then what's wrong?" I asked in Spanish. Both bilingual from childhood, we conversed in a mixture of the two languages, and would have been hard-pressed for an answer if asked which language we thought in.

"This ranch," she snapped at me. "La Rosa. That's what's wrong."

My unwillingness to come home and help her with the management of the place had been a bone of contention between the two of us for years. After I graduated from the university in Austin, I joined the navy and spent three years in uniform despite the family's belief that as the only male in my generation I'd return to La Rosa and assume what they saw as my obligations. After my discharge I secured an appointment as a deputy U.S. Marshal, and the issue became even more sensitive. Then with the deaths of my father and uncle, Carmen thought that at long last I would come home. Indeed, she'd used her position in the South Texas Democratic political machine to ease me out of the Marshals' service. When she learned that I'd foiled her by taking a job as a detective with the Cattle Raisers Association, her rage had been volcanic.

"What about it?" I asked, well knowing what she meant.

"You go off chasing thieves and leave me here alone with all these wild Mexicans and this place to run!"

I couldn't help laughing, even at the risk of getting pounded again. "Please . . . can't a woman of your intelligence come up with something better than that? In the first place you're a quarter Mexican yourself. And secondly, there's not a vaquero on this place who wouldn't cheerfully slit the governor's throat for you. Hell, you're probably safer than President Roosevelt."

"And then there's the politics," she countered. "It would be better if a man —"

"If a man did what?" I asked. "Fronted for you, you mean? Why bother? Everybody knows that you've been the boss of this county since long before Uncle John and Dad died. They weren't interested and you were. Why, I bet the superintendent of schools still sends the young teachers out here to get your approval before he hires them."

She gave me a tight little smile and reached to grab a big hank of my hair. Shaking my head roughly, she said, "Virgil, sometimes I almost hate you."

"Ahhhh . . ." I said with a laugh. "You're crazy about me and you know it."

"All the philosophers say that love and hate are very close together," she said. "Or haven't you ever heard that?"

When I didn't reply she poured a shot of whiskey into each of our cups and asked, "When are you going to quit this silly detective business and come home?" Her dark eyes were fierce now, pinning me to my chair as if I were a bug on a board. "I can't live forever, you know. Do you want to see this place fall apart?"

"No."

"Then when?"

I sighed tiredly and ran my fingers through my hair. "I was going to surprise you in about a month by just showing up one day, but I might as well go ahead and tell you now. I haven't officially resigned, but I've farmed out all my pending cases to a couple of the other association detectives."

"Well, well . . . this *is* news. I hadn't really dared to hope."

I shrugged. "What else could I do? There's the matter of this girl that I have to tend to, and I can hardly do that working full-time. Plus all your pressure, all the letters you keep sending me . . ." I smiled at her with

58

affection. "You're a relentless old bat, you know. It's finally gotten to the point that to get any peace I've either got to give in and come home, or else shoot myself. Even before this thing with Madeline cropped up, I'd planned to make the move sometime this coming spring."

"What happened with the navy?" she asked.

I shook my head. "When I tried to reactivate my commission I was told they really didn't need officers with substandard vision whose training was a decade out of date. They also said I could do the war effort more good by catching rustlers. They mentioned something about the troops not being able to fight on empty stomachs."

"Good," she said firmly. "Stay here and take care of your own world."

"I suppose that's what I'll have to do, but I want you to understand that I intend to have a real say in the management of the ranch. I'm not going to be just a rubber stamp."

"Done. I promise."

"And I intend to hold you to it right now. Beef prices are going to be very high before this war is over, and I think we need to expand."

"How?"

"I want to buy Lester Doan's herd and lease his acreage."

Doan was our neighbor to the north. Several months earlier he'd been felled by a bad heart attack and I'd heard he was anxious to sell out and move to San Antonio to live with his daughter.

"I made a tentative agreement to buy his cattle a week ago."

"You've already talked to him?" she asked in surprise.

"Sure."

"How much?"

"Thirty dollars a head for cows, baby calves thrown in. Fifteen a head for calves over six months. And he'll lease us the ranch for a quarter an acre per year."

"How many head are we talking about?"

"Twenty-two hundred. Do we have that much ready cash?"

She quickly calculated in her head and nodded. "Yes, but if we buy him out we'll probably run a little short of operating money."

"We can go to the bank for a few thousand if we need to," I pointed out.

"And you really think this is the thing to do?"

"Definitely." I said firmly. "I know it is."

She nodded. "All right. I've never doubted

your intelligence, Virgil. Just your seriousness."

"And there's one other thing. Next year I
want to replace at least a dozen of our herd
bulls with that new Santa Gertrudis breed
Bob Kleberg has been developing over at
the King Ranch."

"What! Is he already selling those bulls
commercially?"

"No, but he'll let me have a few for
reasons of his own. He wants to try them
on a herd that's genetically unrelated to his
own cattle."

"Yes, and he'll want too much for them,"
she objected. "You know Bob."

I shook my head. "I don't care. They'll be
worth it. Remember what Grandpa always
said? Your bull is half of the blood line of
your calf crop. Good bulls are the cheapest
way to improve a herd."

She regarded me for a moment, then nodded slowly. "If that's what it takes to get
you home, then we'll try it." She sat down
at the table and drained her coffee cup.

"It's the thing to do. The Santa Gertrudis
was developed for the kind of climate and
pasture we have here in South Texas."

She nodded absently as though she hadn't
heard me. "Virgil," she said musingly,
"please tell me why it's taken so long for

you to take this place seriously?"

"It was because I knew that when I came home and got involved with the ranch, that would be it. I'd never leave. You see, I love La Rosa as much as you do, but I wanted to have some life apart from it before it closed in on me for good."

Her expression softened and she nodded thoughtfully. "I don't suppose I can begrudge you that. When are you moving home?"

"As soon as I get this business with Madeline settled and my apartment in Big Spring closed. Maybe two weeks. Three at the outside. How does that sound?"

She nodded. "Good enough."

"This calls for another drink," I told her. "The prodigal returns."

"You go ahead. I've got to get dressed."

We both stood. As she was about to leave the room I reached out and hugged her tightly against my chest and felt her arms go around me, this tiny, iron-willed woman who, even more than my own mother, had always been the center of my world.

"Say something nice to me, Tía Carmen," I said with a laugh.

"You've got what you wanted, so tell me what a sweet boy I am."

"You're an incorrigible rascal is what you

are, Virgil Tucker," she said as she pulled away and poked me lightly in the belly with her fist. "Have your drink. I've got to tend to this ranch."

"Is Alonzo driving you this morning?"

"*Sí.*"

"How's the jeep working out?"

Instead of answering she whisked quickly from the room.

Thinking she hadn't heard me, I shrugged and splashed more whiskey into my cup. Then I went outside and sat down on the back steps. It was a little cool, but the sun was coming up bright in the east and the day was dawning crystal clear, without a cloud in the sky. I lit a cigarette, and as I sat smoking and sipping my drink, I almost dozed off in the placid freshness of the early morning. Soon I heard the clop of hooves, and the old ranch buggy swung into the drive with Helena's husband, Alonzo, at the reins.

Sixty-five years old, tall and slim, with naturally dark skin that had been baked by a lifetime in the sun, Alonzo looked like he'd been charbroiled on a spit. Rarely far from my aunt, he moved about the ranch as quietly and unobtrusively as a ghost. Dressed as he invariably was in his tattered khakis and ratty sombrero, his Colt single-action revolver and his bullet-filled bandolero, he could have easily been a renegade from Pancho Villa's army.

As well he might have been, I realized the dates were about right. Alonzo had arrived at La Rosa by wagon with Helena and their two children one stormy night thirty-five years earlier, carrying an ancient and well-worn letter from my long-dead grandfather. The essence of the letter was that the family was greatly indebted to this man and his kin for certain unspecified services that had been rendered some time in the distant past. Furthermore, the letter laid a burden upon its author's descendants to give its bearer refuge and aid, regardless of the circumstances.

They spent that first night in the main house. The next morning Helena was at work in the kitchen while Alonzo busied himself with the remuda. Over the next few weeks the family slipped quietly into the gentle rhythms of ranch life. Whatever trouble he'd been fleeing, it was of a lasting nature; I knew that he hadn't set foot off La Rosa in the three and a half decades that had passed since that stormy night.

For many years my aunt had used a buggy to travel around the ranch, sometimes taking the reins herself, but more often than not with Alonzo as her driver. The previous summer I'd accepted a stolen army jeep as payment of a debt of several hundred dollars that I never could have collected any other way. I brought the jeep home and taught Alonzo to drive it in the apparently vain hope that it would replace the dilapidated buggy. That morning the vehicle was nowhere to be seen as the old vaquero guided the buggy up to the back door.

"What happened to the jeep?" I asked as he alighted from the seat.

He took a can of Prince Albert tobacco from his shirt pocket and slowly rolled a cigarette. Placing the cigarette in the corner of his mouth, he lighted it with a match he struck with his thumbnail. Then he regarded me for a moment with his sad, dark, impenetrable eyes as he slowly blew a cloud of smoke from under his drooping mustache. "It was a most wicked beast, Señor Virgil," he said at last.

"What? The jeep?"

"*Sí.*"

"How? In what way was it wicked?"

"It sought to throw us twice."

"Throw you?"

"*Sí.* Me and Tía Carmen. It sought to throw us on the way to the Bolivar pasture. But do not worry. It will do no further

65

harm. I killed it with my *pistola*."

I grinned in spite of myself. "What did Aunt Carmen have to say about that?"

"It was Tía Carmen who instructed me to shoot it, though I would probably have done so anyway. As I said, it was a most wicked beast."

I roared with laughter and felt my heart swell with affection for this formidable old man. Years earlier, when I was a sophomore in high school, a bully, a compact, hard-bodied school yard tyrant named Stubb Martindale moved to town and chose the shy, skinny kid I'd been back then as the prime target of his malice. I fought him twice, losing both times but proving my courage. Still, Martindale humiliated me on a daily basis, and my life at school became miserable. At home I became more quiet and withdrawn than usual. Alonzo was the first to notice, and he drew me aside one evening to inquire about the source of my discontent. At first I was reluctant to speak, but he persisted, and the story eventually poured out. All the while I spoke, Alonzo, who was then about forty-five and in his prime, nodded sympathetically.

"I will tell you what to do," he said once I'd finished. "You must put your boots aside and wear your Sunday shoes to school, the heavy brogues with the thick soles and square toes. Lace them tightly, and the next time this hooligan begins to distress you, kick him hard in the cojones. Not as hard as you can, for you must give up some force for accuracy of aim. But kick him hard. Do not wait once his bullying has begun. Do not converse with him or trade insults or threats as boys are prone to do. Kick him immediately. This will be a great shock to him. He may even vomit. All of this will be very pleasing to you, but you cannot dwell on it."

"No?" I asked, puzzled. I'd never before gotten such advice from an adult.

Alonzo shook his head. "No. You have more to do. If possible, kick him a second time in the privates, then jerk his feet from under him. Or trip him. It doesn't matter how you do it, but you must get him on the ground one way or another. Then kick and stomp him into complete submission. Do not kick him in the head, for this could kill him and this is not what you want. But kick him in the stomach, the back, the kidneys, the soft parts of his body. Kick him a dozen times or so, and kick him with great force. When you are finished, say nothing. Utter no threats about what will happen if he ever molests you again. He will know without being told, and your silence will be even the more intimidating to him."

"But I could be expelled," I objected.

Alonzo smiled coldly at my naivete. Though I didn't know it at the time, he was well aware that the principal of the school could hardly dare to expel the son of the county's largest rancher on so small a provocation as a school yard brawl. But he saw no reason to share that knowledge with me. "That is possible," he lied. "But it is of no consequence. Also, your father will almost certainly thrash you if he finds out, but that too does not matter. You see, to rid yourself of this bully you must convince him that you do not fear the school authorities, that you do not fear your father, that you do not fear anything, and that you will go to any lengths to be free of him. Then he will know you mean business."

The strategy worked. And despite Alonzo's warning, I gave the hulking boy one solid kick in the mouth, knocking out a tooth and splitting his lips so they bled copiously. Left whimpering and humiliated, abandoned by those who a moment before had been his admiring friends, Stubb Martindale never again so much as raised his eyes to meet my stare.

A few weeks passed. Late of a Saturday

afternoon in November, Alonzo once again drew me aside. "Your horse is saddled at the barn," he said. "Let us take a ride down toward the river. We will enjoy the beauty of the full moon, eh?"

At that time the ranch employed only four other full-time vaqueros. All of them were Mexican-American men Alonzo's age or older, and all bore the signs of the cattleman's life in the Texas brush country — scarred faces, broken and badly set bones, missing fingers; one had a missing eye whose empty socket was covered by a homemade patch. All four were descended from people who had worked on the ranch in the days of its founding. And like Alonzo, they were always armed with Colt pistols. Not far from the barn, they joined us.

We rode on slowly, not hurrying, saying little. Our horses were trained cow ponies, sturdy, close coupled and agile, bred from native Spanish stock with strong infusions of quarter-horse blood. An hour later, just as the sun was setting, we emerged into a natural clearing, a meadow of some five or more acres that had been turned into a holding pen many years earlier by cutting and piling the brush along its sides until it formed an impassable wall. At the pen's far side stood an ancient bull — a massive animal of mixed blood, part longhorn, part Hereford, part anyone's guess — its head and shoulders looming huge in the gathering darkness, its horns thick and battered and dull with age. It stood placidly chewing its cud, yet its old eyes were still fierce and proud even now in the winter of its life.

"What are we doing here?" I asked in Spanish.

"I wish to instruct you on certain matters," Alonzo answered in the same language.

"I get plenty of instruction in school," I scoffed.

Alonzo turned to face me, his face full of feigned surprise. "And these schoolmasters, they told how to deal with your bully? Your friend Martindale? How to rid yourself of him?"

"No," I admitted with a shake of my head.

"Just as I thought. Now listen carefully." Alonzo jabbed his finger toward the bull. "This old *toro* here is perhaps the most dangerous beast on La Rosa. I have watched him since his youth. He has fought the other bulls many times, and always he has won. He is especially dangerous now because he has learned never to hesitate. Also, a certain contempt has grown in his heart for those who think him weak and irresolute because of his age, and he longs to see the fear in their eyes in that moment when they learn differently."

I thought he was ascribing a lot of wisdom and insight to a bull, but prudently I said nothing. Instead I asked, "What now?"

"Watch and do exactly as I tell you."

The five of them sat on their mounts for several minutes, the bull staring at them and they at the bull as the darkness gathered and the full moon rose above the horizon. At last Alonzo raised his arm for attention. The others gathered their reins in their hands. "Aheeeee!" he yelled, and the five men raced off across the clearing, riding first toward the bull, then circling him. The mighty old animal whirled in his tracks, following the lead rider as the five rode around and around him, a perfect melding of men and beasts in a blur of motion. Then Pablo, the one-eyed vaquero, tossed his lasso deftly over the bull's neck. At almost the same moment one of the other men roped his horns. Their horses, long trained to do so, skidded to a stop and quickly backed up in opposite directions, taking the slack out of the ropes. The bull thrashed and pawed. Alonzo rode behind and carefully threw his rope under its right hind foot. His horse backed up and the rope came tight, immobilizing the hapless animal. Alonzo dismounted and motioned to me. "Come," he said softly. As he walked calmly toward the bull, he pulled his ancient bone-handled knife from his pocket. The bull struggled against the ropes, its eyes full of rage as it tried desperately to hook the old man with its horns. Alonzo spoke softly to the animal in that magic voice of his that could calm the wildest of horses. "Easy, old *toro*. Easy. You have been chosen for a noble end."

He felt along the bull's neck for a moment, then jabbed quickly with the knife about halfway between the head and the shoulders. He wriggled the knife around until he'd punctured the bull's jugular, and the blood began to spurt out hot and steaming in the cold night air. From out of nowhere there appeared the small silver cup I'd seen several times on a shelf in Alonzo's house. It was held under the wound and filled five times, and each time one of the vaqueros drained it, Alonzo drinking last. Then it was filled a final time and passed into my hands. "Drink quickly," Alonzo said. "Drink while his great heart still beats."

If I'd been asked the day before, I would have replied with a laugh that no, I never expected to be out in the brush in the dead of night drinking raw bull's blood with five wild, crazy old men. But now there was no mirth in me. I saw in Alonzo's bearing the same grave seriousness that was in the priest's eyes at communion time, and I accepted the cup without hesitation. As I raised it to my lips, I felt a weightless freedom possess me as though I'd shed my part of that collective delusion we call civilization. For a few moments the world appeared as it must have been in the very morning of time, and as I drank I was aware of little beyond the hot, salty liquid that filled my mouth and the flat, limitless land that stretched away forever beneath the silver moon.

Afterward, the vaqueros built a small fire. Someone produced a large stoneware jug of homemade tequila and passed it around. When the jug came to me, I hesitated. "Go ahead," Alonzo said softly. "Your father will not mind this one time."

"Did he . . . ?" I began.

"Did he what?" Alonzo asked.

"The blood, I mean . . ." I groped for words for a moment, then shook my head and muttered, "Nothing."

Alonzo grinned, his teeth flashing white in the firelight. The other vaqueros laughed softly. I raised the jug and took the first drink of my life, the fiery liquid burning as it went down. I choked a bit, and coughed, and then drank again, the liquor spreading out to warm my belly.

"Easy," Alonzo said. "You want to go back home sitting on your horse, not draped over his back like a sack of grain. That would be undignified."

The others cackled. "Dignity!" one-eyed Pablo called out. "Let us drink to dignity!"

"Fool!" one of the others said. "Do you not know that one loses dignity quickest by toasting it with the bottle?"

Another shook his head. "No, it goes quickest when dealing with women."

"You are right, my friend," said the third. "Women can take everything if they are of a mind to."

"Bah!" Alonzo snorted.

"Alonzo expresses contempt," Pablo said.

"Alonzo is a wise man," one of the others said.

"*Sí,*" Alonzo agreed profoundly, his voice full of good-natured self-mockery. "Very wise."

"Tell us, Alonzo the Wise," Pablo said. "Have you ever lost your dignity?"

"*Sí.*"

"Relate the story to us."

Alonzo shook his head sadly. "There is little to tell. It was many years ago and the wench is long dead."

"Best not let Helena find out or she'll take her great kitchen knife and remove something more useful than your dignity."

The other men hooted in glee.

"I think not," Alonzo said. "Now that we are growing older she has even less interest in such usefulness than I do."

The others laughed again, and I joined in. The flames leapt and flickered while the moon climbed bright and cold in the eastern sky. The jug went around twice more and I discovered that I was mildly and pleasantly drunk. When at last the fire had died down to embers, we climbed on our mounts and started home. Riding quickly this time, we spurred the horses and shrieked and laughed wildly in the moonlight. I put the quirt to my gelding and shot ahead of the others in a burst of speed. Near the barn I whirled him around and shouted, "*Arriba! Arriba!* Hurry up, old fellows! Get a move on!" I'd never felt better in my life.

They laughed, and as they sped past they called out, "*El hombre! El hombre!* See how he is now the man!"

Once the horses had been unsaddled and turned into the remuda, the vaqueros drifted toward their quarters. Only Alonzo lingered behind. I stood silently and at a loss for words. I was aware that some fine moment was quickly passing away, and I was reluctant for it to end. Finally, not knowing what else to say, I muttered, "I guess I ought to go on up to the house."

Alonzo didn't answer. Instead, he clasped the back of my neck with his hand. It was a fatherly gesture, but his fingers were hard and unyielding. "These men are now your brothers," he said softly. "Do not forget it in the years to come."

Later that night in bed I realized that even though I was an Anglo and the son of their *patrón,* it was not the five old vaqueros but I who had enjoyed the elevation in status implied by Alonzo's quiet affirmation of brotherhood. I shivered and felt small and humble beneath my covers just as I did on those stormy nights when the lightning played across the sky and the loud thunder roared.

"Alonzo," I said that morning as we waited for Aunt Carmen on the back steps, "we may need to take a few precautions in the next few days. I think it would be a good idea for you to send somebody down to close and lock the front gate."

"Certainly," the old man asked. "Trouble?"

"Possibly," I said with a nod. "There is a young woman sleeping upstairs who came here with me this morning. She has had some difficulties in the recent past, and has fled to La Rosa for sanctuary. I think it would also be a good idea to post a guard here at the rear of the house tonight. One of the younger vaqueros, perhaps."

Alonzo shook his head. "Not them. I will see to it myself."

"Then come inside the kitchen where it's warm and stand guard there. If anyone gets in, it will have to be through the back door. The front door is too solid. I don't really anticipate any problems, but I think it best to be prudent."

"*Sí.* I understand."

"You have a key to the house, don't you?"

The old man nodded. I stepped back in the kitchen just as my aunt entered the room from the other door dressed in a split riding skirt and a leather jacket. "I put your friend in the bedroom next to yours," she said.

"The one with the connecting door, I hope?" I asked with a leer, needling her just a little.

"And why not? You're a grown man, and this is your home. It's neither a convent nor a bordello. Do what you wish, but please be discreet and don't rub my nose in it."

"Of course not, dear," I said and kissed the top of her head and she was gone.

With her departure, a bone-weariness came over me. After pouring a couple more inches of bourbon into my cup, I climbed the familiar old stairs to the second floor of the house. I took a quick bath and piled into my bed wearing only my boxer shorts and a ragged old shirt. But despite my fatigue, it was some minutes before sleep came. Madeline Kimbell weighed on my mind. I liked her well enough. Indeed, we'd spent a very pleasant interlude together at the Weilbach after Ollie Marne's departure. Still, almost a decade in law enforcement had given me good instincts about people, and I was convinced that she was not telling me the whole story. Her reluctance to meet my eyes and the slight evasiveness I detected in her manner bespoke some guilt in her heart. I grinned to myself. No doubt. After all, she'd certainly shown me the evening before that she could be a *very* naughty girl. I put the matter out of my mind, and drifted off into an untroubled sleep, convinced that if intruders came, they would come in the dead of night. I was right.

CHAPTER FIVE

I awoke a few minutes before noon, and when I went down to the kitchen I found Helena setting the table. In its center sat a platter of beefsteaks. Around this were ranged dishes of fried potatoes and frijoles and squash, and I could smell corn bread cooking in the oven.

"I have made a cake for your return, Señor Virgil," she said.

"Thanks, Helena," I said and gave her another hug. She knew how much I loved her old-fashioned pound cake.

I poured myself a cup of coffee from the ever-present pot that heated on the back of the great stove. Madeline soon drifted into the kitchen and gave me a sleepy hello. A couple of minutes later my aunt came through the door removing her gloves and her hat. She washed her hands quickly at the sink and we sat down and began to eat without fanfare. When we'd finished, Aunt

Carmen said, "Why don't you take Madeline into town in the pickup? I've got a list of supplies we need."

Coldwell, the county seat of Matador County, was bleak and small, with a few fine homes that were set far back from the street among groves of palms that provided what little shade there was. The remaining residential areas ran the gamut from those struggling to maintain lower-middle-class respectability on down to what were little better than shanty towns. The courthouse was of brown brick, built in the Classical Revival style of the last century, but now it seemed tired and listless, like an old man with nothing left to do but wait for death. As we rounded the corner onto the square, two stake-bed trucks passed going in the opposite direction. Each held a dozen or more Mexicans. Most were middle-aged men, but a few women could also be seen as well.

"I guess the younger guys were all drafted," Madeline said.

"No," I said. "Practically all of them volunteered."

"Really?"

"Yep. They're very patriotic people. Damned if I know why, when you consider what a small slice of the pie they get."

She gazed out the window. On the sidewalks dark faces peered from beneath ratty, wide-brimmed hats.

"Gosh, they're everywhere," she said.

I laughed. "What do you expect? We're fifteen miles from Mexico. Anglos only make up ten percent of the population in this county."

"But how do they make a living?" she asked. "There's no industry. I mean, back home we've got the chemical plants and the refineries and —"

"Ranch work, farm work. And they pick fruit in season down in the lower valley. Anything they can find. Most of them own a little plot of ground and a few goats. They grow plenty of corn and frijoles, so they don't really need a lot of money, at least not to survive. Since the war started there's been some talk of Dow Chemical building a munitions plant here, and that would mean lots of good jobs. But I don't think it will ever happen."

"Why not?" she asked.

"Our politics are too corrupt."

I waved at several people I knew, then pulled up in front of the City Café. The menu, posted on a big piece of signboard just inside the front window, advertised the standard mixing of Southern and border cuisines unique to South Texas — tamales, enchiladas, and chili, along with hamburgers and steaks and country breakfasts. "Let's go get a Coke," I told her.

Inside, the café was narrow and dark with an old-fashioned ornamental ceiling of stamped metal. Over our heads a half dozen ceiling fans turned languidly in the warm air. We took a small table near the rear, and when the waitress came over we each ordered a Coca-Cola.

"You were telling me why the munitions plant won't come," Madeline said once our drinks were served.

"Ahh, yes. The munitions plant," I replied and gave her a cryptic smile. I lighted us each a cigarette, then asked, "What would you say if I informed you that you aren't really in the United States of America right now? Except in a technical sense, I mean."

She gave me a puzzled stare and shrugged.

"Oh, I'm well aware that we're sitting inside the U.S. border. But the truth of the matter is that you've returned to the past for a few days, and Matador County is a sort of medieval barony."

"Virgil, I haven't got the least idea what you're talking about," she said, a little annoyance creeping into her voice.

"Then let me explain how things work

82

down here. Remember all those Mexicans we saw coming into town? Well, they don't make much money. So when they're sick and the family needs a little help with medical treatments at the hospital in Laredo, or when there's a wedding coming up and there's no money for a fiesta, or when a son or daughter has an opportunity for a good job in San Antonio or Corpus Christi but the money for bus fare can't be found — when problems like those arise, they come out to the ranch and they talk to Tía Carmen. If their cause is deserving, and it almost always is, she writes out a little note for them to give to the county treasurer. They take him the note, and he gives them some money."

"But where does he get it?"

"From the county treasury," I said with an indulgent smile. "Where else would you expect a county treasurer to get money?"

"But isn't that —"

"Illegal? Of course it's illegal. Then when election time rolls around, all those same peons turn out and vote for Tía Carmen's favored candidates."

"And?"

I took a long pull of my Coke and regarded her thoughtfully for a few moments before I decided to go ahead and tell her the whole story. "Are you familiar with a thing called a poll tax receipt?" I finally asked.

"Of course."

"Aunt Carmen pays their poll taxes herself, and we keep the receipts in a safe out at the ranch."

"But that must amount to a couple of thousand dollars or more. Where does she get the money?"

"From the same county treasurer."

"Oh . . ."

"Then on election day, the sheriff and all the other county officials go out and round up voters and haul them to the polls. Using county cars and trucks, of course. And county gasoline, too. Then we hand out the poll tax receipts outside the various poling places. They go in and vote, and when they come back out they give us back the receipts to keep for them until the next election. We check them off a master list, and anybody that doesn't show up better have a good reason. For their trouble each one gets a half pint of tequila and the unspoken assurance that the next time trouble strikes, they'll be able to get help from the same source."

"You've actually participated in this kind of thing yourself?" she asked, staring at me with a shocked expression on her face.

"Certainly. I've helped out in practically every election since I was a kid."

She was aghast and I was amused.

"It's called the *patrón* system," I said. "The Spanish word translates to 'patron' in English, but it means a lot more than that. If you were around here long enough you'd hear Aunt Carmen called La Patróna. Or more grandly, La Patróna de La Rosa."

"Do all the other counties down here operate the same way?"

I nodded. "Yes. And we're all loosely allied with one another. That way we can present a united front and have more clout. With all the South Texas bosses and the various county machines acting together, we control over a hundred thousand reliable votes. When a statewide election is obviously going to be close, then we're in a powerful bargaining position. Beyond that, we all give a certain amount of fealty to a man over in Duval County named George Parr because he has influence in national matters. Not a great deal of influence, but some."

"But that's awful," she exclaimed. "I mean, it's contrary to the Constitution and everything we've always been taught in school about how —"

"Yes, it is, isn't it? But let me tell you what the alternative is. Back right after the turn of the century, the fruit and vegetable industry started up strong in the Rio Grande Valley, and real estate developers began attracting a lot of people from up north, people who wanted to escape the winters they have up there, and maybe put their retirement into a little orange grove or a few acres of grapefruit trees. For some reason most of these newcomers were from the upper Midwest. Now as it happens, the upper Midwest was settled largely by people from New England. Not New York or Pennsylvania or the other middle states, but New England. Old Puritan stock. White, English, and Protestant. They came down here and took a good look at the local political situation, and as you might expect, they were appalled. In their view something had to be done, so they began scurrying around, noisily trying to organize things, and before long reform movements began popping up all over the place. There was one in every South Texas county. They were going to clean it all up. Put an end to all the graft and corruption and make everything operate by the book.

"And I'll admit that some things might have been better if they'd won. Probably we would have had better and cheaper roads, because they would have been built by a quarter of the number of laborers we use. We might have better schools and better public buildings, too, because more of the money would have actually gone into the projects themselves instead of make-work patronage jobs for the peons to buy their votes to perpetuate the system. There was only one thing wrong with their approach. Know what it was?"

Madeline shook her head.

"They were completely unwilling to permit Mexicans to participate in the political process, either as officeholders or even as voters. And I mean even well-to-do and educated Mexicans. As you'd expect from the descendants of a bunch of prim New England schoolmarms, they were uplifters who saw Latin culture as inherently inferior to their own. If they'd gotten in the saddle they would have completely excluded the Mexican population for about three generations until they could have educated them and brought them up to their own exalted standards of civic behavior. And probably they would have preferred to make good Protestants out of them as well, if the truth was known.

"So you can see why they weren't able to

change the system. The average Mexican peon down here is illiterate, but don't ever think he's stupid. He knows when somebody is trying to sell him a load of chickenshit by passing it off as chicken salad. Now finish your Coke and let's go. I've got a pretty big load of stuff to pick up at the hardware store."

That evening about eight o'clock Madeline asked for another sleeping pill and then went to bed. Aunt Carmen and I stayed up for another hour. The night was chilly, and I'd built a small fire in the living room fireplace. I was immersed in the latest *Time* magazine while my aunt sat beside the fire in a deep leather wing chair, mending some shirts. At last she said softly, "She wouldn't make a good rancher's wife, Virgil. She's too delicate a flower. Besides, she'd get bored and lonely so easily out here, and we both know the consequences of that."

She was alluding to my own mother, a sweet but weak and neurotic woman from an old Austin family who never adapted to the solitude of La Rosa. A more sensible person would have simply insisted on an amiable divorce, or would have at least spent a part of each year in the city. But the era in which she lived and her intense

Catholicism made such a course unthinkable to her. Instead, her life became a long series of imaginary ailments, all of which required increasing doses of painkillers. My father finally gave up and let her drift off into a dream world, where she was relatively content. In my aunt's estimation, Madeline was cut from the same cloth. That she was probably right didn't make her meddling any less irritating.

"In the first place," I said, my mild annoyance clear in the tone of my voice, "I have no intention of getting that deeply involved with this girl. And in the second place, I don't need you to choreograph my life for me."

"I'm not trying to. I'm just stating the obvious. What's she running from, anyway?"

I filled her in on the details of the evening before, leaving out only the tryst the girl and I had enjoyed after Marne left.

"What do you plan to do with her?" she asked.

"We'll stay here another day or so until she calms down a little more, then I'm going to insist she talk to one of the Rangers."

"I feel sorry for the poor girl," Tía Carmen said. "She's gotten herself into a mess that she may not get out of alive."

"Why do you say that?" I asked with a

grin. "Do you see Santa Muerte hovering over her head?"

In those days many rural Mexicans and even some Anglos in South Texas believed that certain people could see Santa Muerte, the Angel of Death, near those who were fated to die soon. Some said that Saint Death was a white-robed skeleton. Others maintained that she appeared as a mischievous old woman, a sort of puckish jester, full of mockery and malice. Indeed, Tía Carmen claimed to be one of those rare individuals to whom she was visible. It was also a common belief that Santa Muerte ate the souls of the wicked when they died and then took them down into hell, where she delivered them to Satan by vomiting them up at his feet. Of course, I put absolutely no stock in such notions, but my aunt believed strongly in her occasional visions.

"You shouldn't joke about things you don't understand," she replied coldly.

"I suppose you're right," I conceded. "At any rate, I certainly didn't mean to hurt your feelings."

"I know that, but you'd do well to remember what Hamlet said: 'There are more things in heaven and earth, Horatio —' "

"Point taken," I said. "I'm willing to admit that science doesn't know it all. And I know you're an intelligent and well-read woman. It's just that . . ." I groped for the right words, not wanting to say something that would offend her.

She held up her hand to silence me. "Tell me something, Virgil. Do you trust your own eyes?"

"Usually, yes."

"Then why should you expect me to doubt mine? I first saw Santa Muerte two days before Grandmother Rosa died. It was out by the barn, just before sundown. She appeared as the skeleton that time, but I've also seen her as the Old Woman."

"How far away from her were you?" I asked.

She smiled grimly. "No more than ten feet. She turned and looked at me with those great, hollow eyes of hers, and made her teeth chatter like a monkey's teeth. She was laughing at me, Santa Muerte was, and it was a laugh that came straight from the pit of hell itself."

I felt a chill crawl up my spine despite myself. "And you've seen her at other times, too, you say?" I asked.

"Yes."

"Recently?"

"No," she admitted.

"Then see? That doesn't mean Madeline
—"

"Virgil, you must be careful until this is
all over. The inescapable truth is that you
are the sole future of this ranch and this
family. If anything happened to you, all our
years of struggle would be for nothing."

I nodded. "I will, dear. I promise. I'm well
aware that these are dangerous people she's
involved with. In fact, I'm beginning to wish
that I hadn't brought her here. It may have
been poor judgment on my part."

"No, you did the right thing," she said
firmly. "La Rosa is your home. We're safe
here."

"Maybe so, but I'm not taking things for
granted. I told Alonzo to keep watch tonight
in the kitchen."

"Alonzo? In the kitchen?"

I nodded. "Yeah. I heard him come in a
few minutes ago."

She shook her head in annoyance at
herself. "I'm getting old," she said, "and I
didn't hear a thing. I'd better go make him
a pot of coffee."

I knew that Alonzo would tilt one of the
kitchen chairs back against the wall and
doze lightly all night, stirring only to roll
another cigarette or refill his coffee cup
from the back of the stove. His sense of

hearing was still phenomenal and his mind was like an alarm set to awake at even the faintest noise.

"I think I'll turn in," I said.

I rose, stretched, and kissed my aunt good night as she headed toward the kitchen, then climbed the stairs and went into my bedroom. Like the kitchen, it was unchanged since the days of my youth. Both my Parker 16-gauge shotgun and the Winchester lever-action .30-30 rifle with which I'd killed my first deer still hung on the gun rack; the bookcase bulged with my collection of Tom Swift and Rover Boys books; and the two cigar boxes full of Indian arrowheads I'd found at various places around the ranch sat atop the chest of drawers. I pulled one of the books from the bookcase and looked at it for a moment. *Tom Swift and His Motorcycle.* I remembered my father buying it for me in San Antonio amid the armistice celebration that marked the end of the First World War. I'd been ten years old at the time, and motorcycles were still rare enough to be considered the pinnacle of adventure. What was the pinnacle of adventure for me now? I wondered. Bourbon and blondes? No, redheads, I corrected myself.

"I'd probably be better off with a motorcycle," I muttered. I pulled off my boots, then opened the door between the two rooms. Madeline lay sprawled atop the covers in a thin nightgown, her tender, milky white body enticing in the moonlight. I tiptoed quietly into the room and carefully covered her against the cool night air. She barely stirred.

Back in my own room I quickly undressed and slipped between the covers, first carefully placing my .38 Super on the bedside stand.

CHAPTER SIX

Hours later, after it was all over, I kicked myself inwardly for being so slow to react. I was dreaming one of those silly dreams I suppose everybody has at one time or another, a dream where you've been mistaken for someone else, and no matter how hard you protest, no one believes you. In this dream I was the guest of honor at the banquet hall of some long-ago castle, being feted by all the nobles of the kingdom. But I knew I didn't belong there. I was nothing but a simple jester from another country who'd been mistaken for a famous knight. At the peak of the festivities there came a pounding at the door to the banquet hall, and I froze, terrified in the certain knowledge that whoever was on the other side of that door had come to expose me as an imposter. Then I was awake in my own room at La Rosa, convinced for a moment that the knock had actually come from my own hall door. Quickly I checked the radium dial on my watch. It was a few minutes after one o'clock. Then my blood ran cold as I realized the noise had been the sound of gunfire from downstairs.

I slid from bed and grabbed my Colt from the bedside table. Hurrying across the room, I opened the hall door a couple of inches. One of the small but important benefits of having electricity at the ranch was the tiny night-light my aunt always left burning overhead. In its dim glow I could see the silhouette of a man who had just climbed the stairs and now stood on the landing. He held a pistol in one hand, and he was staring so intently at something at the far end of the hallway that he hadn't noticed that my door had opened.

I was just raising my automatic when an enormous blast from somewhere behind the door almost deafened me. The man dropped the gun and grabbed for his belly, then fell forward onto his hands and knees. A second later my aunt glided past me in her night-gown, my father's L.C. Smith double-barrel shotgun held firmly in her hands. The kneeling man looked up with his mouth gaping open and tried to speak. Whatever he had on his mind remained unsaid, because the last thing he ever saw was the tiny, implacable old lady who threw the gun deftly to her shoulder and blew his head to pieces from a distance of no more than three feet.

This second blast left me almost completely deaf. I stepped out into the hall behind my aunt. Madeline's door burst open and she was there beside me in her robe, her hand over her mouth and her eyes wide with fear.

"It's okay," I said, my voice tinny and distant in my ears. Then I remembered Alonzo and the gunfire that had come from below. I took my aunt by the shoulders and turned her around. Her eyes were blazing, and she was clearly ready to shoot somebody else if fate gave her the chance.

"Alonzo," I told her. "I've got to see about Alonzo."

She didn't react.

"Go in your room and reload," I ordered. "You and Madeline both. And stay there until I come to get you."

The girl understood. Showing more presence of mind than I would have expected from her, she took Aunt Carmen by the arm and began to pull her toward the other end of the hall. My aunt shook herself loose from Madeline's grip, her eyes still full of fire. "Go in your room and reload," I said again. "Then stay there."

This time she understood. Madeline grabbed her arm once again and the two of them scurried down the hall toward her doorway. I worked my way around the bloody mess on the landing and carefully descended the stairs. I could see the glow of the kerosene lamp coming from the kitchen. Slowly I approached the kitchen door, my automatic ready, its safety off. Step by careful step I entered the silent room. The outside door was shattered beyond repair where the intruders had burst in. Alonzo lay in front of the stove, his belly covered in blood, his old Colt single action still clutched in his hand. On the other side of the room a second gunman lay sprawled on his back. I approached the man carefully, my pistol aimed at the center of his chest. When I got close enough I saw that such a precaution was unnecessary. His mouth was slack and his eyes glazed, and the .45-caliber hole in the center of his forehead told me he was as dead as he was ever going to be.

I realized my hearing was returning when I heard a faint groan behind me. I turned to see Alonzo trying to pull himself up into a sitting position. Just then a yell came from outside the house. "Señor Virgil! Señor Virgil!" It was Pablo, the one-eyed vaquero.

"Come on in!" I called out.

Pablo appeared in the kitchen doorway, his good eye shining bright in the lamplight. "I need your handcuffs, Señor Virgil," he said in Spanish. "There is a bandito lying on the walk where I clubbed him down, but he is beginning to stir. We must cuff him quickly if we wish to have no further trouble from him."

Five minutes later the intruder was secured and Alonzo sat in one of the kitchen chairs, utterly mortified that Tía Carmen should see him shirtless. The bullet had cut a six-inch tunnel through the flesh of the lower left side of his chest, missing his ribs completely. We found two bullet holes in the wallpaper just above the sink.

"I do not know why I fell," Alonzo said morosely. "I do not believe it was the wound since I did not even feel it until I awakened. But for some reason I fell backwards and hit my head terribly on the great cookstove. It must have knocked me unconscious."

"The dead man upstairs may have knocked you down in his rush," I said. "He was a big bastard."

"*Sí*. That is possible. I was intent upon the bandito I killed."

"Exactly what happened?" I asked.

"I had just lighted a cigarette when the door seemed to explode inward. I pulled my *pistola,* and I thought I shot the first man to come through the doorway, but I could have been mistaken. It may have been the second. Then I fell and that is all I remember."

"We may never know the precise details," I said.

"*Sí.* It is enough that they were stopped, though I think that if I had been younger I could have done a better job of it."

"Who couldn't?" my aunt asked.

"*Sí,* Tía Carmen," he agreed sadly. "We are all growing older. It is time for Señor Virgil to come home and help us take care of things."

"Damn," I muttered. "What is this? A conspiracy?"

I went over to the cabinet and rummaged around until I found a bottle of tequila. After I'd pulled the cork and taken a swig myself, I handed it to the old man. He gave me a nod of thanks and then turned the bottle up to his mouth. By then my aunt had filled a wash pan with water she'd heated on the stove. "I've got to clean this wound, Alonzo," she said. "Then I can pack it with sulfa powder."

"*Sí,* Tía Carmen," he said placidly. "Do

whatever you feel is necessary."

"Do you want me to send for Helena?" I asked.

He shook his head. "Let her sleep. It would only fret her."

Just then Pablo and one of the other vaqueros appeared in the doorway. "What do you wish us to do with the bandito, Señor Virgil?" he asked.

I thought for a minute. "Take him out to the barn. I'll want to talk to him."

"*Sí,*" Pablo said.

"Pablo?" Alonzo called out from where he sat.

"*Sí,* Alonzo. What is it?"

Alonzo's smile was cold and cruel. "It is a chilly night. Make us a fire in the old metal tub in the barn."

The inside of the barn was lighted by a pair of kerosene lanterns. Along one wall ranged a half dozen stalls built of rough planking. The intruder was tied to one of these, his arms spread out as though he were being crucified, his mouth securely gagged with a wadded-up bandanna held in place by a short piece of rope. The floor of the barn was dirt, and in its center sat a galvanized tub filled with mesquite knots that burned briskly. A La Rosa branding iron and a long, narrow steel rod lay in the tub, their ends beginning to glow cherry red. The three old men lounged about, smoking hand-rolled cigarettes and making jests. Their faces were merry and their eyes bright. One-eyed Pablo seemed particularly full of gleeful malevolence. They spoke in English for the benefit of their captive. I stood for a few moments at the doorway and listened.

"What will Alonzo do with this man?" one asked.

"I think he intends to burn his deek off with the branding iron," said another.

Pablo shook his head. "No, I think he has other things in mind."

"Do you know something?"

"Sí," Pablo said with a nod. "I once heard a story of a king who lived long ago. In England, I think it was. For political reasons it became necessary for some of his nobles to murder him. Yet it was also necessary that his body show no signs of violence."

"What did they do?"

"They inserted a hollow reed into his back passage and then ran a red-hot iron through the reed into his inner parts."

"Aheee . . ." one man grimaced mockingly.

"Sí," Pablo agreed. "They were ignorant of the position of the various organs of the

102

body, and the rod had to be reheated and passed through the reed many times before he expired."

"Did this truly happen?" someone asked.

"*Sí,*" Pablo said. "I once asked Padre O'Neal at the church in town, and he said the story was true and this unfortunate king had been named Eduardo."

"But why did they kill him? After all, he was their king."

"He was a sodomite," Pablo said. "One who was very careless, and his activities had become a great embarrassment to the realm. Years ago I told this story to Alonzo, and he was very impressed. I think perhaps he has the same treatment in mind for this gentleman. You see? There is a rod heating alongside the branding iron."

"Then why is the branding iron being heated also?"

Pablo shrugged. "Who knows? Perhaps he will do both. Burn his deek off first, and then minister to his insides."

"That is possible," one of the others said with a sage nod. "Alonzo is a thorough man."

I stepped into the barn.

"Ahhh," Pablo exclaimed happily. "Here is Señor Virgil. Perhaps he will have some ideas of his own."

"*Sí,*" one of the others agreed. "He was a mischievous little *niño,* and everyone knows one's nature does not change."

I smiled and winked at the old men, then walked over to where the intruder struggled against his bonds, his eyes bulging with pure terror. He was a man of medium height and weight, with well-barbered brown hair and what had been a nice gray wool suit just a few hours earlier. I put his age in the neighborhood of forty. On his feet he wore a pair of expensive alligator-skin shoes. A city boy, one who was far out of his element no matter how competent he was in New Orleans or Houston or wherever he'd come from. I stood there for a few silent moments, staring directly into his eyes, then reached up and jerked the gag roughly from his mouth. He began babbling wildly.

"Shut up!" I ordered and slapped his face.

My command had no impact on the torrent of gibberish. I slapped him twice more with the same lack of effect. Then I reached down and pulled the branding iron from the bucket and held it a few inches from the man's nose, its tip glowing fiercely in the barn's dim light. His eyes riveted instantly on the iron and his chattering gradually ceased.

"That's good," I said with a satisfied nod

and tossed the iron back in the bucket.

"You can't let them burn my guts out, mister," he said in a quavering voice, the first truly coherent words he'd uttered.

I smiled coldly. "Oh, yes, I can."

Alonzo appeared in the doorway, then walked on into the barn, moving a little stiffly. He wore one of my flannel shirts, and in his right hand he carried a fresh bottle of tequila. He handed the bottle to Pablo, who drank and then passed it around.

"What do we do with this man?" Alonzo asked me.

"That's up to him," I said. "I want to know who sent him down here. The more he talks the less he has to suffer."

"Then you must tell Señor Virgil what he wishes to know," Alonzo said, fixing the man firmly with his sad brown eyes.

"What's your name?" I asked.

"Lew Ralls."

"Where you from, Lew?"

"South Louisiana."

"Who sent you?" I asked.

The intruder shook his head wildly. "I can't —"

Despite his injury, Alonzo reached down with snakelike agility and jerked the branding iron once again from the bucket. Without fanfare he pressed it to the intruder's thigh a few inches above the knee. It burned through his pants instantly, then there was a faint sizzle as it touched the flesh beneath. The man's body arched forward, the cords in his neck standing out, his eyes bulging. Then he uttered a high-pitched scream that seemed to go on forever. When it ended at last his head fell forward on his chest.

"I believe he has fainted," Pablo said.

"*Sí,*" Alonzo replied. "But he will recover."

"Somebody get a bucket of water," I said.

Pablo took a wooden bucket from the wall where it hung by a peg and stepped outside to the hand pump. A few seconds later he was back.

"Throw it in his face," I said. "That always works in the movies. Maybe it'll turn the trick here."

Pablo doused the man with the water. It proved to be as effective in real life as it was on film. I gave him a few seconds to get his wits back, then I asked, "Are you convinced that we mean business?"

"You're crazy," the intruder gasped. "You can't get away with this."

I slapped him once again then grabbed a huge hank of his hair and twisted his head upward until we were eye to eye. "I can do anything I want to out here, you fool," I snarled. "My family runs this county. The sheriff wouldn't even think of setting foot on this ranch without calling first. I could drive into town and tell him I'd fed you to the snapping turtles down in the river, and he wouldn't give a damn because he knows where his bread gets buttered. Now talk. Who sent you?"

The man's eyes were full of terror. "Carlo Tresca," he finally whispered.

"Who? Speak up."

"Carlo Tresca," he managed.

The name was distantly familiar to me, but I couldn't place where I'd heard it. "Who the hell is Carlo Tresca?" I asked.

"He works for Angelo Scorpino."

Then I remembered where I'd heard Tresca's name.

The year before I'd teamed up with a Louisiana State Police lieutenant while investigating an interstate livestock-theft ring. The man had been a sturdy, aging Creole with an impeccable reputation for honesty, and he knew more about the structure of organized crime along the Gulf Coast than anyone I'd ever met. According to him, Scorpino had been the crime syndicate boss of New Orleans since the early days of Prohibition. Short, squat, and ugly, with a vicious temper, Scorpino's cruelty was noteworthy even in the ruthless criminal world where he lived and reigned. Thus his nickname: the Scorpion Angel. I also remembered that my friend had identified Tresca as one of the junior men in Scorpino's organization, but he'd pegged him as an up-and-comer, a young fellow full of ambition.

"So you work for Scorpino?" I asked.

The man shook his head. "Not steady. I just do special jobs for them every now and then."

"How about your friends. Either one of them on Scorpino's payroll?"

"Not regular."

"So it was Tresca who contracted you for this job?"

"Yeah."

"Why did they pick you rather than some of their own people?"

"I guess they think we're good at what we do."

"Not any more you're not," I said with a cold laugh. "Why do they want the girl dead, anyway?"

"Mister, they didn't tell me and I didn't ask."

"Alonzo, get the iron again."

The old vaquero reached down and pulled the branding iron from the bucket.

"I know you're afraid of Scorpino," I said.

"And I certainly understand why, but you need to consider that I'm here now, and he isn't."

The man's teeth chattered and his voice quavered. "For God's sake, you gotta believe me, mister. I can't tell you a thing more than I already have."

I regarded him speculatively for a few moments. "What do you think, Alonzo?" I asked.

Alonzo motioned for the tequila bottle, then pulled the cork and drank, all the while staring into the intruder's eyes. At last he nodded and said, "I believe this man is telling the truth, Señor Virgil."

"I think so, too," I said in agreement. "It fits what I know of the girl's problems. Besides, I don't believe he's smart enough to dream up a story like this." I turned to Ralls and asked, "How much did they pay you and the others?"

"Two grand apiece."

"Where's your car?"

"We couldn't get in the gate, so we left it there and walked down to the house."

I looked down. The man's fancy alligator shoes were scuffed and the cuffs of his pants were covered in dust. Just then my aunt appeared in the barn's doorway. "Well?" she asked.

"According to this guy, they were sent by some hoods down in New Orleans."

"New Orleans?"

"Right," I said. "Supposedly that Salisbury guy I told you about is fronting for somebody down there."

"I see," she said. "So what do you think we should do now?"

I considered for a few moments. It would be easy enough for three bodies to vanish. I hadn't been joking when I told Ralls the Rio Grande turtles were always hungry. As for their car, Pablo's nephew ran a body shop in Laredo, a place where stolen vehicles sometimes went in one color and came out another, their engine numbers changed, their registration papers brand new and beautifully forged. But to take that course meant murder. Even though Ralls was undoubtedly a killer himself, I didn't find the idea of slaughtering a helpless man appealing.

"Call the law," I told her. "Then have somebody go up and unlock the gate."

CHAPTER SEVEN

The law arrived thirty minutes later in the person of Matador County Sheriff Dalton Polk. He was a tall, thin fellow in his midfifties, with a weathered face and the tired, world-weary eyes of a man who'd already seen it all and expected to again. Dressed in khakis and a fine western hat, he carried a worn old Smith & Wesson .44 in a battered leather holster as a sort of afterthought. He was the first member of his family in living memory to earn his living through anything other than the hardest of physical labor, and his initial instinct in any situation was to protect his job. It also meant that he was a willing tool of the county political machine, as adept at rounding up Mexican voters on election day as he was at tracking down the occasional fugitive that invaded his baili-wick. Of both necessity and gratitude, he acknowledged Tía Carmen's position as virtual dictator of the county. Indeed, it had been she and my father who had approached him twenty years earlier and induced him to run for the office with their backing. He won overwhelmingly, of course, just as he'd done in every election since. Nevertheless, he was a reasonably competent officer, one who preferred diplomacy to force as a means of keeping the peace. Strong-arm he left to his three deputies, chief of whom was the man he brought with him that night, my old nemesis from high school, Stubb Martindale.

Stubb was now a stocky, iron-hard man whose face held a pair of dark, smoldering eyes and a perpetually sour smirk. And he still clung to his bullying ways. He didn't like Mexicans and lorded it over them every chance he got. But his prejudice didn't keep him from extracting frequent favors from the handful of bar girls in town who supplemented their wages by occasionally turning tricks. Even then, he was needlessly rough with them and verbally contemptuous of their race.

The man loathed me thoroughly, and not just because of the beating I'd given him when we were kids. Three years earlier when I was still with the U.S. Marshal's Service, Pablo had taken the truck into town to get some supplies for the ranch, just as he often did. On the way home he stopped at a cantina on the edge of town to buy a case of beer. Martindale accosted him in the bar's parking lot and slapped him around on the bogus pretext that he was drunk and disorderly. Though there was no arrest, the old man's pride had been deeply wounded.

Alonzo learned of the incident and came to me the next time I was home. A couple of nights later, another deputy marshal and I took Stubb for a midnight ride a few miles out into the brush, where we gave him a sound drubbing along with a lecture on the proper treatment of La Rosa vaqueros. Since then none of our people had had any trouble from the man. Twice since the incident I'd spoken to Aunt Carmen about getting him removed from his job, but for reasons of her own she'd put me off.

I greeted them at the front door. Polk shook hands and Martindale gave me a look that was pure venom. I led them up the stairs.

"Damn," Polk said calmly as he surveyed the carnage on the landing. "And who killed him?"

"I did," my aunt replied calmly. "It was me or him."

Polk squatted down and retrieved the intruder's weapon.

"I don't doubt that," he said, handing me a heavy revolver. "Bastard was carrying one of them new .357 Magnums that come out a few years back. Damn thing will shoot through an engine block."

He rose to his feet. "And you said there's another one dead in the kitchen?" he asked.

"Right."

"Let's have a look at him," he said.

I led him downstairs and into the kitchen. He pushed his hat back on his head as he squatted down to peer at the bullet hole in the man's forehead. "Good shooting," he said. "Who plugged this one?"

"One of the vaqueros," I replied casually.

"Which one?"

Neither my aunt nor I said anything. After a few seconds Polk nodded. "I see," he said. "It wouldn't have been that old ghost who lives out here, would it? What's his name? Alfredo?"

"I don't believe in ghosts, Sheriff," I said.

Martindale giggled.

"Shut up, Stubb," Polk said without rancor. "Make yourself useful. Go out to the car and get that flash camera, then take a couple of pictures of each body so we'll have something we can call crime scene photos. And I'd like to talk to the one that survived. You said he was in the barn, is that right?"

I nodded, and as soon as Martindale left the room I led Polk through the kitchen door. "Is that what you keep Stubb on the payroll for?" I asked as we walked across the backyard. "To take pictures?"

"Well, that's one thing he can do. He's awful proud of that camera."

"You ought to get rid of him."

"Why?" he asked rhetorically.

"He's a disgrace to law enforcement."

Polk sighed. "Your aunt got on my butt about that deal with old Pablo, but she didn't tell me I had to fire him. I did have a talk with him, though, and told him to let up on the Mexicans."

"And?"

"He has."

"Good, but he needs to go. One of these days he's going to hurt somebody bad if he keeps carrying a gun and a badge."

"Well, Virgil, now that we're on the subject of abuse of authority, that beating you and that other federal boy gave him wasn't exactly legal either."

"So what?" I asked. "Half of what we do down here in South Texas isn't legal, strictly speaking. That includes stuffing ballot boxes, and you've done your share of that."

"I don't need you to remind me," he said. "But I kept him on because his daddy was half paralyzed from his last stroke, and the boy was his only means of support."

"The old man's dead now, so let him go."

"Stubb ain't all bad. He did a fine job of taking care of the old fellow, and loyalty like that is worth something."

"Then let him get his reward in heaven. You don't owe it to him, and neither does this county."

He shook his head. "If Tía Carmen tells me to fire him, then I will. But until she gives me that direct order, I'm going to leave him be and keep after him about how he treats Mexicans."

"Look, Dalton," I said, making my voice as sincere as I could, "I'm not asking for any special treatment for my people, and you know that. If one of them is drunk and out of line, then any officer in this county is free to handle it. But I expect it to be done in a civilized manner because they're all good men, drunk or sober. Besides, nobody ought to have to eat shit off some pecker-wood deputy just because of the color of his skin."

He stopped walking and turned to look at me. "That's mighty decent of you, Virgil," he said. "Mighty selective, too. There's many a colored man from the Brazos River all the way back to Virginia who'd love to hear a white man say something like that, but I don't notice you standing up for them."

I shook my head in exasperation. "I can't fix the world, Dalton," I said. "But I can take care of my little corner of it. And maybe I'm just a little sensitive on this particular subject because I'm part Mexican myself. You did know that, didn't you?"

"Sure I did," he replied. "And personally, I like Mexicans. I ain't never understood why guys like Stubb —"

"One other thing. I want you to know that I'm moving back home in a few weeks to help run this ranch. And in the coming years, I'll be getting more involved in the political side of things, too."

"I hear you, Virgil," he said tiredly. "But for now he stays."

We dropped the subject and walked on out to the barn. Inside, three of the old men still stood guard over the intruder, but Alonzo was nowhere to be seen. Polk ambled over and greeted them as if they were long-lost brothers, inquiring about wives and children and grandchildren and schmoozing with a practiced ease. When this dismal little ritual was finished at last, he turned to examine the man tied to the wall. "Looks like he burned his leg," he said to no one in particular.

"*Sí,* Señor Sheriff," Pablo said. "He fell on the branding iron."

"I reckon that's why you strapped him to the fence, then," Polk said. "So he wouldn't fall no more, I mean."

"*Sí,*" came the laconic reply.

"You got to help me, Sheriff," the man wailed. "They said they were gonna burn out my guts."

Polk ignored him. "Well, what do you want me to do?" he asked me. "I can charge him with attempted murder if that suits your fancy. For that matter, he's guilty of second degree murder already."

"What?" the man gasped.

"How's that?" I asked.

"Little-known quirk of Texas law," Polk explained. "If you and your buddy go out to commit an armed robbery, and it blows up in your face and he gets killed, then you're guilty of his death. Life sentence is the maximum penalty on second degree. And in this county? Breaking in on you folks?" He shook his head. "Ain't no way in hell he'll avoid getting it."

"God help!" the intruder exclaimed. "What are you trying to do to me? I want a

118

lawyer."

Polk paid him no heed. "What's this mess all about, Virgil?" he asked.

I pulled him aside and quickly gave him an abbreviated version of Madeline's story and the attack in San Gabriel. When I'd finished he asked, "You say the boy that forced his way into your room works for Milam Walsh, huh?"

I nodded. "Yeah. You know Walsh?"

"No, but I've heard a lot about him, and none of it was good."

"Same here."

"What do you plan to do now?" he asked.

"I need to get Madeline away from La Rosa. Otherwise they'll just send somebody else out here to try again."

"They may do that anyway, even if you're gone."

I shook my head. "I don't think so."

"Why not?"

"Because I'm going to call Salisbury as soon as I can and set up a meeting with him in a couple of days. That's the only way to work this thing out."

"How's that gonna help?"

"It will at least keep his goons away from the ranch and my people."

"But why Salisbury?" he asked. "I mean, you said this guy here claimed somebody named Tresca was behind it all."

I shook my head. "Tresca works for Angelo Scorpino. Madeline says the talk is that Salisbury is up here trying to get a foot into the gambling rackets down on the coast for somebody in New Orleans. That has to be Scorpino."

"But how does Walsh factor into the deal?"

"He doesn't," I said. "Except that Sam and Rosario Maceo over in Galveston have been paying him off for years to let their clubs in Jefferson County operate. And so has anybody else who wanted to run a gambling joint."

"So you don't think he's hooked up with this Salisbury guy?"

"I doubt it," I replied with a shake of my head. "That's not Walsh's style. If there's a move on to displace the Maceos, he'll just stand back well out of the way of any falling bodies, and then collect his tithe from the winner after the smoke clears."

"I see," he said with a troubled frown. "But you shouldn't go see this Salisbury all by yourself. I mean, me and you have had our disagreements over the years, but I wouldn't want to see nothing happen —"

I gave him a pat on the arm and a reassuring smile. "I'm not going alone. I plan to take Jim Rutherford with me, or maybe one of the Rangers."

"Okay," he said doubtfully. "I guess you know what you're doing. But what do you want me to do about this mess here?"

I shrugged. "I'd like for it to stay out of the papers, if possible. You got any ideas how we can handle that?"

He stood in thought for a moment, then nodded. "I think we can manage to keep it quiet unless there's a jury trial. Let's just suppose this old boy here could be induced to plead guilty to the lesser charge of unlawful entry of a domicile. That'll get him five years, which is pretty good, considering the alternative is fifty to life. He'll probably be howling for a lawyer even before we get him to the jail, so I'll call Frank Mendoza and have him explain the realities of life down here in South Texas. I think Frank can make him see the light."

"Good," I said with a nod. Mendoza was a capable attorney from Zapata County, which lay just to the north. The descendant of an old aristocratic land grant family, he had a thriving law practice that took him into courtrooms all over South Texas. He was also something of a kingpin in the political apparatus, one who wasn't given to loose talk.

"I think it's our best course," he agreed.

"Then we can get the judge to convene court kinda private-like and accept his plea tomorrow or the next day. After that I can have him in the pen in less than a week. That way we can keep it all nice and quiet, no stories in the newspapers or anything like that."

"Will the DA go along with it?"

He gave me a smile that was full of sad irony. "Hell, Virgil. You know as well as I do that the DA will go along with just about anything Tía Carmen tells him to go along with, the same as me."

"Then call Frank," I said.

CHAPTER EIGHT

The sheriff hauled Lew Ralls away in handcuffs, and I don't think I ever saw a man happier to get into a nice warm cop car. The funeral home in town sent its hearse out to collect the two bodies. After everybody left we all went to work cleaning up the mess. The upstairs landing was the worst. It seemed as though the man had bled at least a gallon onto the floor. By the time we'd finished the sun was up, and we were completely worn out.

Helena made breakfast. Before we all sat down to eat I got the bourbon bottle out of the cabinet and spiked everyone's coffee. Nobody objected. I half drained mine in one pull, then splashed a couple more inches in my cup. I looked across the table at my aunt. Her age and the night's events told on her face. She looked old and tired.

"How are you doing, sweetheart?" I asked her tenderly.

She sighed and shook her head. "I've felt better and I've felt worse. I'll get by."

"I mean about . . ." I let my voice taper off, not knowing how to say it.

"You mean that son of a bitch I shot? Don't you waste a minute worrying about that."

"You're sure about that?"

She regarded me with a smile that bordered on contempt. "You don't think that's the first man I ever killed, do you, Virgil?"

Nothing she could have said would have surprised me more. I could only shrug in confusion while Madeline gaped.

My aunt calmly sipped her cup and watched the two of us with amusement. "I was only sixteen at the time," she finally said. "It was the summer of 1888, and he was a drunken cowboy, an Anglo with a reputation for meanness. He was after something I was determined to keep a little while longer, so he just decided to take it. I shot him in the throat with a little derringer my daddy had given me. It didn't bother me then, and it doesn't bother me now."

"My God!" I said. "Sixteen? I had no idea."

"No reason for you to. We never talked about it." She smiled at Madeline. "The world only appears civilized, dear," she said.

"Underneath the surface it's all savagery, and if you don't fight back, you'll go under."

Obviously not knowing how else to respond, Madeline gave her a grave nod. My aunt turned back to me. "What now?" she asked.

The previous hours had caught up with me, and I realized I was starving. I began to eat in earnest, talking between bites. "The first thing I want to do is get a carpenter out from town and have the kitchen door replaced. And I want a door that's as strong and easily secured as the front door. We should have done that a long time ago."

"I'll take care of that myself," she said.

"Today," I insisted.

"Done. Then what?"

"Madeline and I are going to leave. I want to get her away from La Rosa. If she stays here they'll just try again."

"I see. Where do you plan to go?"

"Press Rafferty's place."

Rafferty was an old family friend who'd fought with my father in the Spanish-American War. He lived in a wooded, remote section of the Neches River bottom a few miles east of Palestine in East Texas, an area whose inhabitants were noted for their clannishness and insularity. If there was anywhere in the state the girl would be safe, it

125

was with Press and his daughter.

"I also intend to get hold of Charlie Grist and probably a guy I know down in the attorney general's office. I plan to call Salisbury, too. I'm going to do my best to convince him that he doesn't want to send anybody else out here. And I guess we better set up a schedule where our people can guard the house in shifts. At least for a while."

She shook her head. "They were up all night, Virgil. And they're getting old, like me. I think I'll call some of our friends in other counties and see about having some guards sent over."

"George Parr?" I asked with a smile.

She nodded. "Why not? I figure he owes us."

"Just make sure he sends people who won't try to lord it over our own vaqueros. Some of his deputies can be pretty high-handed."

"He'll know better than that," she said tersely. "But I'll mention it just the same. When are you leaving?"

"Late this afternoon. I've got to get some sleep first."

"Fine. I'll make arrangements for the carpenters to come about three so their hammering won't keep you awake. How does that sound?"

"Lovely. Can I have a couple more eggs?"

My phone calls took over an hour. No one knew where Charlie Grist could be found, but I left a message for him to call me at a half dozen of his usual haunts. My friend in the AG's office was also out of pocket. But Salisbury, the man I'd expected to be the most difficult to find, answered on the third ring when I called the Grotto Club in Beaumont.

"This is Virgil Tucker," I said.

I'll give him one thing: he had presence of mind. There was barely a pause before he replied with a noncommittal, "Yes?"

"I'm about to tell you several things you need to know, and I suggest you keep calm and listen. It's for our mutual benefit."

Once again there was the barest of pauses. "Go ahead."

"Two of your men are dead and one is on his way to prison."

"I don't —"

"Also you should be aware that Madeline Kimbell is no longer at my ranch, and that my family is being guarded around the clock by commissioned law enforcement officers. Don't send anybody else down here. If you do, you're going to be stepping into something you don't have the capacity to appreciate."

"That's all fascinating, but what —"

"Surely you know somebody who's familiar with the political situation in South Texas," I said. "Get them to brief you."

"I'll look into it," he replied. By this time he was beginning to sound a little wary. For some reason hoods always think they have a monopoly on power and intimidation.

"I'm willing to give you my word that I can guarantee the girl's silence in the future, and anybody who knows me will tell you that my word is good. In return I want your assurance that she and my family will be left alone."

There came a long pause. Finally he spoke. "Well, that would be an interesting proposition if I really knew anything about —"

"You can cut the bullshit, Salisbury. I'll see you in a couple of days."

I hung up and found myself covered in sweat. I'd walked a fine line during our conversation. On one hand, I had to sound firm and tough enough to convince him that I meant business about his thugs staying away from the ranch, while on the other hand I had to appear naive enough to make him think I'd be willing to accept his assurances. I fervently hoped I'd pulled it off. I desperately needed a little breathing room.

We left a few minutes before four that afternoon. Two guards were already posted at the gate, one Anglo and one Mexican, stone-faced, khaki-clad men in their forties who came armed with well-worn Winchester rifles and big revolvers. I stopped and spoke with them for a moment and learned that they were from Starr County. I also learned that a pair of deputies each from Hidalgo and Webb counties were on their way. I thanked them and drove off, then a few hundred yards down the road it hit me how absurd a system it was that my aunt could just pick up the phone and procure public employees to act as private guards as though she were ordering something from the Sears catalog. It was too much; I started laughing and I laughed and laughed until Madeline finally asked, "What on earth is wrong with you, Virgil?"

"Sorry," I muttered and reached over to pat her hand. "Don't worry about it. I was having myself a little fit to break the tension of the last couple of days."

We rode along in silence for a few minutes, then she asked, "You don't like that Martindale fellow, do you?"

"No, I sure don't," I replied, glancing over at her once again. "Is it that obvious?"

She gave me a nod. "What do you have against him?"

I gave her a quick rundown on Stubb. "He's a bully and sadist," I said in conclusion. "And one of these days he's going to really hurt somebody."

"Are there many others like him? People who hate Mexicans, I mean?"

I shook my head. "No, but most of the Anglos subscribe to the idea that Mexicans are an inferior people. Add to that the class system that's in effect in the whole Spanish-speaking world and then you've got something very complex. Take Tía Carmen. She loves the families who live on the ranch. Yet when we got electricity out here she never considered putting it in the vaqueros' homes or the bunk house. At least not until I mentioned it, then she was fine with the idea."

"But why didn't she think about it? I mean, she's part Mexican herself."

"Upper-class Mexican," I said. "Aristocrats. It simply never entered her mind that Alonzo and Helena would sleep better at night in these awful summers we have here if they had an electric fan. But go into Mexico and see how the hands on the big ranches over there live. It's both a class problem and a race problem, and I don't know the answer."

My voice tapered off and I stared down the road, brooding a little, as the Ford's tires sang over the pavement.

"This part of the state is like a completely different country," Madeline said.

"More like a different planet," I said bitterly.

We made good time to San Antonio, but a few miles north of town on the road to Austin we got caught in one of those endless military convoys that were the bane of travel during the war years. At 9:00 P.M. I decided to find some place to spend the night. Finally, just outside San Marcos, I saw a sign that advertised an all-night truck stop café and a tourist court. I turned off the main road, then swung in behind an abandoned filling station and cut my lights.

"What are you doing?" Madeline asked.

"Checking to see if we're being tailed. I don't think we are, but still . . ."

I waited ten minutes, during which time no cars followed us. Then I cranked the engine, and we pulled in at the tourist court a few minutes later just as the night man was closing the office. Three dollars and we had the key to a cabin near the back of the lot where the car couldn't be seen from the road. "We're leaving early in the morning," I told him.

"Fine," he said. "The office opens at seven. If nobody's here just drop the key in the mail slot."

The room was clean with a big double bed and a bathroom with a deep, claw-footed tub. "Hungry?" I asked once we'd dumped our bags at the foot of the bed.

She nodded. "Do you think we've been followed?"

"No," I said, shaking my head. "I checked the rearview mirror pretty regularly since we left the ranch. But if I'm wrong, they'll come at us in the night, and there's not a damn thing we can do about it. So we might as well get a good night's sleep and try not to worry. I figure that if we're still alive in the morning we're in the clear. I also figure this Salisbury guy has enough sense to wait to hear what I have to say. But still, I wish you'd give me the whole damn story."

"I've told you everything, Virgil," she said. Her tone of voice was sincere but her eyes avoided mine.

"Bullshit," I said. "There's more to this business and you know it. I've been aware of that since the first night up in San Gabriel."

I stared at her for a long while. She tried to hold my gaze, but her eyes faltered and she dropped her gaze to the floor. "I wish you wouldn't look at me that way," she said. "I just can't tell you. I'm so ashamed of myself."

"What is it? If it would make the difference between us living or dying, then I have a right to know."

"It won't," she said plaintively.

"Why not let me be the judge of that?"

She looked up at me, her face thoroughly miserable, yet still saying nothing. I continued to stare pointedly at her.

"It's just that I'm afraid that I may have been the cause of Henry DeMour getting killed," she muttered at last. I don't know what I expected to hear, but that wasn't it.

"What?" I exclaimed. "What in the hell are you talking about?"

"Don't ask me anything more about it, Virgil. Please."

"No," I said firmly. "What do you mean you may be responsible?"

She put her hands over her face and shook her head. I knelt down beside the bed and took her wrists and pulled her hands away. "Tell me," I demanded.

133

"I didn't do anything wrong!" she wailed. "I didn't mean for anybody to get hurt. I've never meant for anybody to get hurt, not in my whole life."

She jerked from my grasp and turned and fell across the bed facedown, her whole body shaking with sobs. I was disgusted. I should have pressed the issue, but I didn't. Most people cry at one time or another, and the truth is that women cry more readily than men. But the more honest of them don't hide behind it. Madeline was hiding now, and I liked her a little the less for it. I let the subject drop and stood watching her impassively until she wound down. When she finally stopped I handed her my handkerchief and said, "Wipe your eyes and let's go try that café."

After we'd eaten, we returned to the room, where I gave her first shot at the tub. When she was finished I took a long, hot soak. I came out of the bathroom toweling my hair to find her standing at the foot of the bed in her gown and robe. She looked at me for a moment, then raised her eyebrows inquiringly. "Do you want to . . . ?" She let the question hang unfinished in the air just as she had that first night at the Weilbach.

"Sure," I said, and kissed her gently. I was

134

still annoyed with her, but there was something so pathetic and disarming about the hesitant way she offered herself to me, something that made me think of a little girl lost in the woods. Of course, it could have all been good acting. I never really knew which. There were a lot of things about her I never knew.

Chapter Nine

We left at six the next morning. Gas rationing was in effect and the traffic was light, but it was still a hard, eight-hour drive with only a quick stop for a hamburger in Hearn. A few miles past the little town of Buffalo the Piney Woods began. The terrain gave way to rolling hills and deep woods, a soft, gentle land a world apart from the harsh Brush Country of South Texas. Two miles east of Palestine I turned off the paved highway onto a dirt road that wound gently downward toward the Neches River. On either side loomed tall, dense forest.

"How far out in these woods does your friend live?" Madeline asked.

"Several more miles," I said.

She shuddered. "It's awfully remote."

"That's why you'll be safe."

"What does he do for a living?"

I looked over at her and grinned. "He's a professional scoundrel."

"Virgil, please . . . for once give me a straight answer."

I laughed. "All right. Press runs several hundred head of cattle on land he leases from one of the timber companies. And he gambles. Craps, for the most part. Loaded dice. He's the best dice switcher I ever saw. He's also got a couple of colored families back in Palestine who sell whiskey for him. Which is funny, because he never touches a drop of the stuff."

"Moonshine?"

"No, bonded stuff. Pints and half pints, mostly. This is a dry county."

"You're leaving me with a bootlegger?" she asked, sounding a little horrified.

"I'll have you know some bootleggers are fine people," I said raffishly. "Besides, gambling and bootlegging don't really qualify as crimes in this neck of the woods. Put your worries aside. He's an honorable man where women are concerned. And you'll have female companionship, too. His daughter Nora and her little girl live with him."

"How old is she?"

"Six," I said. "Her name's Brenda."

"No, I mean Nora."

I shrugged. "A couple of years younger than I am."

"Married?"

"Not anymore. Her husband was a cop in town. Actually, he was a lot like your friend Nolan, now that I think about it. An ex-athlete who thought he could bully his way through anything. After Brenda was born, he began drinking heavy on his days off. Finally one night he and Nora were arguing, and he slapped the hell out of her. Then he went in the kitchen to get himself another drink. Nora followed him, and he told her to get her ass back in the bedroom and get undressed and ready for business. She told him to go to hell, and when he drew back to slap her again she put a thirty-eight bullet through the middle of his right palm."

"My God!"

"Right," I agreed with a laugh. "She packed her clothes that night and came home. About a week later he showed up sober and begged her to come back to him. She said sure, she'd give it another try, but that he needed to understand that if he ever hit her again she'd put the next bullet right in the center of his forehead. Apparently the boy didn't trust his own self-control, because he decided divorce would be a safer course."

"Have the two of you ever been . . ."

I glanced over at her and smiled. "Romantic? No. I have wished, though, and I think Nora has, too. Back when we were kids she and Press used to come down to La Rosa for a couple of weeks every summer. But she didn't take too well to South Texas. In fact, I've heard her say a dozen times that she wouldn't live there if she owned it. I knew the day would come when I'd have to move back home to run the ranch, and I saw what living in a place she hated did to my own mother."

We passed over a rattling plank bridge that spanned a narrow creek. On either side of its banks rose great oak and gum trees, and at their bases the ground was covered in a tangle of tie vines and water myrtle. The road up out of the bottom resembled a dark tunnel. Madeline gazed out the window with an expression that approached horror. "Do they even have electricity out here?" she asked.

"Sure," I said with a nod. "Press put in a big Delco generator right after Nora moved back home. And they've got a bathroom and a radio, too. So don't worry. You'll be as comfortable out here as you would be at home."

I took a couple more turns and came to a fork in the road. Taking the left branch, we wound our way down another dark tunnel, then emerged into a clearing of several hundred acres. A few yards down the road a rural mailbox stood beside a well-graveled driveway. I wheeled into the driveway and topped a gentle rise. Ahead of us, nestled in a grove of pin oak trees, loomed a large, tin-roofed house that was surrounded by about an acre of yard and bordered by a tall fence of heavy wire mesh.

"We're here," I announced.

We'd no more than stepped from the car when a half dozen hounds boiled out from behind the house. They were fine-blooded animals, Plotts and redbones, and their baying was deafening.

"Press likes to hunt," I explained above the din. "He's got coon dogs and squirrel dogs and deer dogs, and I don't know what else. He also likes the security of having some of them in the yard at night. The fence keeps them from getting loose and chasing deer."

The front door opened and Nora Rafferty appeared on the porch looking like something out of a New York fashion magazine in a sleek pair of tan slacks and a tailored shirt of red cotton under a cream-colored cashmere sweater vest. Except that New York fashion models rarely carry double-barreled shotguns cradled in their arms.

"Hush, dogs!" she yelled.

The noise slacked off and she waved at us. "Hi, Virgil."

"Hello, Nora," I said. "Are you planning to shoot me?"

"You mean this?" she asked, hefting the shotgun and giving me a big grin. "Nope. I thought it was you when you first drove up, but I decided to be careful and make sure. Daddy killed a twelve-point buck this morning and he's dressing it out down in the shed. Come on in."

"Deer season ended last week, didn't it?"

"Maybe so," she said with a twisted little grin, "but you know Daddy."

Nora was about five-six with a good figure, ash blond hair, and an angular Scots-Irish face that narrowly missed being beautiful and was all the more interesting for it. That afternoon she wore one of those red bandannas in her hair that were popular with women during the war — part of the Rosie the Riveter image, I suppose — and it looked great on her. Everything looked great on her.

"Nora, this is Madeline Kimbell," I said. "She's had a little trouble with an ex-boyfriend and needs to hide out here for a few days."

"Pleased to meet you, Madeline," Nora

said, shifting the shotgun to her left shoulder so she could shake hands. "Glad to have you visit. It'll be fun to have somebody to talk girl talk with."

"I love your outfit," Madeline said appreciatively.

Nora gave her a big grin. "Thanks. I bet you didn't expect to find nobody dressed this stylish out here in these woods, did you? I been to town this morning is the reason I'm all dolled up. Come on inside and let's have some coffee."

She turned and led us back through the house toward the kitchen with a confident, almost masculine walk. It was a cozy country place with hooked rugs and heavy furniture from the past century. Bookshelves stuffed to capacity filled one wall of the sitting room.

"You must read a lot," Madeline said in surprise.

"Yeah," Nora replied. "It's my character flaw, Daddy says. Of course he don't read anything but the Palestine newspaper."

"Haven't you found you a guy yet?" I asked her as we took our places at the big square maple table in the kitchen.

"Hell, Virgil," she answered with an easy laugh, "I can find all the guys I want at the dance hall in Palestine on Saturday nights.

It's just that don't none of them seem worth the effort."

She turned to look at me, her face full of mischief. "To tell you the truth, I've just about decided that I don't want a man in my life on a permanent basis. You have to make too many compromises when you're living with somebody." She shook her head and turned back to the stove. "Nope, it's better just to find you one that's got plenty of energy over the short course. Then when you get done with him you can boot him out and go on about your business."

"How about living with your dad?" I asked. "Aren't there compromises there?"

She lifted a pot from the stove and poured three cups of coffee and set them on the table. "Actually, living with Daddy works out pretty good. When you've got a pair of anarchists like me and him under the same roof, you got two people willing to give each other plenty of latitude."

Just then the outside door opened and Press Rafferty stepped into the room and hung his worn old Savage Model 99 lever-action rifle on a peg beside the stove. He was a tall, thin man with a prominent nose, two darting, mirth-filled eyes, and a small, closely trimmed mustache over a tiny mouth, all of which contrived to make him resemble a lively, intelligent rodent. As always in cold weather, he was dressed in a pair of faded denim overalls, a flannel shirt, and a red checked wool mackinaw. "Virgil, how you doing, boy?" he asked and stuck out his hand, obviously pleased to see me.

I introduced Madeline and gave him a quick rundown on her problems. "I'm positive nobody followed us," I said, "and not a soul besides Aunt Carmen knows where we are."

"Any friend of yours is welcome here," he said, pulling a pack of Camels from the front bib pocket of his overalls. "You know that."

"I appreciate it. But are you sure you're up for something like this? It could be dangerous."

"Me and Nora can handle ourselves if we have to. Don't worry about it."

"I know, but be careful."

He gave me a cold smile. "I've got a pair of Catahoula leopard dogs out back in the kennels that will kill anything, man or beast, that comes inside my fence at night. Just to be safe I'll turn them out into the yard after you leave. How's that for careful?"

"You staying for supper, Virgil?" Nora asked. "Daddy killed another deer last week, and it's aged out enough to start eating it."

144

I checked my wristwatch and then nodded. "Sure. I'd love to."

A few moments later Nora's daughter, Brenda, came into the room and crawled up into her grandfather's lap. She was a miniature of her mother, with the same angular pixie's face and ash blond hair. "Did you get a good nap, baby?" Nora asked her.

The little girl nodded and regarded me gravely for a few seconds, then said, "Hi, Virgil. Who's the redheaded lady? You gonna marry her?"

After a supper of fried venison, baked sweet potatoes, corn bread, and winter turnip greens fresh from the garden, I reluctantly pulled myself together to leave. "I hate to burden you this way, Press," I said as the four of us walked out on the front porch, "but I didn't have much other choice."

"Hush that talk, boy," he snorted. "I've told you before that if it hadn't been for your daddy I'd never have lived through that mess down in Cuba back in ninety-eight. Besides, she'll be good company for Nora."

I hugged Nora, shook hands with Press, and then kissed Madeline good-bye. "Whatever you do, stay here until I come back for you," I told her.

"When will that be?"

"Soon. A week at the outside, I think. But you stay here even if it's longer."

As I drove away I watched the three of them dwindle in the rearview mirror. For the first time since the meeting in the barroom of the Weilbach, I began to relax.

CHAPTER TEN

It was a long, lonely drive, and I was glad to see the lights of Beaumont come into view. Even at night it was obvious the town was booming. The refineries were running full-bore around the clock helping meet the Allies' need for gasoline and diesel, and two new shipyards had opened to build liberty boats. Skilled tradesmen of every kind were in demand, but welders and electricians could practically set their own terms. Despite the chronic shortage of building materials, new construction was springing up everywhere.

I checked into the Creole Hotel, where my family had always stayed in Beaumont. The Creole was nine stories of burgundy-colored brick and wrought-iron trim with a distinct Carribean flavor to it. The bellboy showed me to my room just before 1:00 A.M., and after a stiff shot of Old Charter and a hot shower I piled in bed and fell asleep almost instantly. At eight on the dot the hotel operator called as I'd requested the evening before. I ordered coffee and doughnuts from room service, then I gave her Jim Rutherford's number in Port Neches and asked her to put me through.

Jim answered on the second ring and I quickly brought him up to date. "I wanted to turn her over to Charlie Grist, but I couldn't find him," I explained. "The only thing I could think to do was to hide her some place safe until I could try to sort this mess out."

"You couldn't find him because he's down here on the coast," Jim said.

"He is?" I asked, thoroughly puzzled. I knew that except for a short stint in Austin when he was a young man, Grist had spent his entire career as a Ranger on the border. "This is a ways out of his territory, isn't it?" I asked.

"The whole state is his territory when Colonel Garrison wants it to be."

He meant Homer Garrison, the head of the Department of Public Safety, the man who bossed both the Texas Rangers and the highway patrol.

"So the Colonel sent him, huh?" I asked.

"Yeah. There are things about this deal that you don't know yet, Virgil."

148

"Now, why doesn't that surprise me?" I asked dryly.

His laugh was earthy and good-natured coming through the receiver. "I talked to Carmen last night, and she said for me to expect you today. Charlie is coming by about ten to have coffee. Why don't you pull yourself together and get on over here?"

Rutherford lived with his daughter, Betty, in a neat, white frame house on a shady residential street in Port Neches, a small town about a dozen miles southeast of Beaumont. A few years earlier Betty's husband had been killed in a shrimping accident, and Jim moved back to the coast to help her raise her two teenaged children. Betty worked part-time at the Beaumont library, but had it not been for Jim's savings and his federal pension she would have been hard-pressed to get by.

He quickly answered my knock — a big, shambling man with white hair and ruddy skin, comfortably dressed in wrinkled khakis and a shirt of green corduroy. "Glad to see you," he said in a deceptively soft voice as he stuck out his hand.

The house had the same cozy, hooked-rug ambience as Press Rafferty's place. In one corner of the living room a big gas heater

149

burned against the damp cold of the day.

Rutherford went in the kitchen and put the pot on to perk. By the time the coffee was ready we heard a knock at the door. It was Grist. Sixty years old with a face that was weathered and seamed like Rio Grande mud, he stood about five-ten, with fleshy features and a protruding belly. That day he wore a pair of rumpled khaki pants and a leather jacket over a flannel shirt of dark blue checks. A Colt .45 auto, its grip safety tied down with a rawhide thong, protruded — sans holster — from the waistband of his trousers.

In all the years I'd known Charlie I'd never heard him laugh. Normally I never fully trust a man without a good sense of humor, but with Charlie I knew the reason why and I made an exception in his case. Three decades earlier he'd been living in Brownsville, down on the border, when a late-night call from an informant took him away from his young wife and three-year-old daughter. By happenstance, an escaped convict was on the prowl that evening, a psychopathic rapist named Lucas Redgrave who was already serving three back-to-back life sentences. When Grist returned home in the middle of the morning he found his house full of police. Both his wife and child were dead, and his wife had been raped and savagely mutilated.

The Rangers take care of their own; three days later Redgrave was literally shot to rags while trying to surrender after a lengthy chase through the Southern Pacific Railroad yards in San Antonio. But Grist never recovered. From that day forward he was a chronic depressive whose view of mankind was so bleak as to border on nihilism. My own feeling was that his sole sense of purpose in life was the occasional opportunity to eliminate the violent and the cruel of this world. I personally knew of at least a half dozen such individuals he'd accounted for over the years, but these were all official kills. I wouldn't have been surprised to learn there were at least as many unofficial ones. Still, along the border he was respected by Anglos and Mexicans alike as a fair if often brutal lawman. Or as one cop friend of mine put it, Charlie disliked everybody equally regardless of race or religion. Mostly I think he disliked himself for not being home the night Lucas Redgrave came knocking at the door. That he'd only done what any conscientious lawman would have done in the same situation was meaningless to Charlie. He was guilty in the high court of his own mind, and that was the only verdict that mattered to him.

He shook hands with both of us, and seemed as glad to see me as he ever was to see anybody. Our host went in the kitchen and quickly returned with a battered tray that held three cups and an enameled percolator.

"What brings you to the coast, Charlie?" I asked casually.

"The Colonel told me to get down here and look into this DeMour thing."

"I know who killed him," I said.

"I think I do, too," Grist said. "You tell me your story first."

As we sipped our coffee I filled him in on my meeting with Madeline Kimbell at the Weilbach and the attack on the ranch. "She told me she saw DeMour strangled, and that one of the guys that did it was a hood named Johnny Arno," I said. "She claimed she didn't know the other guy's name."

"It was Paul Luchese," Grist said. "Both of them were fished out of the swampy end of Lake Sabine a little before three this morning. A couple of fishermen checking their trotlines found them about midnight."

"Damn!" I said.

"Right. Somebody's cleaning up loose ends."

"Salisbury?" I asked.

152

"Either him or Angelo Scorpino."

"Exactly how does Salisbury tie in with Scorpino?" I asked.

"He's Scorpino's nephew."

"Really? 'Salisbury' doesn't sound Italian to me."

"It ain't. Scorpino's sister married an English ship captain. But half-breed or not, little Marty is the apple of the old man's eye and his heir apparent. The last couple of years he'd been overseeing the syndicate's bookmaking business, but now he's eager for bigger things."

"Like the Maceo operation," I said.

"Exactly."

"Do you have any idea why they killed De-Mour?" I asked.

"I think so," Charlie said with a nod. "From what DeMour's friends say, he was planning to run for the state senate with the notion of forcing a legislative investigation into the rackets here in Jefferson County. Or more specifically, into the relationship between the rackets and local law enforcement, meaning Milam Walsh. He'd picked up some strong backing from several of the old families in Beaumont, and it looked like he stood a pretty good chance to get elected. With Salisbury and Scorpino poised to make their big move against the Maceos, they couldn't stand that kind of attention. My guess is that they figured they'd just head him off at the pass."

"I need to talk to Salisbury," I said. "I've got to impress on him that he needs to leave my family alone. Besides, there's no reason to bother the girl now that Arno and this Luchese guy are dead."

"I want to get a look at him myself," Grist said. "Why don't we go by his place tonight? You and him can have your chat while I just size things up. And if by some chance he doesn't want to talk to you, I bet I can make him change his mind."

"That's fine with me," I said.

"I wish the governor would quit dragging his feet on this," Grist said. "As soon as I get the go-ahead I'm going to boot Salisbury's ass back across the Louisiana line."

This announcement came as no great shock to me. Such things had happened before. The Italian crime syndicates had never really gained a strong foothold in Texas, largely because, aside from gambling, the mainstay of their income was labor union racketeering. The changing political climate brought on by the New Deal had forced the big Texas oil companies and chemical corporations and the great Brown & Root Construction Company grudgingly

154

to accept unionization beginning in the midthirties. But they were determined that if they had to tolerate unions, they would be honest unions. Or at least unions free of Mob control. Using their enormous influence in Austin, they put pressure on the politicians, who in turn quietly encouraged the Texas Rangers and certain extremely tough local lawmen to give free rein to their darkest urges when dealing with out-of-state gangsters.

"How about Henry DeMour?" I asked.

Grist shook his head. "We'll never be able to pin that on Salisbury, but he should have sense enough to go on back to New Orleans and count his blessings and stay the hell out of Texas. If he doesn't . . ." He stopped speaking and shrugged again.

"One more body in the lake," Rutherford said with a sigh.

Grist nodded thoughtfully. "I could see that happening. A man just never knows what fate has in store."

"Hell of a way to do things, though," Rutherford said testily.

"It's either that or let them get the kind of hold they got on South Louisiana," Grist countered.

"Yeah, but they had help down there," Rutherford pointed out. "Huey Long was hand in glove with Scorpino from the day he started out in politics. He let Scorpino have free rein down around New Orleans, and the Mob gave him their political support."

"We got politicians in this state who'd be willing to do the same thing," Grist said. "Let somebody like Scorpino get his foot in the door, and before you know it we'd have the same situation."

"Yeah, but —" Rutherford began.

I knew they'd yammer back and forth all day unless I sidetracked them. "Charlie, is anybody working with you on this?" I asked.

The old man nodded. "Yeah. A young fellow named Johnny Klevenhagen. He was a deputy sheriff in San Antonio until he made Ranger last year. He's assigned to Company A up in Houston, but the Colonel wanted me to bring him along on this deal. You ever met him?"

"Not that I recall," I replied with a shake of my head.

"He's a good lad. A hill country German from New Braunfels. One of that dark-haired breed of Krauts the old-timers used to call Black Dutch."

"Where does Milam Walsh fit into all this?" Rutherford asked.

Grist shrugged. "I think he's just waiting

156

to collect his tribute from whoever comes out on top."

"Ralls told me they were hired by a guy in New Orleans named Carlo Tresca," I said.

"He's one of Scorpino's top boys," Grist said. "He started out a few years ago as a street-level enforcer, but he's come up the ladder quick."

"I wonder why they didn't send their own people," Rutherford said.

"Because if Ralls and the other two had managed to kill the girl at your place, they would have wound up in the lake just like Arno and his buddy."

"But weren't Arno and Luchese part of Scorpino's outfit?" I asked.

Grist nodded. "Yeah, but after the girl saw them, they became a link to Salisbury. From that point on they were expendable. Besides, they were queer as a pair of loaded dice, and those old-school dago mobsters don't approve of that."

"Ralls and his friends may have been hired by Tresca like Ralls claimed," I said. "But you can bet that Salisbury had his finger in the deal somehow."

"Sure," Grist said. "He went to his uncle, and then his uncle told Tresca to hire them. Layers of insulation between the top boys and the act itself."

"Okay, when do we see Salisbury?" I asked him.

"I'm told that he's usually at the Grotto by nine. Why don't we meet here at Jim's house at 8:30?"

"Good enough," I said. "What are you doing until then?"

"I got a few people to see. How about you?"

"I'm thinking maybe I'll go over to Galveston and poke around a little. Maybe drop in on Sam Maceo."

"I'd shut that bunch down, too, if they'd let me do it."

"I know you would," I said with a laugh. "But that's just because you're against fun of any kind."

"Shit," Grist muttered.

"Sam and Rosario run a pretty civilized operation," I pointed out.

"Yeah," Grist said. "But that kind of flagrant disregard for the law can't lead to no good. If we're gonna allow gambling, then we ought to go ahead and legalize it."

"The politicians can't do that," I said, grinning. "They have to cater to the church crowd."

"Shit. . . ." he growled once again.

I got to my feet and shook hands with

both men. "I'll see you this evening, Charlie."

"Be on time. You wouldn't want to miss
the fun."

CHAPTER ELEVEN

Outside interest in Galveston and its lucrative nightlife was nothing new. There had been at least one earlier attempt to take over the island rackets that I knew of. An old friend of mine, a Galveston County deputy who'd actually been involved, told me the story not long after he retired. In 1928, Chicago crime lord Al Capone decided to annex the Maceo brothers' operation to his own growing Midwest empire. To determine just what would be involved in such a move, he sent his trusted right-hand man, Frank Nitti, down to Texas. Nitti was well acquainted with the island of Galveston and its people. Years earlier he had worked a few months for an old-time Galveston rumrunner named Johnny Jack Nounes. But things had changed since Johnny Jack's day, as Nitti soon discovered.

Friends in Chicago informed the brothers of Nitti's trip. When his train pulled into

Union Station late that night, it was met by a high-level Maceo employee named Anthony Regilla. My deputy friend was also part of the welcoming committee that evening, along with another deputy sheriff and a huge, marginally retarded man everybody called Jimmy the Chop. Regilla told Nitti's bodyguards they needed to take a hike because their boss was going on a midnight tour of the Island.

"Nice car you got there," Nitti muttered nervously as they steered him toward a sleek Packard touring car that sat at the curb, its powerful engine purring softly.

"Belongs to Papa Rosario himself," Regilla said as he opened the rear door for his guest. "He wants us to take good care of you."

The big Packard glided eastward along Seawall Boulevard until at last it came to a stop beyond the north end of town. The five men climbed from the car and stood motionless and silent for a few moments while the moon hung high in the southern sky and the waves lapped gently against the sand. At last Regilla suggested they all take a stroll out on the north jetty. To Nitti it seemed as though they walked the better part of a mile out over the Gulf until finally they stopped at a place where several dark and disturbing stains discolored the jetty's granite blocks. Nitti later admitted that his heart almost stopped beating when the giant, child-minded Jimmy reached under his coat and drew out an enormous meat cleaver whose well-honed blade gleamed like antique silver in the pale light of the full moon.

"Jimmy is fascinated by crabs," Regilla said pleasantly. "He loves to feed 'em."

"That's right," my friend agreed. "It's always the high point of his week when he gets to come out here."

The other deputy dropped a large, paper-wrapped package he'd been carrying. Jimmy quickly slit the package's binding with his cleaver and pulled the paper aside to reveal a fresh beef brisket. It was only a matter of a few swings of the cleaver and the brisket was rendered into pieces. Next, Jimmy pulled a length of heavy cord from his coat and tied one end of it to a large chunk of the meat. Then he threw the meat over into the water on the shallow side of the jetty and waited patiently for a couple of minutes before pulling it gently to the surface. Three large crabs hung from the thick, suety morsel, one of them almost as big as a dinner plate.

"Friends of yours, Jimmy?" one of the

deputies asked.

"Aren't they pretty?" Jimmy asked in an awed voice, his eyes bright and innocent.

"By the way, Frank," Regilla asked, "just what the hell are you doing down here anyway?"

The Chicago hood smiled weakly and muttered, "Sightseeing, I guess you'd say."

"Seen enough?"

"Oh, yes."

They were almost back to the beach when Regilla threw his arm around Nitti's shoulders. "Say, Frank, Rosario wanted me to remind you about that eight thousand you owe him from the old days when you were working for Johnny Nounes. He hoped you might find it convenient to go ahead and take care of it while you're here."

Nitti nodded enthusiastically. "Sure. I ain't got that much cash on me, but I guess I could wire Chicago and have it sent down."

"That sounds great, Frank," Regilla said with a beaming smile.

The men waited at an all-night coffee shop on Avenue A until the Western Union office called to say the money had arrived. Then they escorted Nitti back to Union Station and put him on the morning train.

"Come back and bring your wife, Frank,"

163

Regilla said before Nitti boarded his Pullman. "This is a great town to visit, but you can see the business opportunities are limited."

On my way to Galveston I stopped at the edge of town and bought a Houston paper to read later when I had my lunch. According to the headlines, the battle for Stalingrad still raged on, the casualties enormous in the savage Russian winter. I got back in my car and headed westward down U.S. 87 along Boliva Peninsula toward the Galveston ferry. The land was treeless and flat, its emptiness relieved only by a few beach houses scattered here and there. Traffic was light that morning, and I pushed the little Ford up to eighty, slowing down only through the tiny communities of High Island and Gilchrist. Occasionally off to my left I could see the waters of the Gulf rolling onto the beach in two-foot breakers beneath a sky that was leaden and gray.

It took the ferry about twenty minutes to cross the three miles to Galveston. I drove down Ferry Road over to the Gulf side of the island, and then turned westward on Seawall Boulevard. A mile farther down the casinos and nightclubs began. Off to my right loomed the great Hotel Galvez at

Twenty-first and Seawall, and across the street the Balinese Room sat far out over the Gulf on its pilings, its three-hundred-foot catwalk making it all but impregnable to even the most determined police raiders. Not that any cops raiding the place were likely to be very determined.

Its owners, Sam and Rosario Maceo, had come a long way from humble beginnings since the early days of Prohibition, when a colorful pair named Ollie Quinn and Dutch Voight ran a bootlegging outfit on Galveston Island known as the Beach Gang. They had a fleet of fast speedboats that went outside the twelve-mile limit, met the booze-laden ships coming in from Cuba, and then ferried the goods ashore at night. At the time the Maceo brothers were barely grinding out a hard living. Both were barbers, and both were willing to take a few risks to get ahead in the world. Rosario was living in a run-down beach house on West Beach at the far end of town when Ollie Quinn came to him and offered him fifteen hundred dollars to let his men hide a load of whiskey under his home for a few days. Rosario agreed and then sweated blood the whole time the liquor was in his possession; he'd been born in Sicily and was subject to deportation if he was caught. After Quinn's henchmen picked up the booze, Quinn himself came to pay Maceo. The barber shook his head and told Quinn to roll the money over, that he wanted to buy into the operation. At that point Ollie Quinn made what turned out to be the worst business decision of his life: he said yes. By 1930 he and Voight were out of the action and the Maceos controlled all the illegal liquor coming in through the eastern part of the Texas Gulf Coast.

The brothers prospered during the 1920s and made a lot of money out of bootlegging, but it was gambling that became the mother lode of their empire. In 1926 they opened a place called the Hollywood Dinner Club, the first air-conditioned nightclub in the United States. Next came the Turf Athletic Club. Both were fashionable spots, and each had a casino in the back. Then in the late twenties they bought and remodeled an opulent nightclub that sat several hundred feet out over the Gulf at the end of a long pier. Over the years this place went through several name changes, but right after Pearl Harbor it was redecorated in a South Seas decor and christened the Balinese Room. In a few short months it earned the reputation as the most opulent nightspot on the Gulf Coast, and it, too, had its casino in back.

These clubs were directed toward the carriage trade, but the pair also owned taverns and dives throughout the city and out along Highway 87 all the way into Jefferson County, each with its hidden gambling room. In addition, they owned thousands of slot machines scattered about in grocery stores, bars, and barbershops all over the upper coast — a completely open operation in a state whose laws permitted absolutely no legal gambling.

My father hadn't been a serious gambler, but he loved his Thursday-night poker games in town with his cronies, and each year, in the spring after roundup was over, he made a weeklong trip to the coast, where he played modestly in the casinos. Generally, he broke about even and had a good time. When I was in college he began to take me with him on these junkets, and I met the Maceo brothers on several occasions. I liked both men, though Sam was the more personable of the pair.

I stopped by the Turf Athletic Club on Twenty-third Street, where the syndicate had its main offices, only to be told that Sam was at the Balinese Room.

"Since the remodeling job he's fallen in love with the damn place, mate," said Little

Tommy Trehan, a diminutive Cockney who was the syndicate's oddsmaker for local sporting events. Tommy had been born the unwanted offspring of an East End slattern, and for him the Great War had been a blessing, an easy escape from the slums and a dead-end life. At seventeen he'd wormed his way into the British Army when the ranks began to thin after the Somme campaign and the recruiters stopped being so fastidious about the regulations concerning a soldier's size. In the trenches he took a bullet in the leg, lost part of a lung to mustard gas, and along the way earned a couple of citations for bravery. While recuperating in an Allied convalescent center, he'd met and made friends with a Texan named Jack Amber. The two of them got on so well that when the war ended Trehan came to the States with him to visit and recuperate and wound up staying, and the pair went into business together.

"Mind calling to tell him I'm on my way over?" I asked.

"Be glad to, mate."

I drove back to Seawall and parked on the beach side of the street. The entryway to the Balinese was decorated to look like a beachcomber's shack. Behind the entry an enclosed walkway extended out over the

168

Gulf to the club itself. The door was un-locked, but the joint appeared deserted.

Public places that are normally crowded and full of loud talk always seem eerie to me when they're deserted, and it was a lonely walk down the long, cavernous hallway with my footsteps echoing back at me. At last I came to the mezzanine, where I found a man in a white waiter's jacket run-ning a vacuum cleaner over the carpeted floor. He'd no more than opened his mouth to speak when the door to the South Seas Showroom swung open and Big Sam Ma-ceo stepped out and smiled when he saw me.

A widower nearing fifty, he was tanned and fit in his white knit polo shirt and dark tweed sports coat that looked English and expensive. He had a thickset, muscular body and a round, happy face and exquisitely bar-bered, coal black hair that showed some gray at the temples. An affable man, the year before he'd married a Hollywood starlet named Edna Sedgewick, a tall, classy girl from an old, semiaristocratic Rhode Island family. From what I'd heard, it was a good union.

"Virgil Tucker," he said happily, and stuck out his hand to shake mine. "What brings you up here? Business or pleasure?"

169

"Urgent business, Sam," I said. "We need to talk."

"Sure," he replied, his voice a little puzzled. He turned to the waiter. "Bring us come coffee, will you, Joe?" he said and pushed the door to the showroom back open to usher me in.

We took a table near the stage. The new decor was South Seas splendor, with exotic murals and the most elaborate black neon I'd ever seen. The waiter quickly returned with our coffee.

"This is the first time we've seen each other since your dad died," Maceo said, spooning sugar into his cup. "And I just want you to know that I'm sorry. He was a hell of a guy."

"Thanks, Sam. We appreciated the wreath you sent."

He gave a diffident half shrug. "He was a good customer and a good friend."

I grinned. "You never won much off the old man."

He waved off my objection. "Who cared with a man like that? Hell, I was proud to have him patronize my places. His passing was a loss to the whole state."

"I agree, but from what I've seen here this morning I may be the one sending flowers to your wake if you don't take a few more precautions."

His eyes hardened. "What in the hell are you talking about?"

"Angelo Scorpino and Marty Salisbury."

"How come you know about that business?" he asked, his voice surprised.

"I got dragged into it," I said and went on to give him the whole story from the moment I first saw Madeline Kimbell in the Weilbach barroom, leaving out the damage I'd done to Nolan Dunning. "She claimed Arno was one of the killers," I said in conclusion. "And Grist says both of them work for Scorpino."

He shook his head and stared out across the room. "I'm shocked that they would murder a man like him," he said softly. "The newspapers said it was a robbery. They took about five hundred dollars off him."

"Really?" I said. "I didn't know that. That must have been to make it look like a heist."

"However they did it, it was a stupid move," he said firmly. "That's the kind of crap that can bring the wrath of God down on an operation."

"How well did you know DeMour?"

"Not well at all, really. I heard a lot about him because he was so well known here on the coast, but I only met him a couple of times. I know for a fact, though, that he never gambled, not in our places or any-where else."

"Was he as honest as everybody claims?"

Maceo nodded. "Yeah. Oh, he was hu-man, like all of us, and he had his weakness. But he was discreet about it."

I didn't ask what that weakness was, and that was a big mistake. At the time it didn't seem important. If I had asked, I might have saved myself a lot of trouble.

Instead I said, "According to Grist, some-thing put DeMour on a reform bender. The story is that he was going to run for the state senate and try to force a legislative investiga-tion into political corruption in Jefferson County if he was elected. Which meant investigating the links between law enforce-ment and the rackets. And nobody doubted he could get elected. Grist thinks Salisbury just decided to nip the investigation in the bud by killing DeMour before he got elected and did any damage. It's common knowl-edge that Salisbury is after your operation. If they'd kill a man as prominent as De-Mour just to head off an investigation, then you're sure as hell vulnerable."

"You're right," he agreed grudgingly. "Maybe I need to be a little more careful."

"There's no maybe to it, Sam."

He turned to beckon the waiter. "Joe, call

the Turf Club and have Rosario send Mort and Benny over here. And tell him to keep some people with him until I get a chance to explain."

"Sure, Sam," the waiter replied. "What's up?"

Maceo grinned and nodded his head toward me. "My friend here thinks that somebody may want to poke some holes in this precious carcass of mine. Can you believe it?"

"We can't have that," Joe said, returning the grin. "I've got a rod backstage. Maybe I ought to go up to the door and wait till they get here."

"That's not a bad idea," Maceo said.

"Loyal employee?" I asked once the man had left.

"Cousin."

"Even better."

"You know, Virgil, I never expected this. Salisbury's been over here to talk to me twice, but I thought we were a long way from gunplay."

"What was his proposition?"

"He said that if we took him in as a partner he could double our margin."

"How?"

"Just what you would expect. Rigged tables, magnets, cardsharp dealers. Every kind of crooked crap you can imagine."

"It's the way guys like him think, Sam."

"Yeah, and it's stupid. Treat your customers right and they'll keep coming back year after year. Screw them, and you may make a bundle off them once, but they'll go someplace else the next time they want to gamble. I know what I'm talking about. I've visited with casino operators all over the world. Bali, Hong Kong, Singapore, Rangoon, Monte Carlo. And they all say the same thing. Run an honest operation and over the long run you still win because the odds are in your favor."

"Grist told me he's just waiting for the word from Austin to run Salisbury out of the state," I said.

"I heard the same thing. I got some friends in the capital myself."

"I wonder why it's taking this long."

He rolled his eyes. "What else could it be but politics? Change of administrations. This new governor is in no hurry to give the word to move."

He meant Coke Stevenson, an arch-conservative rancher from Junction who'd been the first house speaker in the state's history to serve more than one term. He'd moved up from lieutenant governor to governor the year before when his predecessor, a consummate clown named W. Lee O'Daniel, had resigned to run in a special election for the U.S. Senate.

"They don't call him Calculating Coke for nothing," I said. "My aunt Carmen claims he keeps his ear so close to the ground that it's full of grasshoppers. Have you thought about dealing with the Salisbury problem yourself?"

He shook his head. "That won't work. We're just not equipped to fight a war against the likes of Angelo Scorpino."

"I hear he's already got his finger in the pie in Dallas," I said.

He gave me a jaundiced look. "He bankrolls an Italian grocer who has two bookmaking joints that operate almost exclusively in the small Italian immigrant community up there. If you want to call that having his finger in the pie, then he has his finger in the pie. But that's as far as it goes. The real action in Dallas and Fort Worth is run by Herbert Nobel and Benny Benion."

"I hear they're at one another's throats," I said.

He nodded. "Yeah, and they have been for three or four years. Barbarism. But that's them. Down here we're civilized, and we rely on the political pressure our friends mount at the capitol. Oh, I admit we've got

175

a few toughs on the payroll, but the truth is they do the community as much good as they do us, considering that they're better than the cops at running the armed robbers and safecrackers and the whatnots off the island."

I laughed. "Yeah, but your boys have an advantage over the cops when it comes to dealing with people like that. They can always feed 'em to the crabs if they don't see the wisdom of leaving when they're told to leave."

He grimaced and shook his head. "All those stories have been blown way out of proportion, Virgil."

"Sure, Sam."

"Honestly, that's how it is, and it's better this way. The people that run this island won't put up with gang wars. And they won't put up with anybody coming in here who's going to fool around with the unions or start up loan-sharking operations."

"I'm surprised you didn't know about De-Mour, though."

He shook his head in annoyance. "I should have. I used to know everything that happened here on the coast, but now it seems like I'm the last to find out." He glanced at his watch. "When did you eat last? I skipped lunch myself, and I'm getting hungry."

"Me, too," I said.

"Good. As soon as those two bodyguards get here, let's go to Gaido's. I owe you one for telling me about this."

CHAPTER TWELVE

Gaido's had opened two decades earlier as a hole-in-the-wall café on Murdoch's Pleasure Pier, and then began its long ascent to its present position as the best restaurant in a town famous for good seafood. The current location was at Thirty-ninth and Seawall overlooking the Gulf. It was mid-afternoon and the dining room was almost deserted, but we got good service. And why not? After all, my companion's casinos and nightclubs were the Island's main attraction, the engines that kept the money flowing in and the town happy and prosperous.

The waiter had just left with our orders when we looked up to see Tommy Trehan's partner headed our way, a strained smile on his lean, hard face. Packin' Jack Amber was a former bootlegger known all over the Gulf Coast. Tall and slim, he was dressed in a tailored suit of gray flannel and a cream-colored overcoat that sported a fur collar.

Jack was a gambler and a bookie, tough and dependable, and to the best of my knowledge he'd never been involved in violent crime or strong-arm. A native East Texan born only a few miles from Press Rafferty's place near Palestine, he'd served honorably in the AEF during World War I and at one time he'd been a competitive pistol shooter. Back during Prohibition he'd been one of the state's premier rumrunners, but in those days he was known as plain Jack Amber. He unintentionally earned the nickname "Packin' Jack" late one December night not long after the Volstead Act was repealed when he dropped by the Crescent Liquor Store on South Main in Houston to buy a fifth of his favorite brand of scotch. That same evening a notorious local hophead named Josiah Henry decided to rob the store armed with a snub-nose .38 Smith & Wesson. Had robbery been the only thing on Henry's agenda that evening, Amber would have viewed the incident as none of his business, an incident from which he could abstain with a clear conscience. But the junkie, a sadist with a reputation for senseless violence, was also one of the state's legendary cop haters. After cleaning out the store's till, he loudly announced to all present his intention of murdering a popular Houston police captain who happened to be buying a box of cigars when the doper had walked in.

Henry had been running on borrowed time long before he decided to hijack the Crescent Liquor Store. For several years every police officer in the area had viewed him as a DOA waiting to happen, and his fate had been unalterably sealed two months earlier when he'd beaten and badly maimed a popular Post Office Street whore known as Sweet Linda Moretti, thereby earning himself the everlasting hostility of Sam Maceo's older brother, Rosario. A prudish and straitlaced man in his own life, Rosario was broad-minded on the subject of prostitution and took a fatherly attitude toward many of the island's working girls. That Sweet Linda was a local Italian orphan girl had been the final nail in the hophead's coffin. After she was attacked, Rosario gave his men orders to shoot Henry on sight, and the story was that any cop from Beaumont to Port Aransas could earn himself a free week in the best suite in the Galvez, complete with the finest whiskey, willing chorus girls, and limitless gourmet food, all by the simple expedient of presenting Papa Rosario with Josiah Henry's head on a platter. Verbally flamboyant in times of anger, Maceo had meant his offer to be taken metaphorically. Nevertheless, everyone close to him knew he wouldn't have turned a hair if some literal-minded beat cop had walked into his office at the Turf Athletic Club with Henry's severed cranium floating around in a bait bucket full of blood.

It was an offer Amber knew about, but one which didn't interest him in the least. But he was a good friend and occasional poker buddy of the police captain, a benign, grandfatherly individual named Leonard Mallory who was one of the best-liked men on the Houston force. And Jack Amber was also armed that evening. His trade as a gambler meant that he often carried large sums of cash, and at such times he kept a small-caliber automatic nestled in a chamois skin holster under his left arm.

If Henry had simply shot Captain Mallory without fanfare he probably wouldn't have had problems, but he wanted to get a few cheap thrills by feeding on the man's fear before he pulled the trigger. When Amber heard the robber tell the clerk to clean out the cash register, he'd been some twenty feet away on the other side of the store, standing behind a tall Schenley display rack. He deftly slipped his pistol from its holster and stood rock-still, prepared to defend himself on the outside chance that the bandit decided to search the room. When Henry announced his intention of murdering someone, Amber's curiosity overrode his caution and he peeked carefully around the corner of the display to see who the prospective victim might be. Much to his displeasure he saw the junkie holding his old poker pal by the uniform collar, the short barrel of the .38 buried in the elderly cop's throat.

Amber took a deep breath, muttered a nearly silent and exasperated "shitfire," and stepped out from behind the display, his Colt Woodsman Target pistol at arm's length, the sights aligned.

Henry had been shooting speedballs that day, a half-and-half mixture of cocaine and morphine. The coke made him mentally alert, but the morphine made his movements slow and overly deliberate. When Amber moved into his line of sight, Henry made a crucial mistake; he decided he needed to turn both his attention and his revolver toward this new, unwanted intrusion. But he wasn't quite quick enough; as soon as the muzzle of his .38 wobbled safely away from the cop's neck, Jack Amber put a Winchester .22-caliber hollow-point into the center of his forehead two inches above the midline of his drug-crazed eyes.

Southern country boy to the core, Amber gave all the credit to his father: "That's where my daddy told me to shoot a hog at killing time," he explained to the investigating officers in a soft, almost apologetic voice. "He said they'd never squeal if you hit 'em right there."

Amber's father must have known his business because Josiah Henry didn't squeal a lick. He just fell to the floor and gave a few languid twitches before he shucked off this mortal coil and passed on to whatever reward he'd earned in his short, unproductive life.

To everyone that mattered Josiah Henry had been bought and paid for long before his fatal meeting with Jack Amber, and the grand jury never heard of the incident. That Amber had been carrying a pistol illegally at the time of Henry's death was tactfully ignored by both the cops and the district attorney. The only jury that mattered in this case was the consensus of law enforcement opinion; the unanimous verdict was that Amber had performed an outstanding public service. From that time on, he'd been known as Packin' Jack, the policeman's friend.

He greeted Maceo first, then wrung my

hand like a long-lost brother.

"Hell, I didn't know you two guys were acquainted," Maceo said.

"Oh yeah," I replied nonchalantly.

"You bet," Amber said. "Virgil helped my sister's boy out of a bad mess."

Everybody who knew Amber, a childless bachelor, was aware that he doted on his widowed sister's three kids — an older boy and twin girls who were just about high school age. A couple of years earlier the boy and another kid had stolen three registered Hereford heifers from a farm near Lufkin. It was more a schoolboy prank than anything else, though the rancher was mad as a hornet. Sensing the boy was redeemable, I interceded with the district attorney and convinced him to drop the charges back to misdemeanors. The judge sentenced the boys to ten days in jail and a heavy fine, and forced them to make restitution. And from what I'd heard, Jack Amber gave his nephew a sound thrashing the minute he hit the pavement.

"How's the kid doing, Jack?" I asked.

"He's on track now, in his second year at A and M, majoring in animal husbandry. He decided there's more future in studying cattle than in stealing 'em."

"Sit down," Maceo said. "What's on your mind?"

Amber laughed a cold little laugh. "The fact is I need to talk to both of you. I was on my way to the Balinese to see you when I stopped by the Turf Club for a minute. Little Tommy told me Virgil was in town and looking for you, too, so . . ."

"What you got for me?" Maceo asked.

"Bad news."

"Let's have it."

"They raided my book in Port Arthur this morning and shut it down."

"Who raided it?" Maceo asked in surprise.

"The sheriff's department. Milam Walsh's boys. And I thought that since —"

"You're right," Maceo said with a nod. "It's my problem." He turned to me and explained. "Jack is partners with me and Rosario in a couple of legitimate real estate projects. Because of that and a few other services he's done for us in the past, he's considered part of our organization. That means that as far as that bunch in Jefferson County is concerned —"

"Not anymore I'm not," Amber said. "They claim that from now on I've got to cut my own deal."

"Oh, really?"

"Yeah. They say the price has gone up and

185

that there's going to be a little competition in the gambling business in the future. I knew he meant this Salisbury guy I keep hearing about."

"So why didn't you go for it?" Maceo asked, winking at me.

"I may not be much, Sam, but I don't screw my friends."

Maceo winked at me again and asked, "Who did you talk to? Walsh?"

Amber shook his head. "Nolan Dunning. And that's why I was looking for Virgil, too."

"Yeah?" I asked.

"Yeah. You have really pissed that boy off. No doubt about it."

The waiter came with our food. "Want something to eat, Jack?" Maceo asked.

The other man shook his head. "Just coffee."

"So what did you do to get crosswise with Dunning?" Maceo asked me.

"He beat him up, is what he done," Amber said with a grin. "Whipped that boy like a one-legged stepchild. Missing front tooth, broke finger, general lacerations and abrasions. And a bad case of wounded pride."

"How did you find out about it?" I asked.

"Hell, I asked him what happened, and he said a dead man named Virgil Tucker did it."

"A dead man, huh?" I said.

"Yeah, and that's why I decided to look you up when Little Tommy told me you were in town."

"I've had people threaten me before, Jack," I said.

"Take it seriously this time," Maceo said firmly. "Dunning is mean as hell and he hasn't got any sense. He thinks that as long as he's in tight with Walsh he can get away with anything. And in Jefferson County he pretty well can."

"He's right, Virgil," Amber agreed.

"I hear you," I said. "But don't forget that I'm carrying an active Ranger commission. That should make him stop and think."

"Yes, it should," Maceo said, "but that boy doesn't have anything upstairs to think with."

"I'll be careful," I said. "All I want is to have a talk with Salisbury and then go on about my business. When I go to see him tonight Charlie Grist will be with me."

"Good," Maceo said. "Don't go near those people by yourself."

"What do you want me to do about the book, Sam?" Amber asked.

Maceo thought for a minute, then said, "Go ahead and pay what he asks. This is just temporary, anyway."

Amber shook his head, a frown on his lean face. "I don't like that, Sam. It makes you look weak."

"It's the best course in the long run," Maceo countered. "Don't worry. This situation will rectify itself once the governor decides to get moving."

"If you say so —" Amber began.

"That's the way it's got to be," Maceo said, and smiled at both of us, caught up in the irony of the moment. "Isn't this something?" he asked. "We have to wait for the damn politicians to run the bad gangsters out of town so the good gangsters can make a decent living. I don't know what this world's coming to."

After we finished lunch, Maceo and his two bodyguards departed for the Turf Club, while Amber gave me a lift back over to the Balinese Room, where I'd parked my Ford.

Most successful gamblers buy a fine new car every year. Not Jack Amber. His vehicle was a 1937 Cord convertible, an exquisite, dark blue machine with pontoon fenders and retractable headlights. It was common knowledge that it was his pride and joy and that he spared no expense in keeping it maintained. "I swear, Jack," I said as I climbed in, "when you die you'll have them haul you to the cemetery in this damn thing."

He grinned. "Yep. And when I get there I'm gonna be buried in it." Then his mood darkened. "This is bad business, Virgil," he said.

"Yeah," I agreed.

"I don't think Sam is taking it seriously enough."

"That's exactly what I told him earlier today."

"Why is the governor so slow in moving against this bunch?" he asked. "Always before when they've tried to horn in over here they've gotten the boot in no time flat."

"Sam says it's political, and I tend to agree. That's the way Coke Stevenson has always operated."

"You know him, then?"

"Casually, yes. How much do you know about South Texas politics?"

"Very little."

"Then let me fill you in," I said, and gave him a quick rundown of how the machine operated in my part of the state.

"Amazing," he said, once I'd finished.

"Right. And Stevenson needed the organization's help when he ran for lieutenant governor back in thirty-nine. It was a close race, and he sent his people down to San

189

Diego to cut a deal with George Parr."

"I've heard the name. What is he, exactly?"

I laughed and shook my head. "It would take a week to explain George," I said. "For one thing, he's the political boss of Duval County. But since he's the one with the contacts in the national Democratic organization, all the rest of the county bosses defer to him and usually follow his lead. Which makes him the most powerful man in South Texas, and one of the most powerful in the state."

"What about the governor?" he asked. "What kind of guy is he?"

"He's an honest man, and basically decent, but he's like every other politician in that he doesn't want it to be too obvious that he cut some of the deals he had to cut to get elected. Or that he's in debt to the South Texas outfit, to say nothing of the big oil companies and the chemical firms. So he thinks that if he takes his own good time making the decisions he's going to have to make anyway, then it'll look like he made them free of outside influence. And maybe he'll even be able to believe it himself."

"So that's why he's moving so slow on this deal, right?"

"That's my guess."

"Maybe your friend George could talk to

him about this mess. Apply a little pressure."

I shook my head firmly. "Won't work. George wouldn't go for it because he'd be spending political capital and not getting anything in return. You see, Galveston's problems really aren't his problems or South Texas's problems."

Amber looked bemused. "I think I'll stick to gambling. Politics sounds a little too cynical for my tastes."

"That's wise, Jack," I said with a laugh as he pulled up behind my Ford. "You'd just be a babe in the woods."

"So you're going to see Salisbury tonight?"

"Yeah," I said. "Me and Grist and some young Ranger named Klevenhagen."

"Give Marty boy my regards."

"Oh, I'll do that, Jack," I said with a sour grin. "I know it will mean a lot to him."

"No doubt," he said and put the Cord in gear and pulled out into a gap in traffic.

CHAPTER THIRTEEN

The Grotto originally opened as the Empire
Club in 1929, the last year of the Roaring
Twenties. Since then it had known several
different owners, but no one had seen fit to
alter its Art Deco interior. It was built with
expensive materials and beautifully fur-
nished, just as you'd expect from a place
planned back in those heady days before
the Great Crash brought the boom of the
twenties to an abrupt halt. The lighting was
dim and subdued, but I could see walls of
inlaid wood with stylized chrome and art
glass decorations. The bar, a long, curving
sweep of chrome-trimmed fruitwood, lay
just beyond the mezzanine. Behind the bar,
etched into the mirror, the Roman war god,
Mars, kept company with a gaggle of hel-
meted warrior nymphs and one lone and
rather lonely-looking swan. An ivory-colored
grand piano dominated the bandstand at
the other end of the room. When we en-

tered, a four-piece combo was accompanying a tall blonde crooner who was doing a good job of "White Cliffs of Dover." One more reminder of the war I wasn't fighting.

Klevenhagen turned out to be a slim man of about thirty with dark hair and intense eyes, dressed in khakis and a worn leather jacket. Right after we shook hands he lighted the first of a string of Pall Malls he chain-smoked that evening. I was later to learn that he practically lived on coffee and cigarettes.

The bartender told us that Salisbury was late that evening. He also mentioned that there was a cover charge. Grist told him where to put his cover charge and ordered coffee for the three of us. We took a corner table near the bar and didn't have to wait long. Ten minutes after we'd sat down the door to the mezzanine opened and three men entered. Two were big men, obviously bodyguards, both dressed in dark suits and unbuttoned raincoats, and both with noticeable bulges under the arm. The third man was smaller, probably about five-nine, and small-boned, with a trim body wrapped snugly in a belted camel's hair overcoat that sported a fur collar. On his head sat a cream-colored fedora with a dark hat band, while an unlighted cigarette slanted down from the corner of his lips. His mouth and nose were small and delicate, and his face was molded into an expression of utter nonchalance that was obviously studied. I immediately noticed that his movements were curious. His head didn't bob up and down a bit as he walked; instead he seemed to glide soundlessly as though he were on rollers.

Sidling up to the bar, he tilted his head toward the bartender, who spoke for a moment into his ear. Then he answered the man briefly, gave him the barest of nods, and glided on toward the office door at the side of the club without even a glance our way, his unlighted cigarette still dangling down from his cherub's lips.

"Well," Grist said, smiling for the second time that day. "We don't seem to rate very high with this boy. Let's go see if we can't raise our standing a little."

As we approached the door the bartender came out from behind the bar and blocked the doorway. He was a big, beefy dullard who carried about thirty years and close to two hundred pounds, with a weight lifter's arms and a face full of self-importance. "Mr. Salisbury wanted me to tell you that he's not seeing anybody tonight," he said.

"Okay, you told us," Grist said. "Now are

you going to push it further, or do you want to let it lie where it fell?"

The bartender stared at the old man's face for a few seconds, then stepped back out of the way and raised his hands placatingly, palms outward. "Just doing my job," he said.

"Then get the hell out of my way and I'll do mine," Grist growled.

Behind the door loomed a short, dimly lit corridor. At its end stood a fancy double doorway manned by one of the bodyguards. As we approached we fanned out so that Grist was in the center with Klevenhagen on his right and me on his left. The guard's eyes darted back and forth between us a time or two, and he raised his hand palm forward like a traffic cop stopping an oncoming car. Then he opened his mouth to speak, but before he could utter a word Klevenhagen had his big Smith & Wesson out and its muzzle poked in the man's left ear just as smoothly as silk. The guard froze and stayed frozen while Grist reached under his coat and pulled out a Walther P-38 nine-millimeter automatic.

"Turn around and face the door," Grist said.

As soon as the guard had turned, Klevenhagen pulled the door open and Grist put his foot in the man's rump and gave a mighty shove. He shot headfirst through the doorway and the three of us were right behind him, guns drawn. The second bodyguard was on my side of the room, just inside the doorway. His reflexes were pretty good, but not good enough. He had his hand halfway to his weapon when I threw down on him and tripped the safety off my .38 Super. "Naughty, naughty!" I said, grinning right in his face.

Klevenhagen disarmed him, and then he and Grist quickly cuffed the pair. I turned to look at Salisbury. Now shorn of his coat and hat, he sat calmly in a great, high-backed leather executive's chair behind about a half acre of polished mahogany desk. Dressed in an exquisitely tailored double-breasted suit of brown silk with faint gold striping, he appeared utterly calm. His head was sleek and seal-like, with jet black hair that was combed down so tightly against his scalp that it appeared to have been painted on. His hands, which were in the process of cupping a kitchen match to his cigarette, were fine-boned, with long, tapering fingers. But his eyes were his most memorable feature. Dark and small and completely void of any emotion, they looked like nothing so much as a pair of tiny, spent coals. "Yes?" he asked, lifting his eyebrows a little, an expression of pure boredom on his face.

"I'm Virgil Tucker," I said.

"Congratulations."

"Ahhh, bullshit," Grist growled in his cement mixer voice. "Any more of your smart-ass mouth and you're one little piggy I'll be taking to market."

This bought a slight widening of the eyes from Salisbury.

Grist indicated me with a nod of his head. "This man needs to talk to you," he said. "And you better give him your time and attention."

Salisbury stared at the old man for a few moments, then shrugged and gave him a faint nod. "Sure. Why not?"

"We'll be outside in the hall, Virgil," Grist said.

He and Klevenhagen herded the bodyguards out the door and closed it behind them. Salisbury took a long pull of his cigarette, then blew the smoke my way. "What's on your mind?" he asked.

"Madeline Kimbell."

"What about her?"

"I'm going to be straight and simple with you," I said. "And you'd better listen and take me seriously no matter who you're connected with down in New Orleans. We both know that Madeline saw Arno and Luchese strangle Henry DeMour. We also know that you were behind it, but I'm aware there's no way to connect you to it. They worked for you, but I seriously doubt that they were ever on the official payroll. As for Madeline, you know her story and what happened at my ranch as well as I do. And if you have any sense you should realize that with De-Mour's killers dead she's no threat to you. As things stand now, I'm no threat to you either. But if you push the issue . . ."

I let my voice taper off while I looked him right in the eyes.

"Yes?" he asked.

"Just be aware that my family is a part of an organization that's ultimately far more formidable than your uncle's gang of cutthroats. Did you make the inquiry I suggested?"

"I asked a few questions," he said offhandedly.

"And?"

There came a long pause before he gave me a brief, acquiescing nod and said reluctantly, "I heard about your friend George Parr and the setup down in South Texas, and about his connections in Washington."

"And?" I repeated.

He wriggled around in his fancy chair for

a few moments before he spoke. "Well, as I told you on the phone this is all very interesting, but . . ." He tried to smile sardonically, but it didn't come off. I continued to stare at him until finally he asked in a soft voice, "What do you want?"

"I want my life back. I want to be able to go home and not have to worry about a crew of goons kicking my door down some night. I want to be left alone. And I want the girl left alone, too, since there's no way she can harm you."

He finally managed a coy little smile. "If I were to agree, I'd be virtually admitting —"

"Cut the crap. I'm not a lawyer or a prosecutor, and Beaumont's problems aren't my problems. I think it's unfortunate that Henry DeMour is dead, but I'm not on a crusade to right all the wrongs of this world. All I want is to be left alone. Now what's it going to be?"

He gave me the barest of nods. "Okay. Go on about your business."

"How about Madeline?"

"Sure," he said. "But what's with you and that girl that you'd go out on such a limb for her? Was she that good in the sack?"

I shook my head in mild annoyance. "That's the way it always is with guys like you, Salisbury. Money and sex. You can't imagine anybody being motivated by anything else."

This didn't even buy me a shrug. He just continued to stare at me impassively with his dead, dark little eyes.

"Before I leave I'll give you one piece of free advice. If Charlie Grist was as pissed at me as he is at you, I believe I'd pack up and leave town."

"Who the hell is Charlie Grist?"

"That old Ranger waiting out in the hallway."

He curled his upper lip a little in contempt and waved his fingers at me like a man herding chickens. "Shooo," he said. "I don't need no cow cop's advice."

"Have it your way. But if my family or the girl either one is bothered, I'll be back with the heavy artillery and you won't like it."

I turned around and left then, thinking I'd said enough. I didn't really have any heavy artillery. Or at least none beyond my friendship with Grist and whatever pressure George Parr and the South Texas machine might be able to mount with the Feds. But Salisbury didn't know that.

CHAPTER FOURTEEN

I had done all I could do. From that point on it was in the hands of fate. Or so it seemed at the time. And I was tired. Exhausted, actually. After Grist, Klevenhagen, and I ate a quick supper at a late-night café, I went back to the Creole in Beaumont, planning to sleep until noon. I put the "Do Not Disturb" sign on the door and piled into bed after leaving instructions with the hotel operator that I didn't want to accept any calls other than extreme emergencies.

When the persistent ringing of the phone dragged me up out of the warm, dark well of sleep ten hours later, a little voice in the back of my mind told me the whole odyssey had taken a new turn. When I heard Nora Rafferty's voice on the other end of the line I was certain of it.

"She flew the coop, Virgil," she said without fanfare.

"You mean Madeline, I suppose?" I asked, a cold sinking feeling in my guts.

"Who else?"

"How?"

"She sweet-talked the mail carrier into taking her to the bus station in Palestine about seven this morning."

"How do you know she sweet-talked him?" I asked in confusion.

"I know that because he's a lecherous fool who's been after me ever since I came back home. Any good-looking woman could talk him into just about anything. So when I looked out the window and saw her getting into his car at the end of the lane I knew what was happening. Daddy left the house early this morning to go hunting, and it took me a while to get Brenda up and fed and dressed. By the time I got to town the bus for Houston had left, and she was on it."

"Where are you now?" I asked.

"At the phone company office in Palestine."

"Which bus did she take?"

"The Missouri Pacific morning express. But she only bought a ticket to Huntsville, about thirty miles north of Houston."

"But why Huntsville?"

"Because she could get a Greyhound connection from there to Beaumont. That was the quickest way for her to get home."

"I see," I said.

"I'm sorry, Virgil," she said. "Daddy and I both did everything we could to convince her that she was safe here, but I'm not a jailer."

"It's not your fault, Nora, and I don't blame you."

"I know that. In a way I'm not too surprised she bolted, though. She was as restless as she could be all day long yesterday. Just walking the floor and peeking out the windows."

"I guess I'm not really surprised, either," I said, my voice sounding resigned to my own ears. "I've suspected all along that she wasn't telling the whole truth about this mess."

"Anything else I can do?" she asked.

I thought for a moment, then said, "Yeah. Call Aunt Carmen and tell her I'm going to be here in Beaumont another day or two. I was going to call her myself, but I need to get moving."

"Okay," she replied. "And if she has a message for you I'll leave it with the hotel operator."

"Good."

"And Virgil?"

"Yeah?"

"For heaven's sake, be careful."

"I will," I said and hung up. I sat on the side of the bed for a few minutes trying to collect what few wits I had, then I stumbled over to the dresser and found my Texas map. A quick glance told me that an express bus would make the trip from Palestine to Huntsville in no more than two hours. It was also obvious that it would take me almost as long to go from Beaumont to Huntsville, which meant that there was little chance of me getting there quickly enough to meet her. So I had no choice but to wait and meet the Greyhound connection when it pulled into Beaumont. After calling to get its estimated time of arrival, I got dressed, then went downstairs to the coffee shop for breakfast. I ate a leisurely meal, and afterward took my time getting to the bus station. Even so, I had a forty-minute wait until the big Greyhound rolled up behind the building. Madeline wasn't on it, of course. I don't know why I'd expected her to be, considering how everything else on this case had gone. Unreasoning optimism, I suppose. How complicated should it have been for someone to get on a bus in one town and arrive in another with only a single connection? But nothing had been simple with Madeline Kimbell.

During the day I called both the Greyhound office in Huntsville and the Missouri Pacific bus station, but no one at either place remembered seeing her. I called the Huntsville Police Department and the sheriff's department and gave them her description and told them she was a possible missing person. I went by her apartment a half dozen times, and I had Jim Rutherford call her parents twice. In short, I did everything a good investigator should have done, and still I couldn't find a trace of her. At least not until Charlie Grist phoned my hotel room early the next morning to tell me that around midnight the previous evening a motorist had found her body a few miles west of town on the Galveston highway.

CHAPTER FIFTEEN

"You did your best, Virgil," Jim Rutherford said. It was an hour later and we were once more having coffee in his living room. The old man's eyes under his bushy brows were world-weary and tired.

"I'm sorry, Jim," I said.

He sighed and drained his cup. "Madeline was always nervous and flighty. And she had trouble taking instructions."

"How about her parents?" I asked.

"I talked to them a little while ago. They're shattered. Just absolutely shattered."

"Was she an only child?"

He shook his head. "She had one older brother. He's a high school football coach up at Lufkin."

"That's merciful," I said. "When's the funeral?"

"I'm not sure. I just know that it's going to be a graveside service. Are you going?"

"Of course. I feel obliged to give her

parents an opportunity to chew me out for doing such a rotten job of taking care of their daughter."

He shook his head. "There won't be none of that. They're grateful that you tried. But would you mind coming by here to take me with you? I just don't drive anymore if I can help it."

"Sure. I'll be happy to. Leave a message at the desk at the Creole when you find out when it's going to be."

Just then the phone rang. Rutherford lifted the receiver and listened for a few moments, then said, "I'll tell him." He turned to me with a cold smile on his face and said, "That was Charlie."

"Yeah?"

"Right. He said you'd left my number with the switchboard girl at the hotel. He wants you to meet him there at the hotel coffee shop about seven this evening."

"What's brewing?"

"The governor has finally given the word. It's time for Mr. Salisbury to go back to Louisiana."

I'd been waiting ten minutes when Klevenhagen and Grist entered the room. I signaled the waitress to bring them coffee.

"The time has come, the walrus said,"

Grist announced as he took a seat. His face was as grim as ever, but there was a happy light in his eyes I'd never seen there before.

"Anything new on Madeline?" I asked.

He shook his head. "No. And we're not liable to get anything either."

"It had to be Salisbury," I said.

"Maybe and maybe not. We can sure as hell put the question to him, though. But nothing we get out of him would stand up in court and you know it as well as I do."

"You're right," I admitted. "But I don't like it. These people always walk on the real stuff. If they get 'em, it's always for some Tinkertoy crap like when they nailed Capone on tax evasion."

"I know," he said with a sigh. "And I have my own remedy for problems like Salisbury, but in this case they won't let me use it. So this is the best we can do."

The Grotto was busy that night. Salisbury wasn't in his office, and we had almost an hour's wait during which we cooled our heels and drank coffee. At last he entered with two of his henchmen. Once again the bartender whispered in his ear, and once again he glided off toward his office without so much as a glance in our direction. We gave him a couple of minutes, then followed along. This time the bartender didn't even look up at us. At the end of the corridor Grist tapped on the office door. A moment later the smaller of Salisbury's two bodyguards swung it open and motioned us inside. Salisbury was in his big, throne-like chair behind his desk, and both guards were standing. The smaller man was rat-faced under oily blond hair; the big man was bald and stolid and looked slow. Grist pushed the door shut behind us. Klevenhagen had his eye on the two thugs and his hand was comfortingly near his sidearm, so I left them to him and turned my attention to their boss.

"So what's up?" Salisbury asked without much interest.

"For one thing Madeline Kimbell is dead," I said.

"Yeah, I heard about that," came his laconic response. "Tough break."

"I thought you guaranteed her safety," I said.

"I guaranteed it from me. But I can't control what other people do. But hell, you take a ditzy broad like that, it's no telling who got crosswise with her." He gave me a dismissive jerk of his head and then turned to Grist. "What's on your mind, old-timer?" he asked.

"I'm glad you asked," Charlie replied. "As it happens the governor sent me down here with a message for you."

"Who?" Salisbury asked, an expression of mild puzzlement on his face.

"Governor Stevenson. He wanted me to give you a message."

"You don't say . . . The governor, huh?"

"That's right. You're getting all sorts of attention these days. Didn't you know that?"

Salisbury gave him a disinterested shrug, the bare wriggling of his shoulders as he fitted another cigarette casually between his lips. "So let's have it," he said.

I knew exactly what was about to happen, and it was going to happen because Charlie Grist was Charlie Grist. He smiled calmly at Salisbury for a moment, then his upper body exploded into action, his right arm coming around in a vicious backhand arc, the long, lead-loaded sap that had been hidden under his jacket now in his gnarled old hand. It caught Salisbury on the side of the face with the sickening splat of a fastball hitting a wet catcher's mitt, and the blow knocked the man's chair over backwards and spilled him onto the floor. I got a quick glimpse of the young hood on his hands and knees, his eyes wide with fear and surprise, his mouth a bloody hole from which one tooth hung by a thread. Then the old man closed in on him like the Grim Reaper, but by that time Klevenhagen and I had our own hands full with the bodyguards.

Both men reflexively grabbed for their guns, even though we were cops. But I'd had the advantage of knowing what was about to happen and had my Colt out and in their faces before they could get a grip on their pieces. Klevenhagen wasn't far behind me with his big revolver. In a matter of seconds we had the pair searched and disarmed and backed up against the wall. While we were frisking them, I could hear Grist behind me, stomping Marty Salisbury to mush. Finally the beating stopped. I looked over at Klevenhagen and raised my eyebrows. "Be my guest," he said with a shrug.

I handed him my Colt and reached into my pocket and slipped my fingers into the heavy pair of brass knucks I'd brought from home. I shucked off my coat and tossed my hat onto the desk and turned and faced the two bodyguards with a happy smile on my face. "Your turn, boys," I said and buried my fist up to the wrist in the bigger thug's belly.

An hour later the three of us stood watching the taillights of Salisbury's big blue Cadillac convertible as they gradually dwindled into the cold, misty darkness of the Louisiana night.

"An old boy just don't never get over a beating like that," Grist mused philosophically. "Down the way he starts to think he's a man again, and maybe he even begins to strut a little. Then the memory of it pops up in the back of his mind, and he sees himself lying on the floor in a puddle of his own puke begging you to stop. From that moment on, he's yours and he knows it. It's kinda like the relationship between a woman and her first lover. You've taken something from him he won't never get back."

An hour earlier we'd pushed the trio out the rear door of the club and stuffed them into the backseat of Salisbury's car. Salisbury and the bigger hood could barely walk. I'd gone easier on the smaller man so he would be able to drive. I took the wheel of the Cadillac with Grist beside me while Klevenhagen followed in Grist's Ford. We crossed the Sabine River bridge into Louisiana and pulled over to the side of the highway a few miles shy of the little town of Vinton. Grist and I got out and extracted the smaller hood and placed him behind the wheel. Then the old man leaned back into the car and shined his flashlight into Salisbury's face, which was so badly beaten that it was barely recognizable. "Can you hear me, boy?" Grist asked. "You understand what I'm saying?"

Salisbury nodded weakly.

"Your days here are over. Don't come back."

The man nodded again, then coughed and leaned forward to vomit on the floor of the car. Both front teeth were missing and his nose had been flattened like a road-killed skunk. Grist slammed the door. "Go," he told the driver.

After stalling the engine twice, the man finally managed to get the car back up on the highway and headed eastward.

"How about Madeline?" I asked.

Grist pushed his hat back and turned to look at me. "I don't believe they had anything to do with it," he said. "After all, what did he have to gain by killing her with Arno and Luchese both dead?"

"Maybe so," I said. "But if it wasn't Salisbury, then who do you think it was? Nolan Dunning?"

"Could be. We may have been looking at the wrong motive."

"You're thinking of a jilted lover rather than a gangland killing?"

"Right. But no evidence."

"And the Jefferson County cops are never going to make a big deal of investigating the case," I said.

His tired old eyes were sad. "You're right about that, and that's the worst thing about this kind of corruption."

I shook my head bitterly.

"And as for you," he said, patting me on the back, "I must admit I admire your energy." He put his tough old hand on my shoulder and gave me a friendly squeeze. "Maybe I ought to talk to Colonel Garrison about getting you a regular Ranger commission."

"No thanks, Charlie. When this mess is over I'm going back home to manage La Rosa."

"If that's the way you want it," he replied with a sigh. "But it's a waste."

"Where now?" Klevenhagen asked after we were back in the Ford.

"Let's go get something to eat," Grist said. "I'm hungry."

CHAPTER SIXTEEN

After that night things moved fast. In mid-morning of the next day I was awakened by the phone. It was Grist once again. "Hello, Charlie," I said sleepily.

"We got their attention this time," the old man said.

"Whose attention?" I asked, a little confused.

"Scorpino and that bunch. His top hand called me about fifteen minutes ago and asked for a meeting this afternoon at a little beer joint just the other side of the state line. I've got to go back to Austin later this evening, but I got time for this."

"Why Austin?" I asked, dumfounded. "Did you get called back?"

"Yeah."

"But what about the DeMour killing? What about the girl?"

"Hell, Virgil, the DeMour investigation is dead in the water, and you know it as well as I do. The killers are in the morgue and the man behind it is out of the state. As for the girl, even if Dunning killed her we got no way to link him to the crime."

"Yeah, but —"

"I know what you're going to say. Salisbury got away scot-free on DeMour. I don't like it, and the governor don't like it either, but there ain't nothing we can do about it. Anyhow, I thought you might be interested in coming with us this afternoon and talk to this guy."

"You bet I am," I said.

"Then get yourself something to eat and we'll come by to pick you up about three."

"Okay."

"And Virgil?"

"Yeah?"

"We scared 'em. This old boy told me that he wanted to assure me that I didn't need to go to New Orleans to talk it over with the head man. And the way he said it gave me the feeling that Scorpino's afraid we'll come down there and do the same thing to him."

The mist had turned to rain about sunup, a slow, steady downpour that showed no signs of abating, and the weather reports said a cold front was supposed to blow in about sunset. I waited under the awning in front of the hotel until Grist's black Ford sedan rolled up with Klevenhagen at the wheel and Grist beside him. I climbed into the backseat and soon we were on our way. "Who's this guy we're going to meet?" I asked.

"His name's Albert Gracchi," Grist said. "He's Scorpino's chief advisor. Kind of an odd duck for a hood."

"How so?" I asked.

"Well, for one thing, he's a college man."

"Really?"

"Yeah. Honors graduate of Tulane. And he claims his family is descended from some bunch of bigwig Romans back about the time of Jesus. Of course I don't buy that because I don't think no family can go for more than three or four generations without somebody's bull jumping the fence."

"Charlie's a little cynical," Klevenhagen said. "I mention that just in case you hadn't noticed."

"Shit," Grist snorted.

"Just because the bull jumps the fence doesn't mean the cows are going to be interested," I said with a grin. "I should know since I'm in the cattle business."

"Enough of 'em are," Grist said. "Anyhow, Gracchi came over on the boat from Sicily with Scorpino when they were just kids, and they've been friends ever since."

"How did an educated man like him manage to get into the rackets?" Klevenhagen asked.

"Nobody really knows. I suspect that he was a hoodlum at heart before he ever went to college, so it was just a case of a dog returning to its vomit. When you boys meet him you'll notice that he looks like somebody stabbed him in the face about forty times with an ice pick. That's because somebody stabbed him about forty times with an ice pick."

"How come?" I asked.

"It was back right after the first war when him and Scorpino were just getting started. A rival gang was trying to make him give up some information. They left him for dead without making sure. Bad mistake. What he and Scorpino did to the other gang is what began their rise to power. Their response was so damn savage that it scared about half their competition slap out of the business."

The joint where the meeting was to take place was a little roadside tavern with a hilly, sloping floor, a half dozen booths, and a poorly adjusted gas heater that barely dispelled the damp chill of the day. We arrived first but didn't have long to wait before the front door creaked open and three men entered. Two of them were younger, obvious bodyguards. But it was the third man who got my attention.

With an air of almost palpable corruption that hung about him like a cloud of gnats, Albert Gracchi looked like about a hundred and sixty pounds of spoiled meat in a fine suit and a five-hundred-dollar overcoat. His skin, which was deeply pitted and gouged from the long-ago ice pick attack, had an unhealthy, reddish purple tint to it. His eyes were two lifeless brown orbs set in irises the color of dirty dishwater, and his nose was thin and beaklike over a mouth that was a wide, lipless slash.

The two bodyguards took bar stools close to the door, while Gracchi walked slowly back to the rickety table near the rear where we sat. He didn't offer to shake hands and neither did we. Instead, Grist said, "Sit down and say your piece."

Gracchi stiffly eased himself into a chair across from the old man and turned to snap his fingers for the place's single waitress. When she arrived he asked for a cup of coffee only to be told, "This is a beer joint. If you want coffee, go to a drugstore."

Much to my surprise, he didn't take offense. Instead he laughed and ordered a

219

bottle of Falstaff. When he spoke his voice was rich and cultured, with an almost lighthearted ring to it, like the voice of a well-traveled and sophisticated man with an easy appreciation for the little ironies of life. That voice was the most disconcerting and spooky thing about the man. It was like hearing a cadaver singing a Verdi aria, and it made me shudder inwardly.

He turned back to Grist and said, "I appreciate your coming."

Grist nodded in acknowledgment. "Let's hear it," he said.

"Mr. Scorpino wanted you to know that he got some very bad advice, and that this whole affair has been an unfortunate misunderstanding."

"Go on."

"And he wants to assure you that as things stand now he has no further interest in expanding his business into Texas."

I decided to get into the conversation. "That's fine," I said. "But me and him still have some problems."

He turned his dead, dishwater eyes toward me and asked, "And who are you?"

"Virgil Tucker."

He gazed at me for a moment with an expression on his ravaged face that seemed like honest puzzlement. Finally he said, "I'm sorry, but that name means nothing to me."

"I'm the fellow whose ranch was invaded by your hoods a few days ago."

His eyes grew wide. "You've lost me."

"Then try this. Have you ever heard of a guy named Lew Ralls?"

He gave me a slow, thoughtful nod. "I believe I've met the gentleman a time or two."

"Well, you won't be meeting him again for a while because he's on his way to the Texas penitentiary."

Another thoughtful nod and a little glimmer of understanding began to creep into his eyes. "Why don't you just tell me the whole story."

"Ralls and two other thugs broke into my house down in Matador County after a girl named Madeline Kimbell. My aunt killed one of them and one of my vaqueros killed another. We captured Ralls alive and —"

"But why were they after this Kimbell girl?"

"Because she'd seen a couple of guys named Johnny Arno and Paul Luchese murder a man named Henry DeMour who happened to be a highly respected attorney and a member of the Beaumont City Council. In case you didn't know, Arno and Luchese worked for your boss's nephew,

Marty Salisbury. And now they're both dead."

"They are?" he asked in surprise.

"Yeah," I said. "They were found floating in Lake Sabine shot to pieces."

"This is all news to me. I haven't heard a damn thing about any of it."

"That's strange," Grist said. "Virgil here was able to persuade Ralls to talk, and he said they were hired by Carlo Tresca. And you know who he is just as well as I do."

"Yes, I do," Gracchi said, his eyes narrowing. He pulled a long, thin cheroot from an inner coat pocket, bit off the end without ceremony, and then lighted it with a Zippo. "And Ralls actually told you that Tresca had hired them?" he asked me.

"Yes, and I believed him."

"Why?"

"Because we'd already been at him with a hot branding iron, and he didn't want any more of it. But there's more than that. Two nights ago Madeline Kimbell was found dead out on the Galveston highway."

He stared down at the table for a few moments in thought. Then he lifted his eyes and said, "I assure you this is not the sort of thing we had in mind with our move into Texas. We expected it to be more in the nature of a merger, a trading of value for

222

value. We were led to believe that the political climate had changed in such a way that our presence here would not be resented. Mr. Scorpino and I had long felt that there could be considerable expansion of the Maceo operation. With their expertise and our capital . . ."

He stopped speaking and looked at the three of us and shook his head. "Killing prominent citizens and invading homes?" He shrugged apologetically. "No. We had nothing to do with either."

"I find it hard to take your word on that," I said, "considering that I got personal assurances from Marty Salisbury that the girl would be safe just one day before she was killed."

He puffed on his cheroot for a moment and then drained his beer. Finally he held up his hands in supplication. "All I can say is that we're quits as far as Mr. Scorpino and I are concerned. And I'm sorry about the girl. I take it she was a friend of yours, and the loss of a friend is . . ." He stopped speaking and shrugged. "Regardless of what you might think of me, I promise you I'm no stranger to grief. So let's end the matter here."

"I'm willing," I said. "I really don't have any other choice. But if my family is bothered again there'll be hell to pay. I promise you that."

"You have nothing we want, Mr. Tucker," he said. "You are safe from us. I give you my word on that, however meaningless it might be in your estimation." He turned his head to look at Grist. "How about you?"

"I don't intend to push it no further," the old man said. "But you have to stay out of this state. There are some powerful interests here that just won't tolerate your kind of operation."

"Done," Gracchi said and got to his feet. "As I said, it was an ill-advised venture, and we want nothing more to do with it."

We rose and followed him across the room. Halfway to the door he stopped and turned to Grist. "Certain people are going to have some explaining to do once I get back to New Orleans," he said. "I want you to understand that."

His vehicle was a big custom-built Lincoln sedan. A few moments later we stood outside the little joint and watched as it glided off into the drizzle. As we were getting back into our own car, Klevenhagen asked, "What do you think he meant about people having things to explain?"

Grist stared thoughtfully at the Lincoln's dwindling silhouette. "Sounds to me like they may have a palace rebellion going on down there," he said.

CHAPTER SEVENTEEN

Grist and Klevenhagen dropped me off back at the Creole. I checked the desk for messages and found one from Jim Rutherford telling me that Madeline's funeral was scheduled for 10:00 A.M. the next morning at Forest Lawn Cemetery.

At breakfast I'd had nothing but toast, and then I'd skipped lunch. Now my innards were making urgent "feed me" sounds, so I decided to take the path of least resistance and get something to eat at the hotel coffee shop rather than going out and hunting down a restaurant. Noticing that the menu said that breakfast was served twenty-four hours a day, I asked for a double order of bacon and eggs. I was just finishing my last biscuit and jelly when the door from the lobby opened, and Jack Amber and Little Tommy Trehan entered the room. I rose to greet the pair and motioned for them to sit. "What's up?" I asked.

"We need to talk to you," Little Tommy said, his face impish beneath his graying red hair.

"Sure," I said and grinned at the tiny Englishman.

Amber signaled the waitress and ordered coffee for himself and his partner. "Refill?" he asked me.

I shook my head. "What's on your mind?" I asked.

"Mr. Simms wants to see you, Virgil," Amber said.

I blinked twice. "Who the hell is Mr. Simms?" I asked.

"You never heard of Deader Simms?" Trehan asked.

I shook my head. "Nope. And I never heard a name like Deader, either."

"*Deader* is a British slang term for 'corpse,' " Amber explained. "Tommy gave Simms the name by accident years ago."

"Aye, mate. He looks just like a deader, he does," Trehan chimed in, his Cockney accent thick. "And that's just what I said the first time I saw the man."

"That was very diplomatic, Tommy," I said. "I bet he really appreciated it. I know I'd sure warm up to a fellow who gave me a fine compliment like that. So why does this remarkable gentleman who impersonates stiffs want to see me?"

"We really don't know," Amber said. "Just that it's got something to do with this Salisbury business."

"So who is he? What does he do?"

"Mostly he finances things," Amber said.

"The rackets?"

"Not in any big way. Back during Prohibition he'd lend us a hundred thousand or so for a shipment from Cuba. Thirty days, ten percent interest. And he did the same thing for the Maceos a few times. But hell, so did the banks over in Galveston, for that matter."

I held up my hand. "I wasn't moralizing. Just curious."

"Sure," Amber said with a nod. "Anyway, stuff like that is really no more than a sideline for him. He's in the stock market and real estate speculation. He owns a bunch of land along the ship channel and a few tracts out at Kemah. He put me and Tommy onto some good stocks back in 1938, right after the Munich settlement. Firms like Westinghouse, Kelvinator, and Douglas Aircraft that became defense contractors once the war came on. Even way back then he said that a European war was coming and that we'd eventually have to get into it."

"What's he like personally?"

"A nice guy," Amber said. "But kinda formal and old-world in his manners, and pretty well educated. And he's a recluse. Lives in a big suite at the Warwick Hotel up in Houston. Nobody goes in his place but him and his maid, and she's a deaf mute who's been with him forever. He has a kind of anteroom where he meets people if he has to see somebody on short notice, or in an emergency. But when he can he prefers to do all his business away from home."

"Aye," Trehan said. "And he doesn't come out of seclusion except for things he considers real important, does he, mate."

"How about it?" Amber asked.

"Sure. I'll be happy to see the man. When and where?"

"You mind driving back down to Galveston?"

I shook my head. "Not a bit."

"Then how about meeting us on Seawall in front of the Balinese Room about nine tonight? Sam Maceo is going to let Mr. Simms use the manager's office for your conference."

I arrived a few minutes early and parked

across the street from the club. The sky had cleared, but a winter cold front had moved in, and the night air felt harsh and brittle against my face. The full moon hung low over the Gulf, and the palms along Seawall Boulevard were listless and still. As I walked across the cold asphalt, the sound of my boot heels seemed discordant in the island's frigid darkness. While I stood smoking on the curb, a few heavy, chauffeur-driven cars — Cadillacs and Packards and Lincolns — pulled up in front of the club and disgorged their passengers. The men, mostly older, thickset, and prosperous-looking, wore tuxes or well-tailored business suits while their glittering women were dressed in slinky evening dresses and swathed in furs.

I had a short wait. Soon a sleek black automobile glided softly up to the curb with Jack Amber at the wheel and Trehan beside him. I couldn't help but notice the car's unusual hood ornament, which was unlike anything I'd ever seen. It was a thick, squat falcon's head that might have been faceted glass, but which I suspected was pure crystal from the way it glittered in the dim light.

Trehan sprang from his seat as soon as the car stopped and opened the rear door for the passenger. A huge man gradually unfolded his great height from the car's dark interior and stood beside me on the sidewalk.

"Virgil, mate, this is Mr. Simms," Trehan said respectfully.

Deader Simms stood at least six and a half feet tall. He was slim, with narrow shoulders and long arms. On his head sat a black homburg, and he wore a heavy greatcoat of dark wool broadcloth that came to midcalf. In the dim light I could see that his head was enormously elongated, with indistinct features, and a face that was a smear of pale, moonlit gray beneath the brim of his hat. He extended his hand toward me. "Please excuse the glove," he said in a soft, whisper-like voice.

"I'm Virgil Tucker," I said, shaking his hand. I pointed at the car. "Beautiful vehicle you've got there. At first I thought it was a Rolls."

"Packard," Simms said.

"I see that now. But the body's a custom, isn't it?"

The man nodded. "Barker and Company of London made it. It's the same firm that builds cars on a Rolls Royce chassis for the royal family. But the exclusive clientele's not what's important to me. It's the styling. I love that conservative British styling."

"Did you have it made for you while you

were in England?" I asked casually.

Simms's almost lipless mouth was far too small for his great head. Now it curled into a brief inverted crescent, the ghost hint of a smile. "You're clever, my young friend. If I said yes, you could get some of your associates in the various federal agencies to run my name through the State Department's passport rolls and maybe find out something about me. I'll save you the trouble. Yes, I had the car made while I was in England. And to save you further trouble, I'll also tell you that State has no information on me beyond the fact that I hold a current passport. No useful information, at any rate."

I regarded the man thoughtfully. In the moonlight his eyes were pearlescent ovals that seemed almost opaque. "I've never been considered very tactful," I said, "and I suppose it's a failing of mine. But I can't help but wonder why you're so obsessed with secrecy when you don't have any criminal record that I can find. I've already checked that out."

Simms shrugged. He put his hand on my shoulder and turned me gently toward the catwalk. "Maybe I'm the heir apparent to the throne of Bulgaria," he said. "Or maybe I'm just another country boy like you and Jack here, but one who likes to play games and has the money to indulge himself. Who knows? I'm not even sure I know myself anymore. Now let's get down to business."

Despite Simms' great height and thick shoes, his movements were fluid and graceful and his footsteps were nearly silent. He glided effortlessly beside me as the four of us moved across the sidewalk and on down the plank walkway toward the Balinese Room.

The club's assistant manager met us in the mezzanine and escorted us down a short hallway to the office. "Would you like anything?" he asked. "A drink maybe?"

"A cup of coffee, if it's not too much trouble," Simms said.

"The same, please," I said.

"Coming right up."

The room was well lighted, and I could see why Little Tommy had called Simms a deader when he first saw him. His skin had the waxen, parchment-like texture of freshly embalmed corpse, and it made for an immediate impression that was mildly repulsive. I couldn't help but shiver a little. He noticed and smiled faintly. "Don't feel badly, Mr. Tucker," he said. "It's a very common reaction people have when first meeting me."

"It's not fair, though," I said. "And I

apologize. A man's appearance doesn't determine his character."

"Oh? You think not?"

"No," I said with a grin. "Take me, for example. There are actually people out there in the world who think I'm a nice guy."

He returned the smile. "Oh, I think that you're a decent enough fellow or I wouldn't have come down here to see you. However, I do sense that you have a cruel streak that you have to work hard to keep in check."

I said nothing. What *could* I say? The man had pegged me accurately, and there was no sense denying it. A waiter came in with the coffee, and Simms eased his great, long body in the chair behind the desk. He didn't remove his hat, but he unbuttoned his overcoat and flipped it open to reveal an elegant English-cut suit of chalk-striped gray wool, probably by one of the best Bond Street tailors.

We sipped our coffee until our cups were empty. I waited patiently and said nothing. Then Simms put his cup down and leaned back in his chair, his hands folded across his belly, his fingers interlaced. "I suppose you're eager to learn why I wanted to see you," he said.

"Sure I am," I replied with a grin. "But feel free to take your time since you're obviously going to anyway."

He grinned back at me, his tiny mouth opening to reveal teeth that were small, white, and pointed. "Tell me something, Mr. Tucker. Do you have many friends?"

I shook my head. "No. Oh, I have plenty of *acquaintances,* but not many people I would call real friends."

He nodded. "It's the same with me. Jack and Little Tommy are my friends, and then there's Sam Maceo. And a couple of people up in Houston, but aside from them, nobody. But Henry DeMour was a true friend to me, my closest friend for better than thirty years. And I understand that you are investigating his death."

I took my time lighting a Chesterfield and putting the spent match into the ashtray on the desk, all the while trying to compose my thoughts. "Investigation may be too strong a word, Mr. Simms," I said. "I don't want to mislead you. I have no official standing of any kind, no resources, and no encouragement from any governmental entity. In fact, I have nothing but a special Ranger's commission and a head full of curiosity."

He nodded thoughtfully. "I know all that, and I can't help but wonder why . . ."

"Why I'm going to the trouble?" I shook

my head in bemusement at myself. "Now that you pin me down, I don't really know. Maybe it's because I've had doubts from the beginning that Salisbury was operating alone when he had DeMour killed. And then there's the girl, Madeline Kimbell. As I'm sure you know, she was found dead two nights ago. I'd left her with some people up in East Texas, where she would've been safe, but she bolted and came home to the coast. Why? The only way her actions make any sense is to assume that she never told me the whole story, and that she was more deeply involved than she'd led me to believe. And then there's Henry DeMour himself."

"What about Henry?"

"It's just that . . ." I groped around for words, trying to articulate what was little more than a vague sense of disquiet. Finally I said, "From everything I've heard about the man, he deserved better than he got. The local cops and the sheriff's department in Jefferson County have just written the whole thing off as an unsolved robbery, and nothing is ever going to change their minds. And even the state brass down in Austin don't seem interested in pushing it any further. Since Grist has been pulled off the case, I'm —"

"You're all that's left," he said.

"That's right. I'm all that's left. And I'd like to think that if I was murdered, then *somebody* would take it a little more seriously than this."

"I see," he said, looking like a man who'd heard something he hadn't expected to hear. "It impresses me that you would feel that way. It's an attitude that's certainly not in line with the temper of the times."

"That may be true, sir. But I have to go by what my own conscience tells me."

"Indeed you should," he murmured and suddenly leaned forward and gazed at me intently with his strange, obsidian eyes. "So how's it going? Have you discovered anything?"

"Not really," I admitted. "I plan to go to Madeline Kimbell's funeral tomorrow so I can talk to some of the people who knew her. Her best friend was a girl named Alma something-or-other. I want to find her and see what she might be able to tell me. But otherwise, I'm at a dead end."

"I see," he said, and paused in thought for a few seconds. When he finally spoke it was to ask what seemed at the time like the most unlikely question in the world. "Tell me, Mr. Tucker . . . have you ever heard of T. S. Eliot?"

"Who?" I was utterly baffled.

"T. S. Eliot," he repeated. "Have you heard of him?"

"Yes, but I don't know anything about him," I said, a little annoyed at this new twist he'd thrown into the conversation. "What does he have to do with Henry De-Mour?"

He smiled at my obvious impatience. "Henry and I both loved literature," he said. "And we enjoyed pretending that we were like those princes of commerce you found back during the Renaissance. Men like the Medicis and their sort who were captains of industry and finance by day and who dabbled in the arts in their spare time. Who wrote poetry and painted and patronized such greats as Petrarch and Botticelli."

Apparently he read some skepticism in my expression. "Does this perplex you, that grown men would indulge in such a fantasy?" he asked.

"I suppose not," I said, not knowing how else to respond. "It's a free country. Or so they tell us."

"Someone once said that all but the most literal-minded among us have to fantasize occasionally or else we'd go mad. And this was our harmless little pretense. But I asked about T. S. Eliot for a specific reason. You see, Mr. Eliot is an American-born English poet and literary scholar, a sort of old maid in pants who's written a lot of overwrought poetry about how civilization is all falling apart. A few years ago he published an essay in which he claimed that Shakespeare's *Hamlet* was an artistic failure. Can you imagine that? A work that's universally acknowledged as one of the world's greatest tragedies, and this man calls it a failure?"

"Interesting, Mr. Simms, but I don't see what's it got to do with —"

He raised a hand to cut me off and said, "Bear with me a moment, please. Now, this Eliot fellow is highly respected for his pronouncements, so just about everybody who read this essay immediately went to the bookcase and began rooting around in *Hamlet* trying to find out if the world's previous assessment could have been wrong and if Shakespeare had indeed failed. But I think they were looking in the wrong place, because I don't believe the source of Mr. Eliot's discontent with the play lay in the work at all."

"No?" I asked. I had no idea where this was all leading.

"Absolutely not," he said with a definitive shake of his great head. "I think the root of Mr. Eliot's problem in respect to *Hamlet* is inside Mr. Eliot himself."

"So you're saying —"

"That you're looking at Salisbury and Scorpino for the answer to Henry De-Mour's death when you ought to be looking at Henry DeMour. And at his personal habits."

"Such as?"

He smiled. "Do you remember Samuel Pepys, Mr. Tucker?"

I was about to roll my eyes in annoyance at another oblique literary reference, when I realized it wasn't oblique at all. "The great English diarist," I said. "You're telling me that Henry DeMour kept a diary?"

"Precisely," he replied with a satisfied smile. "And he'd been doing it for many years. Beautiful things, they were. Bound in red Moroccan leather with their pages edged in gold. He got them special from a stationer in New York and went through a volume about every six months or so. I used to rag him about a twentieth-century man carrying on such an old-fashioned practice. He always pointed out that all the famous diarists in history were just obscure eccentrics until somebody discovered their journals and saw the literary value in them, usually long years after they were dead."

"Where in the name of God are they?" I asked.

"In his library, at his home, locked away in a fireproof safe. Or at least that's where he always kept them, and I don't see any reason they should have been moved."

"Is there any way I can get at them?"

"I believe so. Go see DeMour's wife. In the meantime I'll call her and tell her that I think she should help you."

"Are you on good terms with this woman?" I asked skeptically.

"Of course."

"Then why don't you go to her yourself and ask for the diaries?"

He shook his head. "That won't do. I know that Henry wrote some humorous things concerning me, and I wouldn't want to invade his privacy by reading them. Besides, actively involving myself in a murder investigation is just not the sort of thing I do."

"All right," I said. "I'll go see her. But it will have to be tomorrow afternoon at the earliest. I've got to go to Madeline Kimbell's funeral in the morning at ten."

"Good enough," he said and rose to his feet. We shook hands across the desk, and he said, "And you are right. Henry did deserve better."

"Just please don't expect miracles," I said.

"I don't," he replied and reached into his

inner coat pocket to pull out a small gold card case. He slipped out a business card and handed it to me. It was a piece of stiff linen paper that said, SIMMS, HOTEL WARWICK, HOUSTON, and gave a phone number.

"If there's anything I can do, either now or in the future, you just call," he said. "I'm almost always home. This business could get dangerous, and I'm not without resources."

I slipped the card into my wallet, and I'd just risen from my chair when the door swung open to reveal Sam Maceo framed in the doorway, his face pale and his eyes hard and full of fire. "My brother Rosario has been shot," he said.

"When?" I blurted out.

"Not more than an hour ago. They just called me."

"Who did it?" Simms asked.

"Who knows?" Maceo replied. "Five shots fired from a gray Dodge sedan just as he was coming out of his office at the Turf Club."

"Is he —" I began.

He shook his head. "No. He took a bullet through the fleshy part of his right arm. But one of the bodyguards got it in the lung. He's in surgery at John Sealy Hospital right now, and he may not make it."

"Where's Rosario?" Simms asked. "Isn't he at the hospital, too?"

"No, he's at his penthouse at the Buccaneer. The doctor's taking care of him there."

"Even better," Simms replied. "Keep him there and tell him I'll call him tomorrow."

"Sure," Maceo said, shaking his head in bewilderment. "But I wish I knew what the hell is going on. This doesn't make any sense."

"Apparently Salisbury was only the tip of the iceberg," Simms replied with a grimace as he buttoned his coat. "Take care, Sam. This business appears to be far from over."

CHAPTER EIGHTEEN

It rained again during the night and the morning dawned gray and cold. I skipped breakfast and then drove by Jim Rutherford's house to take him to the funeral. We arrived at the cemetery about ten minutes before it began. There were around fifty mourners present, most clustered around a half dozen chairs that had been set up for the family under the funeral home's tent. A plain gray steel coffin with bronze handles sat on a catafalque over the grave. The service was short and simple and dignified. A young Baptist preacher read from the Bible, then gave a brief eulogy in which he spoke of the tragedy of such an untimely death. Thankfully, he knew when to stop and didn't belabor the point. Then a tall, slim young woman he described as Madeline's best friend stepped forward and did a magnificent job of singing "Amazing Grace" in a crystal clear soprano voice.

After a short prayer it was over.

I asked Rutherford to introduce me to Madeline's parents. They were a tired-looking, graying, sixtyish couple who looked like they hadn't slept in days. "I'm Virgil Tucker," I said. "And I'm deeply sorry this happened."

The woman nodded and shook my hand then buried her face in her handkerchief and turned away.

Madeline's father said a quiet, "Thank you for trying, Mr. Tucker," that came close to breaking my heart.

"I'm going to do more than that. I plan to do my best to find out who was behind this."

"Do you have any idea . . . ?" he began, only to let his voice taper off.

There was no reason they shouldn't know. "She witnessed a murder a few nights ago. I think she was killed to silence her."

"Was it Henry DeMour's killing, by any chance?"

I nodded.

He shook his head sadly. "I told her she was involved with the wrong sort of people when she first started seeing that Dunning boy. Young people don't listen, do they?"

Not knowing how to respond, I muttered something I hoped sounded decent and got away from them as gracefully as I could.

245

Glancing around, I spotted the soprano headed for a small Ford coupe that was parked about fifty yards away. Moving swiftly, I caught up with her and gently took her arm. "Is your name Alma, by any chance?" I asked.

She stopped and turned and peered at me with guarded eyes. "Yes," she said. "I'm Alma Copeland."

"I'm Virgil Tucker. Is that name familiar to you?"

She was dressed in a pair of well-tailored wool slacks and a matching coat. Her hair, which had been bobbed at ear-bottom length, was combed simply to one side and she wore only a little pink lipstick. She paused a moment before she answered my question, then gave me a hesitant nod and whispered, "Yes."

"Then you know I'm the man who was trying to help Madeline?"

Chameleon-like, her mood changed and she pulled away from me. "You obviously weren't very good at it," she spat and turned and began hurrying toward her car.

I caught up with her just as she was opening the door and pushed it gently shut with the heel of my hand. "No, I suppose I wasn't," I said. "But then it wasn't really a paying job, now was it?"

"Oh, I'm sure you extracted enough from her to make it worth your while."

I stared right into her eyes for a few seconds before I spoke, then I said gently, "Isn't that just another way of saying your friend was promiscuous? Or that you knew she wasn't above using her body to get what she wanted?"

Her mouth fell open in amazement. "Why, why . . . ," she sputtered. "How can you say such things about —"

"About the dead?" I asked, interrupting her. "That's always puzzled me. That business of not speaking ill of the dead, I mean. If you say something bad about someone who's alive it could conceivably hurt them. But criticism has never damaged a corpse that I know of."

"You're hateful," she spat.

"And you're being childish. If you'd think for a moment you'd realize that I didn't have to help her in the first place. And if I didn't care what happened to her, would I be standing out here in this drizzle right now?"

She lowered her eyes and shook her head. "No, I suppose not," she admitted reluctantly.

"Then will you help me?"

"I don't see how I can."

"I just want to ask you a few questions."

She stared off across the cemetery until I thought I'd lost her.

"Miss Copeland . . ."

She turned and gave me a curt little nod. "Let's get in the car where it's warm," she said.

Once we were inside the Ford she cranked the engine and turned on the heater. "What do you want to know?"

"She told me there was a girl with her at the Snake Eyes the night Henry DeMour was killed. Was that you?"

She shook her head.

"Then who could it have been?"

"I don't know. She never said."

"But you do know about DeMour?"

She sighed a long sigh. "Yes, and I wish I'd never heard the man's name."

"Tell me about Madeline. What was she really like?"

"She was my best friend, and she was a nice girl. A little confused, maybe. Looking for love, like everybody. And looking for a good time."

"Had you known her long?"

She nodded. "Since grade school."

"Okay, then what about Nolan Dunning?"

"A bastard of the first order."

"So you don't like him?"

"No, I don't, and I told Madeline he was worthless when they first started dating. But she was taken in by his looks."

"I see," I mused. "But she'd recently broken it off with him, hadn't she?"

"Yeah. Say, do you have a cigarette?"

I pulled my Chesterfields from my coat and lighted us each one. "Thanks," she said, drawing the smoke deep into her lungs. "I'm trying to quit. My doctor thinks it's bad for people."

"He's probably right," I said. "But back to Dunning. She told me he was a real caveman. Tried every way in the world to get her back, including intimidation."

"That's right."

"Do you think he might have killed her?"

She shook her head. "I can't see it. I really believe he was too nuts about her."

I stared at her for a few moments. Something didn't fit. Her voice was strained and the whole conversation seemed somehow awkward. Reluctant to meet my eyes, she kept looking off across the cemetery. Finally I said, "I had her safely lodged with some reliable people up near Palestine, but she bolted and took a bus to Huntsville. She was supposed to get a Greyhound connection there for Beaumont, but she never made it. Somebody must have picked her up at the bus station in Huntsville. You wouldn't have any idea who that might have been, would you?"

She shook her head absently.

"Is there anything you can tell me that might help me?" I asked. "After all, she was your best friend. Please believe me when I say that I'm just trying to do the right thing."

"No, nothing," she replied in a soft voice.

"After she broke up with Nolan, did she start seeing anybody else?"

"No. Why do you ask?"

I shrugged. "She was a pretty girl, and I can't see her being by herself for very long. I just thought that maybe —"

She shook her head. "Nobody."

I watched her thoughtfully for a moment, convinced that she was lying on that one point at least. Maybe about other things as well. I felt like slapping the hell out of her. Instead, I took one of my cards from my pocket and wrote Jim Rutherford's number on its back. "If you think of anything else," I said, "either tomorrow or a month from now, please call. This man can get a message to me."

"Okay," she said in a bare whisper.

I opened the door and climbed from the car. Then I leaned down and looked at her once more. "Madeline didn't tell me the whole truth," I said. "And we both knew it at the time. I believe in my heart she would still be alive if she had. That's something you should think about."

She gave me a nod without meeting my eyes, and once I'd closed the door she put the car in gear and was gone. I stood and watched the little coupe as it made its way out of the cemetery, convinced that I was no nearer to the solution to the puzzle than I'd been when I first saw Madeline Kimbell in the barroom of the Weilbach hotel. I was wrong.

CHAPTER NINETEEN

I dropped Rutherford off at his place, then got a light lunch of Gulf shrimp at a little seafood place only a block from my hotel. Henry DeMour's home turned out to be a huge, two story, high French Victorian with a mansard roof of gray slate. It sat on a half block of deeply shaded yard of ancient magnolias and moss-hung oaks. A pair of oleander bushes at least ten feet high flanked the front steps. I climbed up to the deep, shady porch and rang the old-style doorbell. A few seconds later I heard a faint stirring inside. After about a minute a severe-looking Negro maid opened the door. "I'm Virgil Tucker," I said.

But before I could explain my business, she stepped aside and commanded in an imperious tone, "Come in, suh. She's expecting you."

I had no more than stepped across the threshold when my hostess appeared before me. There was something annoyingly schoolmarmish about Lucinda DeMour, something of the well-heeled and aristocratic old maid who takes a job teaching in the public schools out of a sense of obligation, then spends her lifetime making young people miserable by drumming the more esoteric points of English syntax into their reluctant skulls. She was tall and slim, with graying brown hair worn in a style that could only be called severe. Her gray dress was severe, too, both in cut and fit, its austerity relieved only by a small cameo broach at her throat. She reminded me of my own tenth-grade grammar teacher, and I was well on my way to disliking her when she smiled. It was the sort of tired smile you'd expect from a woman not a week past her husband's funeral, but still there was a world of sunlight in it. It was a smile that made you think of bees and jonquils and tender green grass and the fragrance of wisteria floating in the early spring air. So instead of disliking her, I decided that Henry DeMour had been a very fortunate man.

"Mrs. DeMour —" I began.

"I've been expecting you, Mr. Tucker," she said, extending her hand. "Simms called me on your behalf this morning. And yes, you may see my husband's diaries if you wish. But there are a few things I need to tell you first."

"Sure," I answered, my voice gentle. "And I appreciate this very much."

"Let's go back to the kitchen and have a cup of coffee, shall we? I was just making a pot when you knocked." She waved the maid off. "I can manage coffee without help, Lucy," she said. The woman gave us a nod and disappeared somewhere back into the recesses of the old house.

"I have two servants who've been with me forever," she said over her shoulder. "They've been treating me like an invalid ever since Henry was killed. It's gotten to the point that I feel like strangling them both, but they are so devoted. . . ." She shrugged.

The kitchen would have served a medium-sized restaurant. On a gas range even bigger than the one at home a large ironstone percolator bubbled away. To one side of the room sat a large maple table surrounded by a half dozen captain's chairs.

"I'm afraid Emily Post wouldn't approve of my entertaining guests in the kitchen," she said as she began to pour the coffee. "But I feel more comfortable here than anywhere else. Please sit down."

"It's fine with me, Mrs. DeMour. Sometimes I feel like I grew up in the kitchen back home."

"And where is your home, Mr. Tucker?"

"Matador County, right down on the border. My family are all ranching people."

"A reassuring activity," she said. "I'm from Savannah. By the way, do you like old-fashioned pound cake, by any chance?"

"It's my favorite."

She placed a large pound cake in the center of the table along with two small plates and two large, steaming cups of dark, chickory-laced coffee. We sipped our coffee and ate pound cake for a while, making small talk, then at last she asked, "What have you heard about my husband, Mr. Tucker?"

"That he was a good man. Very civic minded, a person who cared a great deal about the community where he lived."

"That's all true. And he'd been disturbed about the public corruption in this county for years."

"You knew that he was thinking about running for the senate, then?"

"Of course. We had discussed it at length. We talked about everything."

"I see," I said. "Then he must have mentioned the name Marty Salisbury to you."

"Yes. He's a hoodlum who runs a night-club here."

"Not anymore. An old Ranger named Charlie Grist beat him to a pulp and ran him out of the state two days ago. At first I was convinced that Salisbury was responsible for your husband's death, but I'm not so sure anymore. He was involved, but I'm beginning to think there's more to it."

"Really? Why?"

"I'll get to that in a minute," I said. "But first, do you know who the Maceo brothers are?"

She nodded. "Certainly. My husband was acquainted with them both. He said they were reasonably decent men, when you consider that they operate outside the law."

"They are. Now, what you need to understand is that Salisbury is the nephew of a very powerful New Orleans gangster named Angelo Scorpino. Apparently he was sent up here by Scorpino to take over the Maceo brothers' operation. It was equally apparent that your husband was about to get in their way. Grist and I both assumed that was the reason he was killed. Then after Grist ejected Salisbury, we met with one of Scorpino's top men just over the Louisiana line and he assured us that Scorpino had come to realize that the whole thing had been a mistake from the first, and that as far as he was concerned the hatchet was buried."

"Did you believe him?"

I grinned at her. "Yes, because I think the beating Grist gave Salisbury actually scared Scorpino enough that he was afraid the old man would come down to New Orleans and do something to him."

"Really?"

"Yeah. You see, most cops handle these Mob people pretty gently even when they arrest them and make cases on them. But Charlie Grist is a law unto himself. At any rate, that meeting should have put an end to it, but last night five shots were fired at Rosario Maceo outside his office. Obviously somebody still has their eye on the Galveston gambling rackets."

"Who could it be?" she asked.

"I've got a notion, but it's pretty far-fetched. I'd really rather not say anything until after I've looked at your husband's journals."

She nodded and sighed a long sigh. "Then I'd better tell you what I have to tell. Mr. Tucker, my husband had a serious character flaw, and that flaw was younger women. Over the years he had numerous affairs."

"Mrs. DeMour, there's no need —"

"Yes, there is, and for more than one

reason. In the first place, I'm convinced that Henry's philandering contributed to his death."

"Really?" I asked.

"Yes. But I also want to tell you because my house was burgled two nights ago, and I feel sure the intruder was after those diaries."

"What makes you think so?"

"Henry's library was rifled, but not a single thing was taken. They came in through the porch window and went straight to the library and searched it thoroughly. I didn't even discover the burglary until the next morning, and nothing else was disturbed in any way. That's why I'm convinced they were looking for his journals."

"Did you call the police?"

She looked at me sharply. "Are you joking? With the kind of law enforcement we have in this county? What good would that have done? And I don't mind telling you that I haven't slept securely since then, but what can I do? My bedroom door is sturdy, and I keep a pistol beside my bed. Beyond that, I just trust in God."

"I see your point," I admitted with a nod. "Who else knew about the diaries?"

"All his friends, I'm sure. He talked about them a great deal. They contained his observations on national affairs and what-not, and he was really quite proud of them." She smiled sadly and put down her cup. "But back to his womanizing. The first time it happened we'd been married fifteen years. I was terribly hurt, and almost left him. He begged me to stay, and I did. Oh, it's not what you're thinking. He didn't promise to do better and then backslide later on. Quite the contrary. He told me that it was almost certain to happen again. You see, tender young female bodies were like an intoxicant to him. And he was handsome and very charming and able to get almost any woman he wanted."

"I'm sorry," I told her.

"It was not your doing, Mr. Tucker. Henry told me that I was the one real love of his life and that his attraction to other women never went beyond the physical. He also said that he regretted it, but that he knew himself well enough not to make any rash promises he couldn't keep. He pointed out that he'd never lied to me, which was true, and he told me that he didn't want to start."

"Mrs. DeMour, there's no need —"

"Yes, there is, because I want you to know. You are dealing with some very dangerous people, and you are entitled to the whole story."

I shrugged and nodded and she went on with her story.

"So I had a choice between divorcing a man who was an ideal husband in every other respect, as well as being a devoted father to our two children, or putting up with his childish philandering. And that's what it was. Childish. So I chose to stay. Actually, such an arrangement really isn't all that uncommon among the people we socialized with."

She stopped speaking for a moment and looked at me with eyes that were a little sad. "I suppose you think I was a fool," she said.

"No, I don't," I said gently. "Besides, it's not my place to pass judgment on you."

"At any rate, I did stay, and we raised our children and were active in community affairs, and he was discreet in his romantic activities, never causing me any embarrassment or shame."

"I appreciate you being so frank with me, but I don't see what this has to do with his murder," I said.

"At the time of his death Henry was involved with a young woman, and he had gone to meet her that evening."

"Are you sure about that?" I asked.

"Of course I am. I'd been married to the man for thirty-five years. Besides, as I said, he never lied to me. When he left the house that night I asked him if it was a business call or a social call he was making, and he said a social call, so I knew what he meant. It was a sort of code we had. That means that at the very least, being out with this young woman when he could have been safe at home put him in the place where he was killed. And deep down I can't help but feel that somehow she lured him to that nightclub."

"Do you have any idea who she was?"

She shook her head. "None whatsoever. But I wanted to tell you this because you may find some mention of it when you read his diary, and I didn't want you to feel you had to protect me from the truth. Most of all, I didn't want you to feel sorry for me."

I nodded. "I would never presume to do that, Mrs. DeMour. And I really don't want to pry into your private business. It's just that —"

"Why *are* you doing this anyway, Mr. Tucker?" she asked. "Looking into Henry's death, I mean."

"Like I told Mr. Simms last night, I'm not really sure myself. Part of it is that your husband seems to have been too decent a man to be written off the way he's been written off by the officials in this county.

Then there was this girl who saw the murder. I was supposed to be protecting her, but —"

"The one who was found out on the Galveston highway a couple of days ago?"

I nodded.

She gazed at me thoughtfully for a few moments, then rose abruptly. "Follow me," she said. "I imagine you are anxious to see those journals."

Henry DeMour's library was what one would expect from a wealthy man who loved books — dark wood paneling and deep leather armchairs, built-in bookshelves floor to ceiling, books everywhere. She opened a door in the paneling to reveal a large safe. After fooling around with the combination dial for a few seconds she swung the door open to reveal a neat stack of leather-bound books. "Take your time, Mr. Tucker," she told me.

I thanked her and she left the room, closing the heavy door behind her. The top book was the most recent one. I sat down in one of the big leather chairs and began to read. It took me only a few minutes to find what I was looking for, and, when I did, its implications almost curled my hair. I sat for a while, thinking furiously, truly frightened for the first time since the night the goons had come to La Rosa.

Finally I came to a decision. I went out into the hallway and found it deserted. Wandering back through the old house, I discovered Lucinda DeMour once more installed at her kitchen table, coffee cup in hand. "Did you —"

"Mrs. DeMour, you told me you were from Savannah. Do you have any relatives there?"

"Several, including my brother and his family. Why do you ask?"

"You need to go there now."

She appeared more exasperated than shocked. "Mr. Tucker, I don't see how —"

I can be extremely persuasive when I put my mind to it. But in this case I didn't have to be. Instead, I simply put her husband's open journal on the table in front of her and said, "Read this, please."

Her eyes quickly skimmed over the book, then she turned the page. When she'd finished she looked up at me with a stricken expression on her face.

"You see?" I asked. "There's no doubt in my mind that your life is in danger. The next time they won't bother with burglary. They'll just force their way in and demand to know where the journals are. Then they'll kill you afterward."

"You think?" she asked, alarm in her eyes.

"I'm certain of it. Please pack a few things and let me take you to the depot."

"All right. I'll trust you, though God knows why. I guess with Henry dead I don't have anybody else to trust."

"Do you need to call your brother?"

She shook her head. "No, I'm welcome there any time, and he and his wife asked me to come last week when they were here for the funeral."

"Fine. Just get whatever you need as quickly as you can and let's go."

She nodded and went to the door.

"And Mrs. DeMour?"

"Yes?" she asked, turning back to me.

I held up her husband's journal. "I'm going to need to keep this," I said.

"By all means. I'll feel much better with it out of my house."

She took no more than a half hour to get packed. After she'd sent the servants home, I put her bags in the trunk and headed for the Southern Pacific Depot.

"You should be able to get a connection in New Orleans without any trouble," I said as I pulled up out front.

"Don't worry about me, Mr. Tucker. I've made this trip many times before. When do

264

you think I'll be able to come home?"

I shrugged. "I have no idea. Why don't you plan on staying a couple of weeks, at least."

"What are you going to do?"

"I'm going to get back in contact with Charlie Grist. He was working this case, but he got called back to Austin. I think this will renew his interest. And then I think I'll talk to a friend of mine who works for the attorney general's office."

"Good," she said. She opened her purse and took out a pen and a small notebook. "I'm going to give you my brother's address and phone number. Please let me know what happens."

"I promise."

She had her ticket in a matter of minutes and we had only a half hour wait until the eastbound *Sunset Limited* pulled into the station. Once the porter had taken her bags, she turned to me and held out her hand, and for just a moment there was a plaintive expression on her face. "It may seem rude to you for me to ask such a question on so short an acquaintance," she said, "but I would like an outsider's opinion. Do you think I was a fool for staying with Henry all those years?"

I took her hand and bent down and kissed

it, and I felt like Clark Gable. "Mrs. De-Mour," I said, "I don't believe you could ever play the fool. You make me wish I was thirty years older."

Her eyes misted and she leaned over to kiss me gently on the cheek. "You are a true gentleman, Mr. Tucker. A lesser man would have said he wished I was thirty years younger."

The porter helped her into the coach and a few seconds later the train rolled away into the misty gloom of the winter afternoon.

CHAPTER TWENTY

From the depot I went downtown to a Kress's variety store and paid a quarter to get DeMour's journal snugly wrapped for mailing. Then I drove to the main post office and mailed it to Frank Russell, the president of my bank back home, along with a note asking him to hold it safely in the vault until I came by to pick it up. After that, I breathed a little easier. Besides being a fellow rancher and political ally, Frank was a trusted friend. Once the diary was in his hands it would be safe, since he was so closed-mouthed he wouldn't even discuss routine bank business with his wife.

Next I stopped at a Texas Company service station to gas up my car and have the oil checked. I asked to see the phone book, and in a few seconds I had Alma Copeland's address. This was a relief. For all I'd known she might have been married or living with her parents, which would have made what I had in mind considerably more difficult. Her place turned out to be a small bungalow in one of the older residential neighborhoods on the west side of town. There was no sign of her car in the driveway, but a small porch light burned against the deep gloom of the afternoon. Ever mindful of my blood sugar, I found a mom-and-pop store a few blocks away where I bought three Cokes, a box of crackers, and a small jar of peanut butter.

I went back to the bungalow and parked on the opposite side of the street about thirty yards from her driveway so that my car was partially screened by a large privet hedge. It was a long wait. My peanut butter was half gone and it was nearly dark when her little coupe pulled into the drive. I slipped out of my car and hurried up the street. Moving as soundlessly as I could, I mounted the porch behind her and slipped my hand under her arm just as she was unlocking the front door. She jumped a foot high and almost dropped her purse. "God, you scared me!" she cried out.

"Good," I said roughly. "It's about time something did."

"What do you want? I thought I told you —"

I took her by the arm and pushed the door

open with my other hand, then shoved her through the doorway and closed the door behind me.

"You can't do this —"

"Yes, I can."

"I, I —"

"Shut up," I snarled and pushed her across the room and threw her down on a small sofa that sat against one wall. "You're going to tell me what I want to know if I have to beat it out of you. In fact, after the runaround I've gotten on this case, knocking you around a little might be fun. Or maybe I'll just arrest you as a material witness and take you to Austin this very night to talk to some investigators from the attorney general's office. How would you like a week or so in the Travis County Jail with the state boys going over you?"

"You're awful!" she said, near tears.

I looked at her coldly, my eyes meeting hers. "Probably," I said. "But diagnosing my personality quirks isn't going to help you a bit."

"I've told you everything."

"What you've told me is a pack of lies. I think your motives are innocent, but that doesn't change things. So talk."

She was crying freely now. I stood staring

down at her implacably. Finally she wound down.

"Talk," I repeated. "Make it easy on yourself."

"What do you want to know?" she whispered.

"Let's start with Madeline's breakup with Nolan Dunning. She was seeing somebody after that, wasn't she?"

"Yeah, I guess so," she muttered with a reluctant nod.

"You know so. Now who was it?"

She heaved a great sigh. "You're going to think this was so cheap."

"Never mind what I may think. Who was it?"

"Henry DeMour."

I nodded. "That's just what I've suspected since I talked to his wife earlier in the afternoon. Give me the whole story."

She wiped her eyes and took a deep breath. "Mr. DeMour came to her school with a tour of local business and civic leaders, not long after the fall semester started. Apparently he was quite the ladies' man. They met and talked and he asked for her phone number. She gave it to him and he called a few days later. Not long after that she broke up with Nolan and started seeing DeMour."

"How did Nolan take it?"

"How do you think he took it?"

"All right, tell me about the night De-Mour was killed."

"Nolan had been badgering her continuously about coming back to him, even threatening her. But finally he quit. Then after about a week he called her and told her he was reconciled to the fact that she was gone, but that he wanted her to help him with one thing. He promised her that if she would, he'd never contact her again. He said some friends of his needed to talk to DeMour about a business deal, but he'd been reluctant to see them. Nolan wanted Madeline to bring DeMour to the Snake Eyes Club so they could meet him. He told her that it was a great deal for DeMour, and that later on he'd be grateful that she'd done it."

"And she believed him?" I asked in amazement.

She nodded.

"Why?"

"Because she wanted to, I guess. I mean, she and Nolan had been together for over a year and they'd had some good times. And if he was telling the truth about this, then maybe she could convince herself she wasn't so stupid for getting involved with him in the first place."

"It never occurred to her that Nolan might want to get DeMour off where he could do something to him?"

She shook her head. "She thought De-Mour was too important for a deputy sheriff to mess with. Besides, Nolan could be really smooth and convincing when he put his mind to it."

"So she said. But I've also heard he was too stupid to come in out of the rain. Which is it?"

"He's pretty dumb in some ways, but he has a sort of animal cunning where women are concerned. I can see where he'd have a certain appeal to girls like Madeline."

The way she put it puzzled me. "What do you mean, 'girls like Madeline'?" I asked.

She looked up at me with eyes that had gone cold and hostile. "Girls who like men."

"Don't you —" I began and then a lot of subtle, little things fell into place and it became clear to me. That she'd worn a slacks suit to a funeral; the no-nonsense way she combed her hair; a certain mannishness to her bodily movements, minimal makeup. "I see," I said softly. "Go on. What hap-pened that night at the Snake Eyes?"

She shrugged. "As soon as she and De-Mour got out of the car, those two hoods were on him. She ran and got away from them."

"So there wasn't another girl there with her that night?"

"No, just Henry DeMour."

"Go on."

"Then a couple of days later Nolan called her and told her he'd make it right with the people behind it if she'd come back to him."

"So she told the truth about that much, at least."

"She told you as much of the truth as she felt she could," she said plaintively.

"Why didn't she tell me about DeMour?"

"She was afraid her parents would find out she'd been fooling around with a married man who was a lot older than she was."

"That seems rather trivial, really, when you consider the number of people who've gotten killed over this business."

"You don't know her parents. They're old-fashioned and very religious. She would never have heard the end of it. They might have even disowned her."

"Do people really do that?" I asked. "I thought it only happened in Victorian novels."

"Like I said, you don't know them."

"How did she get from Huntsville to Beaumont?"

"She called me from Palestine, and I went over there to meet her."

"That's what I thought," I said with a nod. "Did she give you any reason why she bolted?"

"She just said she was so nervous with dogs barking at odd times and guns everywhere. She said that your friend Nora kept a thirty-eight in her pocket and that the old man never stepped outside the house without his rifle."

"But that was why she was safe there. Didn't she have sense enough to realize that?"

She just shrugged.

"Why didn't you just tell me at the cemetery that you were the one who picked her up in Huntsville?"

"Because she asked me not to."

"What happened after the two of you got back to Beaumont?" I asked.

"I don't really know. She had me drop her off at her place and that's the last I ever saw of her. She was supposed to call me the next morning, but she never did."

"So you have no idea what she did or where she went after she got home?"

She shook her head firmly. "No."

I stood regarding her thoughtfully. "I hope you're telling me everything you know," I said. "It's to your benefit to come clean."

"I have."

"If that's true I won't be bothering you anymore."

I was across the room and just reaching for the doorknob when she said, "Thank you."

I turned back, a little puzzled. "For what?"

"For not asking about me and Madeline. I mean, if we ever . . ." She gave me a wan smile.

I shook my head in wonder that she could think such a thing important at such a time. Or that she could think I really gave a damn. "Good-bye, Alma Copeland," I said softly and stepped out into the darkness of the night.

I should have had my mind on my business instead of on the sad screwball I'd just talked to, but I didn't. So I fell for the oldest trick in the book. Or at least it's a trick as old as the backseats of cars. I'd climbed in my Ford and pulled the door shut and was just fitting the key into the ignition when the blow came. It must have been a padded sap of some kind or it would have killed me. As it was it slammed me forward into the steering wheel and almost — but not quite — knocked me out. It did render me helpless, and they had me hustled out on the street in a flash. I remember being on unsteady legs for a moment with two men holding me up while somebody drove away in my car. Then a big Buick four-door sedan materialized before my eyes. It had fancy whitewalls and a Jefferson County Sheriff's Department seal on the door, and I recall thinking that was strange since cop cars were always plain-Jane Fords and Chevys and Plymouths with blackwall tires. Suddenly the back door of the Buick was magically open, and they shoved me inside.

That was when I noticed that somewhere along the way I'd acquired a pair of hand-cuffs on my wrists. I felt something sharp at the base of my rib cage and looked down to see a big, long-barreled revolver. Its muzzle was buried in my side, and its other end was attached to the arm of an exquisite gentleman who was wearing several hundred dollars' worth of hand-tailored silk suit and a camel's hair overcoat. I saw a handsome matinee idol's face with wavy hair that was going gray at the temples, a pencil-line mustache, and manly features. He looked like Errol Flynn, but he wasn't. He was Milam Walsh, and his smile was the smile you'd expect to find on a mako shark.

CHAPTER TWENTY-ONE

The Buick whisked off down the street, picking up speed. Within a mile or so my wits were starting to come back. I recognized the driver as Nolan Dunning. But I almost fainted dead away when the man in the front passenger seat turned around so I could see his face. "Hi, Virg!" chirruped my old nemesis Stubb Martindale. "How's tricks?"

I sat motionless for a long moment, then lunged desperately for the door, only to find that its handle had been removed. I tried bursting it open with my shoulder, but it was useless. Almost wild with fear and rage, I was turning to attack Walsh when I sensed movement above my head and saw Martindale's arm coming my way. There was no pain; just a flash of dull orange behind my eyelids and the last thing I remember was the floor of the car coming up to meet my face. This time I was out for the count.

I have no idea how long I was unconscious, but I think it was about ten minutes. When I came to, the windows were dark, and I knew we were beyond the edge of town and away from the streetlights. My breathing must have changed noticeably and alerted them, because Walsh reached up and turned on the dome light. "Hello, Tucker," he said in a voice that was full of good-natured self-confidence. "You've become a real nuisance. Did you know that?"

I could only groan.

"Headache?" he asked cheerfully.

"Screw you," I managed despite my throbbing head.

"Oh, come now, Tucker. There's no point in being childish. Get off the floor and sit up like a man."

Martindale reached over the seatback and grabbed the collar and shoulders of my coat and hauled me up and pitched me back against the rear seat. "How's everything going, Virg?" he asked.

"What in the name of God are you doing here?" I asked, rubbing my head.

"I finally figured it out, Virg."

"Figured what out?"

"The big secret."

I had no idea what he was talking about, but the pain in my skull was gradually receding. "Good for you," I said.

"Not curious about the big secret, huh?"

I only grunted at him.

"I think I'll tell you anyway, Virg. The big secret is that them who gets the prizes in this life are the ones that open the door when opportunity knocks."

"You're not making any sense."

He giggled. "You see, Virg, I got some talents that you high-and-mighties down there in Matador County never did know nothing about. And that's because you don't know me. Oh, you recognize me when you see me on the street, but you don't really *see* me. Not as a man, anyway. To you and your kind, fellows like me ain't nothing more than fence posts. You don't even notice us till we ain't there any longer. Then somebody asks, 'How come there's a hole in that fence?' 'Awww, ole Stubb, he up and left and the cows done got out.' "

He was right, but I didn't feel in the mood to be apologetic about it. "Tough shit," I said.

"Yeah, and you gonna find out how tough in a little while. Anyhow, we were talking about my talents. One of them is that I can hear a gnat sneeze a half mile away. Bet you didn't know that, did you? You just wouldn't believe how good my ears are. So that night back at the ranch I didn't go get no camera like Dalton Polk told me to do. Shit, he wasn't never gonna look at them pictures no how, so why bother? I just followed the two of you out to the barn and hung around outside the doorway and listened while you talked. Heard every damn word you both said, too. And another talent of mine that comes from being a nobody at the bottom of the heap is that I don't dismiss things as quick as you do. You wrote Sheriff Walsh off as a kind of high-toned security guard for them fellows down in New Orleans, but I got to studying, and I figured out that maybe he might be just a little more important in this gambling deal than you thought he was. I also reasoned that he might have some use for a sharp fellow who could tell him you were coming his way. So I lit out for Beaumont the next morning. And it didn't take him no time at all to see my value as a man. Ain't that right, Sheriff?"

"Indeed it is," Walsh agreed.

"Say! How 'bout that redheaded gal? Was she a pretty good piece?"

"Hey!" Nolan yelled from behind the wheel. "Watch your mouth."

Stubb giggled again. "Nolan ain't too

280

happy you wound up with his girl, Virg."

"Piss on you, you white trash pecker-wood," I growled.

He was raising his sap again when Walsh stopped him. "Enough, Stubb!" he said curtly. "Let's leave a little something to tell us what we need to know."

"Which is?" I asked.

"Mr. DeMour's journal," Walsh said.

"Come clean on who you're fronting for and I might just give you the damn thing," I said.

"You're hardly in any position to bargain," he replied.

"As long as you don't know where that journal is, I am."

"Oh, I think we can get that little piece of information out of you. I fully believe that Stubb here will prove most adept at that sort of persuasion."

He was probably right, but I saw no reason to agree with him. So for lack of anything better to do, I kept talking. "I've been wondering ever since Rosario Maceo was shot just who could really be behind this whole business."

Walsh sighed. "Behind it all? Why, some people who are intent upon seeing the Gulf Coast realize its full potential."

"Full potential?" I asked. "What on earth

are you talking about?"

"Think for a minute. Imagine a string of resort towns and casinos from Beaumont to Brownsville. Galveston, Port Aransas, Corpus Christi, Padre Island. Why, Texas could become the playground of the nation. A nation that's going to come out of this war rich beyond imagining."

"And you're their waterboy?"

In the dim glow of the dome light I could see his well-kept teeth gleaming as he smiled indulgently. "You're not going to get under my skin with a meaningless little insult like that. I'm the man who can provide a certain type of protection, which makes me a major factor in the whole plan."

"How long have you had somebody tailing me?"

"Ever since you hit town."

Martindale turned around to look at me once more. "There you go again, Virg," he said. "Too high and mighty to cover your own back. It just never entered your mind that somebody as important as you are could be under surveillance, did you? I mean, with that Ranger commission and all."

"You're sure right about that, Stubb," Walsh agreed. "That's something I've noticed about the Rangers. They pin on that badge and they think everybody who sees it is going to roll over and play dead for them."

We fell into silence and the big Buick sped onward into the night. I saw a sign that said, SARATOGA 5 MILES, and I felt my heart sink. I knew where they were taking me — into the heart of the Big Thicket — the Pine Island Bayou drainage basin — one of the most impenetrable parts of the whole state. Sparsely populated with only a couple of small villages and a few dozen subsistence farms, it was about fifty miles long and half as many miles wide — a low, flat, alluvial jungle of ancient gums and oaks and magnolias, many of which were too big for two men to reach around, their trunks rising from tangles of vines and undergrowth so dense that it was joked that the bears and panthers that had once roamed it by the hundreds had to use the trails to get around.

The Thicket had been settled in the years between the Texas Revolution and the Civil War by the last of the old Southern frontiersmen, people who neither wanted nor needed the benefits of civilization beyond gunpowder, lead, salt, coffee, and what few other things they couldn't make for themselves. Three generations of Texans had grown up on stories of people who had wandered into the Thicket and never been seen again. I didn't want to be one of them, but it was my guess that Milam Walsh and his cronies had other ideas.

I once knew an old Oklahoma deputy sheriff who'd enjoyed one of the most interesting careers of anyone I ever met in law enforcement. After more than three decades of chasing moonshiners and other assorted felons in Oklahoma's notorious Cookson Hills, he'd been one of five experienced lawmen hired to teach pistol shooting to the agents of the FBI after Congress passed the bill that allowed them to carry firearms in the mid-1930s. Besides being a man of great courage and vast experience, he was blessed with a native wit and one of the most brilliant, if untutored, minds of anyone I had ever encountered. One of his maxims — and it is a maxim I have come to believe myself — is that criminals are fundamentally stupid no matter how high some of them may score on an intelligence test. And some do score quite high.

Walsh and his cronies were true criminals despite their badges. They were men with criminal minds and criminal attitudes, subject to all the criminal shortcomings that keep the prisons full. Had they cuffed my hands behind my back, which is what any reasonably prudent officer would have done, I would be dead today. But they didn't. And they should have known better. Stubb Martindale because of the skinny kid I'd once been who fought him three times, the third time committing what amounted to a felony assault; Nolan Dunning because of the beating I'd given him up in San Gabriel; and Walsh because he was supposedly an experienced lawman. But through the hoodlums' combination of arrogance and sloth, coupled with the unshakable belief that they had the monopoly on violence and intimidation, they'd cuffed my hands in front of me, and it proved to be their undoing.

I made no conscious decision. Indeed, I suppose the decision had been made thirty-five years earlier when I was born with the same bullheaded determination that drove my ancestor, Isaiah Tucker, all his life, a determination that was rooted in our genes. There was no doubt in my mind that my ultimate destination that night was meant to be a shallow grave, but I didn't intend to go easy because it just wasn't in my nature to do so. So I did what only a fool would have done.

On either side of the car rose dark walls of forest. A couple of miles back we'd turned off the paved road onto a gravel trail that led deep into the heart of the Thicket, and since then I'd been looking for my chance. At last I saw what I needed. Ahead the road forked, and in the apex of the fork sat an ancient gum tree, its trunk nearly three feet in diameter at the base. At that precise moment Walsh began to blather on once again, building his air-castle casinos along a golden Texas coast that would never be. I noticed that the car's speedometer read twenty-five miles per hour just as I lunged over the back of the seat and wrestled the wheel out of Nolan Dunning's grip.

The Buick was the big four-door model, just one step down from a limousine. The back passenger compartment sported a footrest on either side, a sort of flattened bar fixed to a U-shaped mount that held it a couple of inches above the floor. As I sprang forward my right foot slipped under this metal contraption, and a little voice in the back of my mind told me that any triumph I might enjoy that night was going to be tempered with sorrow.

Dunning had good reflexes, but they weren't good enough. He managed to get his foot on the brake, but the car hadn't shed more than a small fraction of its speed when I steered it headfirst into the gum tree. The results were dramatic. Stubb Martindale flew halfway through the windshield as neatly as a man slipping his foot into an old and well-loved boot. At the same time Dunning slammed into the steering wheel so violently that it came apart in my hands, his head whipping forward like a puppet on a broken string, while Walsh piled into the back of the front seat in midsentence. Stubb was motionless and the other two stunned. As for me, for just one unworldly moment, I felt like I was suspended in space, held aloft by some great hand holding my left foot, which was firmly wedged under the footrest. Then I felt a crystal clear *pop* as the bone in my instep behind my big toe broke just as cleanly as Dunning's finger had broken that day back in San Gabriel. A dozen thoughts raced through my mind, most of them having to do with chickens coming home to roost and quid-pro-quos and devils getting their due. But I didn't have time to dwell on the irony of the moment. Like the man in Frost's poem, I had miles to go before I slept.

CHAPTER TWENTY-TWO

I wound up spending the night in the woods. It was cold and damp and lonely, and at times it was frightening. What more is there to say? All the stories I'd heard about panthers, which is what woodland cougars are called in that part of the world, came back to haunt me when I heard a large animal somewhere behind me in the underbrush lapping water with a feline intensity. I had Walsh's .38 Police Positive, but I had little confidence in it being adequate for a varmint that size. At last the sky grew light in the east, and the day began to dawn foggy and gray. As soon as I could see a few yards I stood up. During the night I'd had to slit the side of my boot with my pocketknife where my foot was swelling horribly, and it was agony to get on my feet again. But I had no choice.

I was on a narrow dirt road. I had absolutely no desire to go back toward the car, so instead I went in the opposite direction. Each step sent a burning pain shooting up my leg. After a few hundred yards I became dizzy and almost passed out. I hadn't had a thing since the peanut butter and crackers I'd eaten the evening before, and my blood sugar was getting low. I stood with my hand braced against the trunk of a tree until the dizziness passed, but still I felt weak. Nevertheless, I pressed on.

A quarter mile farther down the road I came to a mailbox that stood beside a lane that was really no more than a pair of well-worn car tracks. The mailbox was reasonably new, and the grass was worn away where the mail carrier had been driving off the road to get to it. That told me there had to be people who went with the mailbox.

The lane wound its way into the woods for maybe an eighth of a mile, then made a sharp bend to the left and opened into a clearing of about three acres. In the center of the clearing, surrounded by a half dozen mammoth oak trees, stood a large house with a roof of wood shingles. Perched at least three feet off the ground on brick piers, it had a long gallery across its front, an open dog-trot hallway, and brick chimneys at either end. Though it was void of paint and its wooden shingles were green with age, it was trim and square and its yard was neat. From one of the chimneys a wisp of wood smoke curled upward into the chilly air, and under a shed in back I could see a Ford pickup that looked no more than a year or so old.

I was about two-thirds of the way across the front yard when an ancient, liver-colored pit bull emerged from beneath the porch and made its way toward me, its golden eyes full of curiosity. Its tail wagged languidly, and its progress was slow and deliberate like that of an old gentleman with all the time in the world. Then a man came around the corner of the house. He appeared to be a few years older than me and wore a battered felt hat, khakis, and a denim coat. Like the dog, his eyes were more curious than hostile. When he saw me he stopped, but the dog sauntered on until it stood at my feet. Then it sat back on its haunches and looked up at me expectantly. I reached down and let it smell my hand. After a moment's hesitation, it licked my fingers and thumped its tail on the ground. Thus encouraged, I scratched it carefully between its closely cropped ears. Its muzzle, head, and neck all showed masses of scars beneath its reddish coat. I examined it closely for a few moments, then asked, "Is this a Lightner dog, by any chance?"

The man nodded slowly. "Yes. It's an Old Family Red Nose out of William Lightner's stock. You know pits?" he asked.

"Some."

"A fellow named Dan McCoy picked the sire for that animal. I've heard he's dead now."

"He is, but I knew him well," I said.

"Really?"

"If we're talking about the same man. The Dan McCoy I knew was an itinerant fry cook and full-time alcoholic who rode the rails all over this county. Had a talent for breeding bulldogs that's never been equaled. McCoy's eaten at my father's table many a time."

"That's him," he said and paused to reflect for a moment before he spoke, then tilted his head quizzically to one side. "Are you a dog fighter?" he finally asked.

I shook my head.

"Me neither. I'm too tenderhearted about dogs. But my daddy . . ." He smiled and shook his head ruefully.

"Mine too."

He raised his hat and scratched his head for a moment, then asked, "Mister, I know it's changing the subject, but you look a little peaked. Is there anything I can do for you?"

I straightened up from petting the old dog, and when I did, the world spun and reeled all around me once again. "I don't know," I muttered. "Something to eat before I pass out might help. I think I'm about to faint."

Ten minutes later I was seated at a big pine table in a big clean kitchen, halfway through a stiff bourbon toddy, with my spirits beginning to lift. My host's name turned out to be Frank Riddle and his wife was Nan. She was a small, sandy-haired woman with a ready smile and a good figure under a gingham dress and ruffled apron. They both had direct blue eyes and faces unsullied by either guile or suspicion.

I'd told them I was an officer in the middle of an investigation. My badge and ID lay on the table. I'd given Walsh's Colt to Riddle outside because I didn't like the idea of entering the man's house armed. It now rested on a shelf near the door. In the far corner of the room loomed a large coal-oil cookstove where Nan Riddle busied herself with breakfast. Her husband sat across the table from me nursing a cup of coffee. After putting a cookie sheet full of biscuits in the oven, she sat a pan of hot steaming water in front of me, along with a washcloth, a towel, and a bar of soap.

"You're an angel from heaven," I told her. "I feel as nasty as a buzzard. This will help a lot."

She gave me a quick smile and asked, "What's wrong with your foot?"

"It's broken," I replied.

"Don't it hurt?"

"Lord, yes, it hurts," I replied and raised my toddy glass. "But this whiskey is helping."

"I've got something better than that," she said and went out the kitchen door. By the time I'd finished washing my face and hands, she reentered the room and set a prescription pill bottle beside my glass. "Half-grain codeine," she said. "I broke my arm a couple of years ago, but I couldn't take this stuff. It made me crazy. You're welcome to it if you think you can handle it. There's about twenty of 'em left."

"Now I *know* you're an angel," I told her.

"Better start off with two," she said and poured more bourbon into my glass.

A few minutes later I tore into a plateful of sausage and buttered biscuits and ribbon cane syrup, eating like a man who hadn't been fed in a week. By the time I was halfway through my meal both the codeine and whiskey had started to kick in, and I felt better than I had since I heard about Madeline's death. I looked across the table at my hosts. "This is so kind of you," I said.

"Heck, we're glad to have company," Frank Riddle said. "It gets lonesome out here."

"Where are we exactly?" I asked.

He grinned. "A little north of Batson and a couple of miles south of Kaiser's Burnout. Does that mean anything to you?"

"No," I said. "But I saw a sign last night that said we were five miles from Saratoga. I've been there. So we must be . . . what? About twenty miles west of U.S. Sixty-nine. Right?"

"That's about it." He sipped his coffee in silence for a few moments, then said, "You know, it truly surprised me that you recognized a Lightner dog a little while ago."

"We had some of them," I replied. "Some of John Colby's stock, too."

"You say your dad was a fighter?"

"In a small way. He had a few dogs and couple of Mexicans who took care of them for him. He was a rancher by occupation."

"Where you from?" he asked.

"Matador County."

He nodded thoughtfully and forked another piece of sausage onto his plate. "My daddy fought dogs all over Southeast Texas and southern Louisiana. Gamecocks, too. That old fellow outside is the last good pit dog he had. Won seven straight fights in record time, and killed one of Floyd Bedding's best dogs in under five minutes. I don't hold with it, though."

"Me either," I said. "I'd get real attached to one of the dogs, then Dad would take it off and get it killed. I'm still half mad about some of the animals I lost."

"I understand," he said with a nod.

"What do you do?" I asked. "If you don't mind my asking."

"He hunts," his wife chimed in with a grin.

He smiled at her easily. "I farm some. And like she said, I hunt a lot. You see, my family had some land in the Batson oil field, and we've got a little money. As long as we're careful with the checkbook we do fine."

"I see."

"I guess you wonder why we don't move into town where living would be easier."

I shook my head and grinned. "It's no mystery to me. I live way out in the country, too. We've only had electricity and running water at my ranch for a couple of years."

We ate on in silence, and finally he pushed

his plate aside and lighted a Camel. I dug around and came up with my Chesterfields and got one going.

"I know you're bound to be curious about all this business," I said. "I mean, what I'm doing out here in the woods in the early morning with a broke foot and torn-up clothes."

He nodded thoughtfully. "Yeah, but a little curiosity never killed a man." He glanced at his wife and winked at her affectionately. "Or a woman either, though I've known some that thought it would."

"I feel obliged to you," I said. "And I think you have a right to know what you've gotten into by taking me in. Do you know who Milam Walsh is?" I asked.

"Sure."

"How much do you know about him?"

"I know that he's sorry, and that he's a big-time crook who's capable of just about anything."

"He's all of that," I agreed with a nod. I went on to relate how Walsh and his goons had kidnapped me in front of Alma Copeland's house, and how I'd rammed the car into the big gum tree, and how I'd held the muzzle of Walsh's own Colt Police Positive ground into his belly with about three pounds of pressure on the trigger until he

296

carefully unlocked my handcuffs. I told them how I'd fled, leaving the three Jefferson County lawmen in the wrecked Buick, and how I'd spent the night shivering in the cold darkness before stumbling onto their place.

"Why did they grab you?" Riddle asked.

"Because I've got evidence squirreled away that links Walsh up with some New Orleans gangsters, and he wants to get his hands on it."

"So they were going to beat on you until you told them where it is . . ."

I nodded.

"You're lucky you got loose from them. After they got what they wanted, they'd have left your carcass somewhere out in the bushes just as sure as taxes."

"I know that," I replied. "And you may be in danger, too. They could come here looking for me."

He smiled wryly and shook his head. "No, they won't. They might sneak up here by the dead of night and kill somebody, or throw a body out in a ditch, but you couldn't pay him or any of his people enough money to come in the daytime and bother a man. Especially not me."

"Why's that?" I asked.

"Because this is Hardin County, and my

uncle has been high sheriff here for nearly thirty years. He'd as soon kill Walsh as not."

"Really?"

"You bet. My uncle John is a Campbellite elder with fixed ideas about how lawmen ought to act, and Walsh don't measure up to his standards. In fact, the two of them done had one little head-butting incident."

"What happened?"

"Walsh come up here trying to throw his weight around about an old boy from Port Arthur that Uncle John had locked up in the jail. He slapped the fire out of Walsh in front of about a dozen people, right there on the street in town."

"What did Walsh do?" I asked.

"He tucked his tail between his legs and went on back to Beaumont. So you just relax and don't worry. You're as safe here as you'd be at home. My uncle ain't got no more use for that man than he has for a cut dog, and Walsh knows it. Want another shot of this whiskey?"

CHAPTER TWENTY-THREE

Every time I find myself on the verge of giving up on the human race, I meet somebody like Frank and Nan Riddle. Then I'm forced to pull up a few inches short of the simon-pure misanthropy my instincts tell me is the only sane response to my own species. People like them are what everybody could be if we'd all just practice a little common decency. I also suspected that what he'd said about being careful with the checkbook was modesty on his part. Either that or the desire to keep his dollars-and-cents business to himself, something my dad always claimed was a sound practice for anyone, man or woman. I knew that with the war on and oil at an all-time high, even a few acres in the Batson Field would yield very generous royalties, and my guess was that they had money enough in the bank to buy just about anything they wanted. But they also had something that was almost as important: sense enough not to want much.

After breakfast he offered to take me into the county seat to a doctor.

I shook my head. "They're bound to have seen me limping off last night, so I'd just as soon not have it known around town that a stranger with a broken foot was looking for medical attention."

Instead I asked him if he'd drive me to the nearest phone to make a call. "Be happy to," he replied. "But if you're not going to see the doctor, why don't you stay here and rest and let me make it for you? That is, if it's not too personal."

I thought for a few seconds. I'd already decided to take Deader Simms up on his offer of help. It was either that or call the phone company office in Palestine and leave a message for Nora to come get me. But I reasoned that Simms could more easily afford the time and the gasoline. Of course I could have called Jim Rutherford, but that would have meant going back to Jefferson County, something I didn't intend to do. But there was no reason Riddle couldn't deliver a message to Simms for me. And I was utterly exhausted. "Okay," I said. "But you need to understand that if he's not at home you may be stuck with me until tomorrow."

He waved off the possibility as not worthy of concern. "Always glad to have a little company. Don't you worry about it."

I gave him Simms's number and tried to pay him for his trouble. He acted mildly insulted at the suggestion, which was exactly what I had expected. He did agree to take my unlimited gas rationing card and fill his truck up while he was in town. A few minutes later I dozed off into a dreamless sleep between sparkling white sheets that smelled faintly of wood smoke and lye soap.

They woke me shortly before the noon meal, which consisted of home-cured ham, winter turnip greens, hot corn bread, and more ribbon cane syrup.

"Your Mr. Simms answered on the second ring," Riddle told me as we sat down at the table. "He said he'd send somebody to take you wherever you needed to go, but he thought it would probably be late in the day or maybe even early evening when they got here."

"Thanks. I appreciate it."

"He also asked me if you'd made any progress."

"What did you tell him?"

He gave me an ironic smile. "I said you'd made so much progress that you'd got your foot broke and your car stole, and that you

301

probably didn't need no more progress right now."

I laughed. "You're right, you know. I sure don't need any more cases like this. Which is why I'm quitting law enforcement and going back to ranching."

"I don't blame you. I did tell him that you said you'd call him in the next few days, and that you had part of the answer."

After we ate I took two more codeine tablets and spent the bulk of the afternoon dozing in a rocking chair beside the fireplace. Riddle was in and out as he did his chores around the place. They had a battery radio, and a couple of times I heard the strains of fiddle music and once I caught a Cajun-tinged voice that identified the station as one in Lafayette, Louisiana. A little after four Nan came in with a mug of fresh coffee for me and noticed me gazing at the picture of a young man in an army uniform that sat on the mantelpiece. "That's our boy, Sam," she said.

"You don't look old enough to have a boy in the army," I said.

"I was fifteen when we got married," she replied with a girlish laugh. "We get started young down here."

"Do you have any other children?"

"One daughter. She's married to a fellow

that works at the Texas Company refinery in Port Arthur. He does some real important something-or-other that keeps him out of the army. I reckon they figure he's worth more where he's at than he would be carrying a gun. I wish Sam had something like that. I worry about him all the time."

She left the room and I drank my coffee, then dozed a little more. About an hour before sundown my host helped me hobble out onto the porch for a breath of fresh air. It was chilly, but being out-of-doors lifted my spirits. The sky had cleared during the day, and the dying light of the setting sun gave the remote clearing an unworldly feel. The land we were on had never been logged. All around us loomed a great forest of tall climax hardwoods. It was a setting that made it easy to imagine what the whole country had been like before the white man came. We sat in a pair of rough-hewn hickory rockers and talked. I told him about Isaiah Tucker's journey to Texas and about the founding of La Rosa, and he recounted to me how his great-grandparents had come to the Big Thicket in the 1840s, and I learned that Kaiser's Burnout got its name when a Confederate officer named Kaiser torched several hundred acres trying to flush out draft resisters during the Civil War.

We talked of dogs we'd hunted behind and deer we'd killed and men we'd known, now all gone from this earth. Finally our conversation lapsed and we sat in silence enjoying the timeless peace of the gathering twilight. Then, just as we were rising to go inside, Jack Amber's Cord glided softly up the drive and stopped in front of the house.

Chapter Twenty-Four

I said good-bye to Frank and Nan Riddle on the front porch.

"Come back next fall and we'll get us some deer," Frank said.

"I'll do it," I replied as I shook his hand, knowing that in his world such an invitation was about as high a compliment as he could pay a man. And I meant it. But first I had to manage to live through the next few days.

Once we were in the car, I asked Jack to take me to Press Rafferty's place. Going to La Rosa would have meant an all-night drive, and I just wasn't up to it.

"What in the hell were you doing that caused you to wind up way out here in the shape you're in?" Jack asked as soon as we were back on the road.

I quickly gave him an abbreviated version of the previous day's events, ending with my arrival at the Riddle home early that morning.

"So Walsh is in this mess up to his eye-balls?" he said.

"Right. And as a principal, not just as the after-the-fact leech we thought he was. Or at least he thinks he's a principal. The people behind him may have other ideas."

"But who in hell could he be fronting for?"

"Beats me, Jack. I spent the whole after-noon trying to figure that out. But whoever it is, they think big." I went on to tell him about the string of resort casinos Walsh had bragged about the evening before.

"Amazing," he muttered.

"So how are things going with your book in Port Arthur?" I asked.

"Oh, just great," he said bitterly. "I'm back in business, and they're taking twenty-five percent right off the top."

"How about the one in Houston?"

He shook his head. "They can't touch it."

"And the Maceos?"

"Nobody's approached them either."

"How's Rosario?" I asked.

"He's okay, but the bodyguard died."

"Did you know him?"

He nodded. "Yeah. He was an ex–high school football star at Texas City. Got a scholarship to UT, but got hurt his first year. The boy wasn't too bright. Rosario took him on just to give him a job."

"Pity," I said.

"By the way . . . I went by the Creole and took care of your bill."

"Thanks, Jack," I said in relief. "I'm glad you thought to do that. I'll send you a check as soon as I get home."

He shook his head. "It's on Mr. Simms. And I picked up your clothes and suitcase and stuff. It's all in the trunk."

"Thank God. I've been wearing what I've got on for two days. Now if I only knew where my car is."

"I don't think you're likely to ever see it again, Virgil."

"Me either, but I can always hope."

Press had already gone to bed, but Nora was still up reading by lamplight. She came to the door in her robe, shotgun in hand, and I lunged from the car and yelled out my name lest she shoot us on general principles. Once she saw who I was, she quelled the dogs long enough for us to get in the house unmolested. By that time the commotion had brought her dad out of bed, and I introduced them both to Jack. Press took one look at me, shook his head sadly, then went outside to crank the Delco so I could get a bath. While I soaked, Jack ate a quick supper. Just as I was getting out of the tub he stuck his head in the bathroom door. "I'm off, Virgil," he said.

"You're not driving back to the coast tonight, are you?"

He shook his head. "I'm going to stay at the O'Neal Hotel in Palestine. Your friends offered me a room here, but I'm always more comfortable in a hotel."

After he left, I dried off and limped out into the hall. Nora appeared and tried to get me to eat. I shook my head. "Just a toddy and then sleep," I said. "I'm dead on my feet."

She steered me into the guest room, disappeared, then quickly returned with a bottle of brandy and a glass, both of which she placed on the table beside my bed. "Sleep tight," she said. "If you need anything in the night, just call out. I'm in the next room. And by the way, there's an old pair of crutches out in the barn Daddy said he'd find for you tomorrow."

Jack had put my suitcase on the end of the bed, and I quickly changed into fresh underwear and a clean undershirt.

I downed two more of the codeine tablets with about three ounces of brandy, climbed into bed, and was asleep before I knew it.

The doctor was a barrel-chested GP.

Though it was Sunday morning, the man was dressed in a shirt and tie under a clean white lab coat. His practice was in one side of a big Victorian house on Highway 79 in Palestine. He and his wife, who doubled as his nurse, lived in the other half. Nora had known the man for years and said he was one of the better doctors in town.

"Some people are born fools, Mr. Tucker," he said. "And some people have to work hard to get there. Which is it with you?"

"Both," Nora said, answering his question for me. "He came into the world crazy, and he's done his best to improve on what God gave him."

"I believe it," he said, shaking his head. "Why didn't you do something about this foot when it first happened?"

"Some men were trying to kill me, and I had to hide in the woods all night."

He never batted an eyelash. "Well, such things do happen, I'm told. But whatever your reasons, there's nothing I can do for you except give you some more pain medication. Your foot is swollen far too much to put a cast on it. The pain would drive you crazy, then when the swelling went down the cast would be too loose."

"So what can I do?" I asked.

"Let it heal the way it is, then have it re-

broken under surgical conditions by somebody who knows what they're doing. Where
are you from?"

"Matador County."

"Go to San Antonio. They've got some
good bone men there."

He wrote me a prescription for a hundred
of the same codeine tablets I'd been taking.

"That's a pretty big prescription, isn't it?"
I asked.

He shrugged. "A man's either going to be
a dope fiend or he isn't, and the size of a
bottle of pills doesn't have much to do with
it. I see no reason for you to have to pay
some doctor down in South Texas another
three dollars to prescribe some more of the
damn things. Don't take them except when
you have to, and put what's left in your
medicine cabinet for emergencies. Soak that
foot in epsom-salts water twice a day, and
keep it elevated as much as you can."

We stopped by the telephone company office so I could call Tía Carmen. She spoke
with me and Nora both, and the outcome
of the whole matter was that the Raffertys
were to bring me back to La Rosa and stay
through Christmas, which was only a few
days away.

That night, after Press and Brenda were

asleep, Nora came into my room with a tray that carried a kerosene lamp, a bottle of brandy, and two glasses. "Like a little company?" she asked.

"Sure," I said. "How did you know I was awake?"

"I didn't. I was going to rouse you if you weren't."

She set the lamp on the bedside table and adjusted its wick as low as it would go. Then she poured us each a glass of brandy. After giving me mine, she crawled up on the foot of the bed facing me and curled her legs up under her Indian style. "How you doing, Virg?" she asked.

"Okay," I said offhandedly.

"No, I mean how you *doing*?"

"In respect to what?"

"Madeline."

I drew in a deep breath and sighed a long sigh. "Mostly I feel sorry for her. If she had stayed here she would still be alive today. But like your doctor friend said, some people are born fools."

"So you're not wallowing in guilt?"

I shook my head. "I think I did the best I could have under the circumstances. Besides, I've never been much of a hand at beating myself up over what's already done."

She grinned at me. "No, I remember back

when we were kids you were always the first one to forgive yourself, and you expected everybody else to hop on the bandwagon."

I grinned back at her and said nothing.

"Did you know she was halfway in love with you?" she asked.

"I'm not surprised that she would lead you to believe that. It may have even been true." I went on to tell her of Madeline's affair with Henry DeMour, and how she'd kept it from me. "So you can see that she wasn't above using people to get what she wanted."

"Who is?"

"You, Nora," I said honestly. "Everything's out in front with you."

"Yep," she said, sipping her brandy. "I'm the original pay-as-you-go girl. I don't like debts, and you start piling them up the minute you start misleading people. Which is why I wanted to know how you felt about Madeline. I didn't want to be accused of seducing a man who was pining away for his dead sweetheart."

"Huh?"

"You heard me," she said as she rose from the bed. She quickly drained her brandy and dropped her robe to the floor. "I think we've earned this, Virgil. And I suspect we'll never get another chance." She pulled her gown over her head and slid into the bed beside me. "That is, unless you've taken too many of them damn codeine pills."

"I think I can manage," I said softly and turned toward her.

CHAPTER TWENTY-FIVE

It was the best Christmas in recent memory, and there is no doubt in my mind that having Brenda present made all the difference. When we arrived, a tall cedar tree already stood in the corner of the living room ready to be trimmed, the first one we'd had in years. My aunt had been shopping in town, and she showered more presents on Brenda than any little girl needed. Alonzo and the other vaqueros doted on her and argued among themselves about which one would get to ride her around on the front of his saddle. After the second day, Nora pronounced the kid completely ruined by all the attention. It was a fine time, and I was able to forget for a while the dark cloud that hung on my horizon.

The night before they were due to leave, Nora entered my room quietly through the connecting door and slipped once more between the covers beside me. Later, over brandy and cigarettes, we talked for a while, me reclining propped up on my pillows, she leaning against the footboard of the bed, her legs stretched out in front of her. She was wearing one of my old shirts, her hair was disheveled, and her eyes were sleepy. But she looked gorgeous anyway. I finished my brandy quickly, feeling it warm my insides, then poured a couple more inches into my glass.

"I just want you to know, Virgil," she said, "that I believe Madeline was basically a good kid, and I think it was really decent of you to do what you did for her. Not everybody would have."

I grinned at her. "I'll accept a verdict of decent," I said, "but I don't want anybody thinking I'm some kind of starry-eyed idealist."

She laughed. "That's never gonna happen, Virgil. Not anybody who knows you, anyway."

"I hope not. But, I think I'm getting even worse the older I get. Almost as cynical as old Charlie Grist, in fact. When this war first started I was all cranked up to go do my duty. I tried to get my naval commission reactivated, but they wouldn't have me. And to tell the truth, I felt guilty as hell that I wasn't in uniform. But in the last few days I've been thinking about the war, and I realize now that in my heart I've known all along that it's just another damned catastrophe brought on by rascals and fools. When you put aside all the political crap they spout to justify themselves, Hitler and the Jap warlords are really no different from Scorpino and Walsh and Salisbury."

"Virgil . . ."

"And if that's not disgusting enough, add in the half dozen or so big American banks who were doing business with the Japs and the Germans both, and who used every bit of political clout they had right up to the day Pearl Harbor was bombed to keep us from breaking off diplomatic relations with them so's not to kill the goose that was laying the golden eggs. Then on top of that put the munitions makers and the chemical firms who wanted war just as bad as the banks wanted peace because that's where *their* profits were going to be. So when you get right down to it, why should I give my life to pay for their stupidity and greed?"

"You sound like my daddy," she said.

"Really?" I asked. "Well, did he ever tell you that the human race is just a great big buzzard perched at the top of a rotting tree waiting for an opportunity to pick its own carcass clean?"

She'd been amused by my little tirade, and her eyes were full of mischief in the lamplight. "Not in those exact words. But he got the idea across. And I suspect there's a lot of truth in what you say. But when you boil it all down, the human race is all we've got."

"I'm afraid you're right," I said. Then at that moment it hit me just how many years her face and her ash blond hair and her impish smile had been lurking in the back of my mind. So long, in fact, and so omnipresent that I'd become unconscious of it. I realized, too, how much I cared for her and how hopeless it all was. "Nora, let's get married," I said impulsively, all but certain what her reaction would be.

She shook her head sadly. "We can't, Virgil."

"Is it the climate down here in South Texas?"

"Partly. But there's more to consider than that."

"What?"

"Daddy. I can't take Brenda away from him. Besides, he's getting older, and we're all he's got. The time will come —"

"Hell," I said, "bring him down here, too."

She got out of bed and poured more brandy into her glass, her flanks under my old shirt shining golden in the dim lamp-light. Then she took a long pull of her drink and turned to face me. "Virgil, up at home Daddy's *somebody.* He's known in a half dozen counties as the best hunter and dog man in the Neches River bottom. People come to him for advice and small loans and all kinds of help, and even the Liquor Control Board officers and the game wardens who try to catch him respect him. But down here?" She shook her head and grimaced. "Down here he'd just be another old geezer with a bunch of stories nobody wants to hear."

"So maybe I could move up to Palestine," I said, knowing even as I spoke that it was a fool's notion.

"Now there's a really fine idea," she said sarcastically. "Then a few years from now you could start sitting on the front porch and brooding all the time because Tía Carmen had died and you'd sold off La Rosa and thrown away your birthright. What good would you be to me then? Hell, I'd have to start having affairs just to have somebody to talk to."

"You're right, of course," I said, smiling a little at her blunt honesty.

She drained her glass and set it on the bedside table, then said, "There are things in this world that outweigh romance, Virgil. Family and place and a person's obligations are all more important. And you know it as well as I do."

We dropped the subject and talked on for another half hour until finally she came around the bed and climbed in. I turned off the light and spooned her up against me, pressing her back close to my belly. After a little while we both drifted off to sleep. About an hour later I half awoke as she slipped from my bed and went back to her own room. Early the next morning she and Brenda and Press left for Palestine, and except for a few quick hugs over the years, I never held Nora Rafferty in my arms again.

CHAPTER TWENTY-SIX

"We'll hear something from Walsh soon," I told my aunt over our midmorning coffee. "Either that or they'll attack the ranch. Which I can't see them doing since the guards are lawmen."

"You feel sure he'll try to contact you?" she asked.

I gave her a thoughtful nod. "The fact that I haven't gone to the Rangers with the journal should tell him I'm willing to deal."

"But why haven't you gone to the Rangers? Not that I think you should, you understand. I'm just curious since you've always trusted them."

"Because we don't have any idea who's behind Walsh. Hell, it could be the governor for all I know. Going to the state boys right now might just dig us in deeper. My hope is that I can give him the damn thing and be shut of the whole mess. Like I told Jack Amber, the coast's problems aren't our problems, and I want to convince Walsh of that. I hate to see Sam and Rosario put on the spot, but there's nothing I can do about it. At the moment they're under guard and at least as safe as we are. In the long run, it might be in their best interests to make a deal, but that's not my decision to make. I just want out."

"But you know as well as I do that the journal may not satisfy him," she said.

"If that's the case, then we'll have to deal with the problem ourselves."

The call came on the last day of the year, and it came from an unexpected source. Tía Carmen picked up the phone when it rang, then after speaking for a few moments, handed me the receiver. I listened, then said, "Thanks," and hung up.

My aunt looked at me inquiringly.

I nodded. "Monday at the Windmill Café in San Diego."

"Is Walsh going to be there?" she asked.

"No, but he's sending me a proposition."

"Can you drive?"

I shook my head. "I'll get one of the vaqueros to take me over in the truck."

She nodded. I leaned down to kiss her forehead. "What do you think will happen?" she asked.

"I think there's a chance Walsh will take the diary and call it quits. If not . . ."

"If not, it's nothing we can't handle."

The man who'd just come through the door of the Windmill Café stood five feet eight inches tall. He had a sturdy, compact body and wore a well-cut double-breasted suit of blue wool, a fine white cotton dress shirt, and a silk tie of mottled reds and golds. His thinning brown hair had been carefully combed straight back from a broad forehead that loomed above a pair of mischievous brown eyes behind rimless glasses. To all the world he looked like a prosperous small-town banker. But this man was no banker. He was *El Patrón* — George Berham Parr, the Duke of Duval, the Boss of Bosses in South Texas politics.

As always, he was guarded by a trio of deputy sheriffs. All three were Mexican-American men in their midthirties, and all three were dressed in cheap gabardine suits, scuffed boots, and ratty Stetsons. Two of them were tall, and thin to the point of emaciation. They wore Colt pistols slung low on bullet-filled belts, while the third, a short, stolid individual with a jailhouse swagger, carried a sawed-off pump shotgun and stared out at the world with the dead-fish eyes of a cut-rate mortician.

They were but three of a hundred or more similarly armed and hard-bitten border men he could call on in times of need. Now forty-two years old and nearing the peak of his career, Parr was preeminent in a group of ruthless political bosses that included — besides my own aunt — such individuals as Ed Lloyd, the virtual dictator of Jim Wells County; the Guerra family of Starr and Hidalgo counties; and Judge Manuel Ramon of Laredo, a figure so spectral and illusive that it was joked that not even his own wife recognized his voice. Through these interlocking alliances, he controlled an enormous bloc of votes, a bloc large enough to make his support the deciding factor in any closely contested statewide election. Consequently, all the state's major politicians, even silver-haired patrician senators from the old cotton counties, eventually found themselves waiting hat in hand in the anteroom of his fortress-like office a block from the decaying courthouse in San Diego.

Parr came over to the table where the kid who'd driven me to the café and I sat while the two skinny deputies took up positions near the door. The shotgun man followed his boss and stood nearby the whole time we talked. "Virgil," Parr said, his voice high-pitched and happy. "How you doing?"

"I've been better, George," I replied, shaking his hand.

"So I heard. You gotta be more careful."

"I plan to once this business is all over."

He stared at me quizzically. "Just what the hell's going on?" he asked.

"Do you really want to know?"

"Sure," he said firmly. "But let's have a hamburger while we talk. Best burgers in the state."

"Okay," I agreed.

Parr motioned for the waitress, then turned to Juan, my driver, and broke into a stream of fluent Spanish. "I need to talk to your *patrón* privately," he said. "Why don't you go on back in the kitchen and eat?"

"*Sí,*" the man said with a shy nod and rose to his feet.

"Order anything you want," Parr told him. "And have them put it on my ticket."

"So you want the whole story?" I asked once Juan was gone.

"Hell yes. I want to know as much as I can about everything. Half of mastering politics is just learning to listen and knowing how to use what you hear."

"And the other half?" I asked, still grinning.

He made motions with his hands like a man dealing cards. "Spread that moola around. But you know how it works as well as I do. By the way, how's Tía Carmen?"

"As bossy as ever."

He cackled and slapped his hand down on the table. There was a boyish exuberance about the man that made you like him despite what he was. Which was as crooked as a snake. Two years earlier he'd bought the famous Dobie Ranch, making the first payment with a check he simply drew on the Duval County treasury. But in politics his word was good, and he was loyal to his friends.

The waitress appeared and took our orders. When she'd left, Parr leaned forward and said in a low voice, "Like I told you on the phone, this concerns Milam Walsh. What I didn't tell you is that he came all the way over here to see me, and asked me to arrange a meeting between the two of you. Said he had something you needed, and you had something he needed, and he was willing to trade."

"Is he still here?" I asked in surprise.

"No, he went back home."

"Why didn't he just call and tell you what he wanted on the phone? Why go to all the trouble of driving down here?"

Parr smiled coldly. "My guess is that he doesn't entirely trust the security of the telephone system."

"Oh," I said. "I get it. He's worried about the Feds?"

"Maybe," Parr said with a shrug. "Or maybe he was just unsure of himself and wanted to look me in the eye. But anyhow, I thought the whole thing was pretty strange since he's the big dog over there in Jefferson County, and you're really just a private citizen. And why come to me? I've never even met the guy before."

"He's smart, George," I said, "and he knows how things work. Which means he realizes that you're the man to see if you want to get something done in South Texas."

"Yeah, but why didn't he just drive out to the ranch if he wanted to talk to you?"

I gave him an offhanded shrug. "I guess he just didn't feel free to."

"Oh? Have the two of you had some trouble?"

"You might say that," I replied with a sour smile. "The bastard tried to kill me."

His eyes widened but he remained silent while the waitress poured our coffee. Once she'd left the table he leaned forward and said, "Maybe you need to tell me the whole story . . ."

■ ■ ■ ■

We parted an hour later, shaking hands on the sidewalk in front of the café. "You sure this is the way you want it, Virgil?" Parr asked.

I nodded. "This is the way it has to be."

"I could do better by you if you'd let me," he said.

I shook my head. "Just call Walsh as soon as you can, and convince him that I jumped at his offer. And tell him to come out to the ranch three days from now, in the late afternoon, about five — and somehow manage to let him know all the out-of-county deputies have gone home. Tell him we were having to pay for them, and that I'm glad to get out from under the expense or something like that."

He nodded. "Don't worry. I can manage it. Anything else?"

"Forget we ever had this conversation."

"Sure."

As Juan drove off up the street I looked back and saw El Patrón gazing after us, a troubled frown on his face. I didn't blame him; I didn't feel too cheerful myself.

CHAPTER TWENTY-SEVEN

That evening about eight as Aunt Carmen and I sat before the fire the phone rang. I picked it up, listened a few seconds, then said, "Thanks."

"Who was that?" she asked as I hobbled back to my chair.

"George Parr."

"It's set then?"

I nodded. "Late Thursday afternoon."

"So be it."

I sighed. "I'm just so damned sorry to have brought all this trouble down on your head," I said.

She shook her head. "You've brought nothing down on me. Where there is life, there is trouble."

"Still —"

"No! Listen to me this one time and for once accept what I tell you. It will be all right. We are safe here."

I smiled at her and asked, "You really

believe that, don't you?"

"Certainly. Hasn't it always been true?"

"I suppose so," I admitted.

"And it always will be."

I said nothing. I really didn't know how to reply. She stared at me for a few moments, the expression on her face close to exasperation. "Virgil, ownership is a sort of fiction when it comes to land. We no more own this ranch than it owns us. If you love the land and treat it with respect, it will take care of you."

"What? La Espirita de La Rosa?" I asked with a smile. "You think the spirit of the ranch itself will rise up and smite our adversaries?"

"Perhaps," she replied softly.

I regarded her with bemusement. She knew as much equine and bovine medicine as many veterinarians, to say nothing of her grasp of scientific stock breeding. She read good books, *The New Yorker, Atlantic Monthly,* the San Antonio paper, and kept up with world affairs. Yet there was no doubt in my mind that she was serious.

"You've got that faraway look in your eyes," I said. "Just like you had back when I was a little kid and you told me about Santa Muerte eating the souls of the wicked. That scared the hell out of me, you know. That, and your almost going into a damn trance when you talked about it."

She took no offense at my teasing. "Think what you wish. The time will come when you know that what I say is true. Which is why you are so important to the continuation of the family. All that we possess, we received in trust, and we must pass it on. We *must*."

"But for how long? Surely you don't expect this ranch to be in the family a thousand years from now."

"And why not?" she asked, her eyes full of fire. "Some of the great estates in Spain have lasted at least that long. And there's certainly no disgrace in trying."

"Provided we're alive a week from now," I said.

"We will be. You've spoken with Alonzo?"

"Yes," I said. "If Walsh has any sense at all he'll realize that he's out of his element down here."

"Either way, it's in the hands of God."

I decided then to broach a subject that had been on my mind ever since I'd come home. "Tía Carmen?" I asked.

"Sí?"

"Since you mentioned things being in God's hands, I want you to do something for me."

"If I can, I will."

"From now on, every time you go to mass, I want you to light a candle and say a prayer that a boy named Sam Riddle will get safely back home from the war. Will you do that?"

"Certainly. I take it he's the son of the people who helped you?"

I nodded.

She looked at me for a few moments, her eyes soft. "You surprise me, Virgil. You haven't been to church in so many years that I assumed you'd stopped believing anything at all."

"Maybe I have and maybe I haven't. I'm not even sure I know myself. But you believe and maybe God will honor that."

She nodded. "I will pray for this boy. And I pray for all the boys we know who're in the service. I pray for them all the while knowing that some of them won't make it."

We sat quietly for a few minutes, saying nothing, both lost in our own thoughts. Then I laid my book aside. "Tía Carmen, do you have any idea why Alonzo had to flee Mexico?" I asked.

"*Sí*," she replied with a nod. "He killed a highly placed police official who had raped Helena."

"Really?"

She nodded grimly. "In Mexico back in

those days it was not uncommon for a strongman to set himself up as the virtual dictator of some town and then rule for a few weeks or months until he was overthrown by someone even stronger. One such individual was a captain in the *federales.* Helena was very beautiful when she was young, and she caught his eye. At first he tried to seduce her, but being a virtuous woman, she refused him. So he simply took what he wanted."

"How did Alonzo kill him?"

She shuddered a little and looked away. "I don't want to speak about that. I don't even want to remember it."

"What's Alonzo's last name?"

"De Alejandro."

"*De* Alejandro, eh?" I asked musingly.

"*Sí,*" she said.

"I'll be dammed. I've known him all my life and never knew his last name until now. He never told me, and somehow it never seemed important to ask."

"Many generations back his ancestors were Castillian gentry. Then afterward, he fled north to La Rosa, and he and his family have been safe here ever since. Just as you will be if you love the land and treat it with respect."

CHAPTER TWENTY-EIGHT

Besides Alonzo and the other old men, the ranch had four full-time hands, two Mexicans and two Anglos, young, unmarried men who lived in the old bunkhouse a half mile from the main house. On Tuesday morning I gave them each a fifty-dollar New Year's bonus and told them to take the remainder of the week off. Within the hour they had all departed for the fleshpots of Nuevo Laredo.

On Wednesday afternoon I sent the guards home. Thursday morning dawned bright and clear. I had breakfast, then whiled the day away alternately reading and working on the ranch's bookkeeping. In the early afternoon I had a final word with Alonzo. We were as ready as we were ever going to be.

Finally, a few minutes before sunset, I heard the throaty purr of a heavy car coming up the lane. I hobbled to the front door in time to see a big Packard convertible sedan swing up in front of the house. It was one of the top-of-the-line models, a huge, looming machine, its dark green paint and shiny chrome gleaming brightly in the last dying rays of the setting sun. Three men emerged and started up the walk, and I felt my heart sink.

The healing remnants of several small cuts dotted Stubb Martindale's face, and his hair had been shaved back a couple of inches from his forehead where his scalp had taken a dozen or so stitches to close a deep gash. Nolan Dunning didn't show any outward damage beyond what I'd done to him in San Gabriel, but he moved slowly and stiffly like a man with a couple of broken ribs. Walsh was his usual confident, smiling self, dressed in a pair of gray slacks, a leather jacket, and a shirt of sparkling white.

As they started up the steps, I said, "If this visit is really as amiable as you claim, why don't you come in and have a cup of coffee? I think I've earned the right to ask a few questions."

"Gladly," Walsh answered. "There's no need for hard feelings. In fact, if you're interested, I imagine a place could be found for a man of your talents in the organization my friends and I are putting together."

"That might be something worth considering," I said.

Moving ponderously on the crutches Press had given me, I led them back through the house to the kitchen and flopped down gratefully in a chair on the far side of the table. "Have a seat," I said.

Dunning's face was impassive, but Stubb Martindale had been staring daggers at me since he'd come in the house. I winked at him and said, "Hi, Stubb. New hairstyle?"

He opened his mouth to speak, but Walsh cut him off brusquely. "I believe you mentioned coffee?"

"Right you are," I said.

The two younger men took seats on either side of their boss. My aunt came in the room and I introduced her to Walsh. He was polite, but paid no more attention to her than he would have a waitress in a restaurant. She reached for the big percolator on the back of the stove, and after she'd poured us each a cup, I found myself staring across the table at the man.

Some might have said that Milam Walsh had come a long way from the decaying blue-collar neighborhood in Port Arthur where he'd been born and raised. Personally, I don't think he ever left it, at least not in his own mind. Underneath his silky exterior and charm-school manners still lurked all the sullen, poor-boy resentments that had driven him so ruthlessly upward. Drafted into the American army not long after Wilson's declaration of war, he'd shipped to Europe with Pershing's force and seen a fair amount of combat.

Despite the democratic rhetoric and the successes of the occasional Stonewall Jackson or Ulysses S. Grant, the American officer corps has always been dominated by men from prosperous, well-to-do families. I suspect that it was there, in the trenches of France, perhaps chafing under the inept leadership of some high-born CO who was his equal in neither brains nor ability, that Walsh first understood that the class distinctions he'd suffered growing up back in Texas were likely to be permanent. Unless, of course, he took matters in hand himself.

Then after the war came a taste of the splendors of Paris. But a common soldier's plebeian amusements wouldn't have satisfied him completely, and in my mind's eye I could see him standing beside some broad Parisian boulevard in the gathering twilight, gaping at the fine Renault limousines that whisked by, and at the stylish women and finely dressed men and high-ranking officers who entered the nightspots where a

336

month's worth of his pay wouldn't even meet the cover charge. Then he was back home again and struggling to put himself through college by bussing tables, the Twenties beginning to roar all around him, with the rich young swells he'd known in high school decked out in their Stutz roadsters, their sexy and compliant girlfriends beside them, passing him as he plodded homeward late at night on the rain-slicked streets, and then gliding off into the night while their mocking laughter rang in his burning ears.

My earlier comparison of him to Errol Flynn was more accurate than I realized. His physical appearance, his style of dress, his demeanor, even his way of phrasing his sentences — all were straight out of Hollywood. There was nothing left of the real Milam Walsh except his hidden resentments and his boundless ambition. He was like a man who wasn't there. Only he *was* there, and he was my problem as he sat sipping his coffee and returning my stare. "So what do you want to know?" he asked me at last.

"Let me give you a theory I've come up with," I said, "and then you can tell me how close I am."

"Sure, why not?" he replied with a smile.

I returned the smile. "It was you, wasn't it? You were the one behind the whole thing.

You and nobody else."

His face lighted up as though I'd paid him a compliment, and he asked, "What makes you think so?"

"Well, I kept trying to figure out who those 'powerful individuals' behind you could be, the ones you told me about that night in the car. But there was nobody that fit. I've got a pretty fair grasp of how the various power structures in this state operate, and there just wasn't anybody with that much clout who would have been interested. They were all too busy frying other fish. Then finally a couple of days ago it hit me, and I realized that it was you all along. You were the one who dreamed up the idea of taking over the gambling in Galveston. It was you who approached Salisbury instead of the other way around. And that's what got this whole mess started."

He gave me another film-idol smile and said easily, "You're pretty smart to have figured that out, Tucker."

"Thanks," I said dryly. "And your being a county sheriff was a perfect cover. Oh, people expect a certain amount of corruption in law enforcement, and I've even known a couple of peace officers who owned part interest in gambling joints. But for one to be a boss cop and a kingpin gangster both at the same time? Who would have believed it?"

"I would have been the only complete man in the business," he said with a cynical smile.

"Congratulations."

"But you are wrong on one point. It wasn't Salisbury I talked to first, even though I'd heard that he was eager for bigger things. It was Scorpino, and in all modesty I must say that I was instrumental in convincing the man that the move was feasible. With my protection, of course."

"But then you found out that Governor Stevenson was under pressure to eject Salisbury, and you didn't want that. At least quite yet. So you came up with the idea of going to DeMour and offering him a piece of the action. You knew he had enough influence with the governor to keep the state boys off Salisbury until the two of you could deal with the Maceo brothers and consolidate your hold on the upper coast. Then when they finally did run Salisbury out of the state, you would have been left with the whole pie. Or maybe, just maybe, if your timing was right, you could have killed Salisbury and convinced his uncle the Rangers did it. Oh, you would still have had to kick some of the money back to Scorpino, but it wouldn't have been a lot. With DeMour's influence you would have been in a strong bargaining position. What I don't understand is why you thought that after you'd killed Sam and Rosario you could just saunter into Galveston and take over their operation."

"And why not?" he asked. "What was there to stop me? Without Sam and Rosario the organization would have been nothing. The island's influential families might not have liked it, but they would have gone along with anybody who could guarantee peace and prosperity. And I could have guaranteed it."

"And then you could have started expanding on down the coast. Because the one part of what you said that night that was true was your dream of a string of resort casinos all the way down to Brownsville."

"That's correct," he said.

"What do you intend to do now?"

"Wait awhile till the dust settles, and then begin again on my own."

"But why?"

He looked at me with an expression that was close to pity. "You should know the answer to that."

"No, I really don't."

"Because it's all possible. After all, why

did Caesar conquer Gaul?"

"Because he was an asshole," I said.

He gave me the sort of patronizing smile you might give an idiot stepchild. "You lack vision, Tucker," he said.

"If I thought vision would make me like you, I'd take myopia every time."

This bought me a mild scowl, but I ignored it and plunged on. "But let's get back to Henry DeMour," I said. "He's a lot closer than Caesar and Gaul. As it turned out, you misjudged him completely. Because of all his womanizing you thought he was bound to be crooked, too. Or barring that, you believed you could blackmail him into coming around. Whatever you thought, you didn't take into account that he was old money, old family, or that he had a sense of personal honor that ruled out graft and murder. A man with his values just wasn't conceivable to you because you think everybody has an angle. Nor were you aware that in his social class there's no great stigma attached to having a mistress on the side. So when you broached him, he told you to go to hell. And he probably did it in a way that made you feel like something he'd scrape off the bottom of his shoe before he went in the house."

His remained impassive but his face reddened a little, and I knew I'd hit a nerve.

"And he wrote it all in his journal," I went on. "Just the same as he'd been doing for years. And it was there in his own handwriting, the handwriting of a man who would be believed if word of it ever got out. It wouldn't have been enough to convict you of anything, but think of what Sam Maceo's friends at the Houston and Galveston papers could have done with it. You would have been ruined politically at the very least, and probably the attorney general's office in Austin could have used it to subpoena all your records. So after you learned about DeMour's journal, you knew you were vulnerable. If I hadn't come across it, somebody else would have. Some reporter, maybe. Or some of his family. I don't know for sure how you found out about the thing, but according to his wife it was common knowledge among his friends."

"Go on," he said.

"The only thing I don't know is how deeply Madeline Kimbell was involved. And I'm still not sure who killed her or why."

"Well, I guess there's just some things you won't ever be able to figure out, smart-ass," Dunning said contemptuously, the only time he spoke.

"I don't suppose it really makes any difference," I replied.

"You're right about that," Walsh said. "And now I need that diary, as we agreed. Then we can be on our way."

I took a deep breath and looked at my aunt, and our eyes met in understanding. "Would you mind?" I asked her. "It's in the safe in the office."

"I'll get it," she said. "But let me light the lamp first. It's getting dark."

She rose from the table and went over to the cabinet and pulled out one of the old kerosene lamps and struck a match and touched it to its wick. Then she fumbled around getting the shade back on the lamp while I lived through the most nerve-racking moments of my life. To distract Walsh and his two henchmen I began babbling. About what I don't remember to this day, but all the while I was trying desperately to keep my eyes glued to his face and not give the whole thing away by glancing over his shoulder where Alonzo had just emerged, specter-like, from the kitchen closet's dark interior. The old man moved soundlessly in his sock feet, his bald head gleaming in the lamplight, his weathered face as serene as the face of a nun at her prayers, while in his hand he clutched the same ancient, stag-handled knife with which he'd punctured the bull's jugular so many years before.

He was almost within striking distance when something — perhaps some small noise — gave him away. Stubb's eyes widened, and Dunning jerked his head around to look behind him. But before he could raise the alarm I pulled my silenced .32 automatic from where it rested on a little shelf I'd built under the table and quickly shot him twice in the right temple. He didn't topple over as I'd expected. Instead his body went rigid and began to quiver and twitch, his feet beating a dancelike tattoo on the floor while his hands jerked and grabbed spasmodically at the tablecloth. Walsh turned to gaze stupidly at his now-defunct deputy, but by then Alonzo was on him and had one iron-hard old hand buried in his carefully combed hair. Quickly he jerked the man's head back so that his eyes stared upward at the ceiling. Then the knife flashed silver in the soft glow of the lamplight, and a moment later Walsh's exposed throat lay gaping open from one side to the other.

All at once the room seemed full of blood. Dunning crashed to the floor, a crimson stream spurting from the side of his head. Martindale finally reacted and began to grope for his pistol. I pointed the .32 at his face and pulled the trigger, but the gun didn't make a sound. I looked down and saw that the cartridge casing from my second shot had hung in the gun's ejection port. I was feverishly trying to pull back the slide to clear the jam when my aunt raised her arms above her head, the old meat ax that had resided for years unused in the cabinet now clutched tightly in her hands. Where she'd hidden it that day, I don't know, but her face was the face of an avenging angel as she brought it down with all her might and buried its blade to the hilt in the top of Stubb Martindale's head.

For what must have been at least a couple of seconds he sat motionless, staring at me with eyes that were sad beyond knowing, and for one dreadful moment I felt a sharp stab of pity for him deep in my heart. Then he slapped both hands down on the table and made one abortive effort to rise before he collapsed beside his chair and lay there jerking and snorting like a hog in heat.

I lunged to my feet. Alonzo had Walsh pinned to the floor, where he held him for the short time it took him to become unconscious. Nolan soon quit moving, but Martindale continued to quiver and twitch for what must have been a full minute.

Then it was all over, and the deep silence

of the winter twilight descended on the room. Soundlessly, as though they were materializing from the very air itself, the other old men appeared beside us in their sock feet, their pistols in their hands. No one said anything. We all stood frozen in a moment that seemed to stretch outward into eternity. Finally I came to my senses and hobbled over to the cabinet and pulled out a fifth of bourbon. I took a long pull and handed it to Alonzo, who drank and passed it on. With trembling hands I lighted a Chesterfield and offered the rest of the pack to the others. After Pablo had drunk, he pointed down at the three lifeless bodies on the floor, his single eye shining bright and baleful in the dim light of the kerosene lamp. "Santa Muerte will feast tonight," he said softly.

CHAPTER TWENTY-NINE

To many people South Texas presents a bleak and unforgiving landscape. Most of the trees are stunted and gnarled, and in places the undergrowth forms an impenetrable barrier against all but the most determined of men and beasts. I hadn't exaggerated when I told Madeline that anything out in the brush that didn't bite you would sting you or stick you. Rattlesnakes and scorpions abound, and the iron-hard spikes of the blackthorn bush are everywhere. Yet it has its own rough charm. The wildflowers seem brighter there than anywhere else, perhaps because you instinctively realize that their fragile splendor is the only color that ever comes to an otherwise drab and colorless land. And in the spring of 1943 they were magnificent, though I can't swear they were really better than in other years. I know that I took more pleasure in them than I ever had before.

Coming within an inch of being murdered will do that to you.

My foot had to be rebroken in the surgery of the San Antonio hospital, and it was a long time healing. It was the middle of summer before I could walk without a limp. In the intervening months I rested and read a great many books and often took the reins of the old buggy beside Tía Carmen as we made our daily inspection tours of the ranch. The price of beef skyrocketed, just as I'd predicted. When all the bills were paid after roundup, the books showed that 1942 had been La Rosa's best year in over half a century.

Some nights as I lay in my bed in the dark, my mind wandered back to that late afternoon when Walsh and his two goons came to La Rosa with their hard eyes and their big guns. If I had it to do all over again, I would slaughter them the minute they stepped out of their car. But until that moment I'd had some lingering uncertainty in my mind. I'd thought that Walsh might be content to take the journal and call it quits. But when I saw Stubb Martindale with them, my doubts faded away. Walsh and Nolan were already partners in crime, each with enough on the other to send him to the chair, and they had to stand or fall together. But they had no real hold on Martindale beyond his participation in my abduction, something they could have claimed was a legal arrest. This made him both dangerous and expendable.

When we searched the bodies we found the Colt .38 Super they'd taken from me down in Beaumont. It was in Nolan's overcoat, and I knew then what they'd had in mind. They intended to murder my aunt and me, and then one of them would have shot Martindale with my gun and arranged things to look as though he and I had killed each other in a shootout that had its roots in our mutual hatred from years past. I have no idea what they'd planned to do if their gunplay brought the attention of the vaqueros. But if Milam Walsh was anything, he was a skilled improviser, and he had brass. No doubt he'd thought he could pull it off.

The bodies went into deep pools in the Rio Grande, weighted down with old chains and stripped of anything that could identify them. I knew that before a week passed the turtles and the catfish would do their work. Two of the old men took the John Deere tractor far out into brush and bored three deep holes with the auger. Into these holes went the men's clothes and rings and watches and wallets. Then they filled the holes, and within a few days even they would have found it impossible to return to the exact spot. Shortly after midnight that same evening a heavy car with Mexican license plates rolled up to the international bridge at Laredo. At the wheel sat a well-dressed but tired-looking man of middle age who carried documents that identified him as a medical doctor from Sonora. Traffic was light and the guards were tired. After waving him across with no more than a cursory inspection of his papers, they stood watching sleepily as Milam Walsh's fancy Packard vanished forever into the bowels of Old Mexico.

CHAPTER THIRTY

Late in January, Charlie Grist came calling. It was a warm day, and Aunt Carmen and Alonzo were out in the buggy. I brought the coffeepot out on the front porch, and he and I sat in tall-backed rockers and drank strong coffee and talked about nothing in particular until at last he said, "Carlo Tresca's dead."

"That was to be expected, I suppose," I said. "The attack on the ranch was a complete botch, and that kind of failure is a capital offense among those people."

"What you probably didn't expect is that they killed Marty Salisbury, too."

"What?" I asked, utterly dumfounded.

"You heard me. Salisbury's dead. They put a forty-five bullet in the back of his head and dumped him in Lake Pontchartrain."

"And you think Scorpino had it done?"

Grist nodded. "I know he did."

"But —"

351

"There's been a power struggle going on inside the New Orleans Mob, and Salisbury was up to his neck in it. Once Galveston and Beaumont were in the fold, he and Tresca planned to do away with old Scorpino, and probably Gracchi as well. If they'd been successful, Tresca would have set himself up as the kingpin. Then with Salisbury running the Texas operation, they would have controlled all the coastal rackets from Galveston to New Orleans. A few of the other young Turks in the outfit were involved, too." He grinned. "They tell me that there's a lot of dead men floating around in the lakes and canals down there."

"Imagine blood kin doing one another that way," I said in wonder, not doubting that it was true, but still finding it difficult to accept. There is a point at which the mind rebels, a point where we learn things we don't want to know about our fellow man, and by inference, about ourselves.

"Beats anything, doesn't it?" Grist said. "They damn sure named old Angelo right."

"How's that?"

"The Scorpion Angel. Scorpions eat their own young if they get the chance."

I shuddered. "But how did you find all this out? Who was your informant?"

"You'd never guess. Not in a million years."

"No, I probably wouldn't," I said. "The whole thing has me baffled."

"Gracchi."

"You've got to be joking!" I almost yelled. He shook his head.

"But why?"

"He was real open with me because he wanted me to know that all the problems had been taken care of. Of course, he didn't actually tell me they had killed Salisbury and Tresca, not in so many words, at least. But he let me have the rest of it in a roundabout way."

We sat and rocked and sipped at our coffee for a couple of minutes while I tried to digest what I'd just heard. At last Grist broke the silence. "And I guess you read in the papers that Milam Walsh has disappeared," he said.

I nodded. "Yeah, I've been following the story pretty closely."

"What you don't know is that the attorney general's office down in Austin was fixing to move on him pretty soon when he up and vanished. And that the IRS was looking into his finances, too."

"I'm not surprised. He'd gotten too blatant."

"His wife's squealing like a stuck pig. He left her without much cash in the bank, and on top of that she claims that he had a young woman over in Lake Charles. Seems he's been squirreling money somewhere overseas, and now she thinks him and this Louisiana gal have run off together. She's going to court to try to get some of his other assets freed up so she can support herself."

"Well, Charlie, if he thought the attorney general and the Feds were about to jump him he may very well have bolted."

He nodded and sipped at his coffee, his hard old eyes regarding me thoughtfully over the rim of his cup. "I could buy that except for one thing," he said.

"What's that?" I asked.

"His chief deputy is missing, too. Nolan Dunning. You remember him, don't you?"

"Of course."

"And Walsh had just hired a new deputy named Stubb Martindale who folks say came from down here in Matador County. He's vanished, too."

"But what does all this have to do with me?"

He sighed a long, tired sigh. "You see, I'm the one the governor picked to investigate the whole thing. He thinks there needs to be some official disposition in the matter, considering that Walsh was an important county official, even if he was a crooked son of a bitch. And since you —"

"So what do *you* want to do?" I asked, cutting him off. "Personally, I mean."

He leaned back in his chair and sighed once more. "Given half a chance I'd go along with the notion that Walsh flew the coop," he said speculatively. "It's this business with the deputies that holds me back."

I nodded and stared off into the yard for a while, saying nothing, just thinking. Then I asked, "Would you feel more comfortable with that conclusion if you had evidence that Walsh and Dunning were involved in murder?"

"That bad, huh? I knew Walsh was a thief, but —"

"Oh, he was a lot more than that," I said.

"Who did they kill?"

"Henry DeMour."

"But Salisbury —"

I shook my head. "Walsh just used him and his goons to get it done."

I got to my feet and retrieved the journal from the safe in the office. Coming back out on the porch I opened it to the pertinent pages and handed it to him and said, "Henry DeMour's diary."

He read quickly. When he'd finished, he

turned and fixed me with his eyes and asked, "Virgil, are you absolutely certain that DeMour wrote this? It's not a forgery?"

"It's his, Charlie. His best friend told me about it, and his wife gave it to me."

"But why —"

"Because it was Walsh who was behind Scorpino's move into Texas in the first place."

He looked at me for a moment, his eyes big with incredulity. "You're not joking, are you?"

I shook my head and smiled. "Not at all. He convinced Scorpino that they could pull it off. With his help, of course."

"I guess that must be the bad advice Gracchi was talking about when we met with him."

"Exactly," I said. "But of course, what Walsh really wanted was to use Scorpino and Salisbury to get rid of the Maceos. After which he'd use DeMour to get the governor to have the Rangers kick Salisbury's butt out of Texas, just like you did anyway. Then he'd be the kingpin."

"Well, I'll be damned. If that don't beat all. He's certainly not the only sheriff to take bribes in this state, but to think —"

"Right," I said. "It's a first of sorts. The man planned on a grand scale. You'll have to give him that."

"So this is why DeMour was killed?"

"Not the diary, exactly. Walsh didn't know about it until after DeMour was dead or he probably wouldn't have had him killed. See, it was Walsh's visit that got DeMour on his reform tangent, and that's what did him in. Walsh misread the man completely. He thought he could force DeMour to help him because the guy was having an affair with a younger woman."

"Really?" Grist asked in surprise. "You don't happen to know who she was, do you?"

I nodded and gave him a smile that was full of irony. "Madeline Kimbell," I said.

His mouth fell open and he stared at me in shock. "Damn," he said at last.

"They used Madeline to lure DeMour out to that parking lot behind the Snake Eyes Club where Arno and Luchese killed him. You see, it was Dunning who got her to do it. He told her a big story about a business deal they had for DeMour, and he promised her that if she'd get DeMour to come out there, he'd leave her alone for good."

"How did you find this out?"

"From Alma Copeland, her best friend."

"So Madeline was lying about the reason Dunning was after her when you met her out in San Gabriel, right?"

"Yeah. I think Dunning really intended to let her go, but Arno and Luchese jumped the gun and killed DeMour right there in the parking lot in front of her. From that point on she was a terminal liability to Dunning. However much he may have cared about her, he cared more about his own hide, and her testimony was his ticket to the electric chair."

"What a mess," he said, shaking his head sadly.

"Yes, but what really caused Walsh to bolt wasn't the diary by itself, and that's why I believe Nolan went with him. Think about it for a minute. Walsh had to either take the kid along or kill him, because Nolan had enough on him to hang him."

"How about Martindale?"

"Stubb? Oh, he's a fly-by-nighter anyway," I said casually. "He probably just flitted off somewhere when Walsh flew the coop."

"I wonder why DeMour didn't just go ahead and file attempted bribery charges on Walsh."

"You know the old saw about not getting into a pissing contest with a skunk? Well, it just wasn't Henry DeMour's style to make public accusations and engage in that kind of open controversy. He wanted to do it the right way, through a senate investigation. His wife said he'd been disgusted with the corruption in Jefferson County for years, but I think that when Walsh tried to drag him into it he felt so insulted that he decided to make it a personal project to clean things up."

"But if it wasn't the journal that made the two of them run, what was it?"

I grinned at him. "They kidnapped me the night Mrs. DeMour gave the damn thing to me."

I almost laughed then. The old man opened his mouth and closed it about four times, utterly shocked, unable to decide what he wanted to say. At last he managed to croak out, "Kidnapped you?"

"Yeah. They'd heard about the journal and got somebody to break into DeMour's house looking for it even before I went to Mrs. DeMour. But it was in a hidden safe in his library and the burglar couldn't get to it. After that they figured out that she must have given it to me because I took her to the depot and put her on a train to Savannah. You see, Walsh had one of his detectives following me ever since the night you ran Salisbury out of the state."

"Why?"

"Why not? After all, I'd been with Madeline Kimbell for three days and he didn't know but what she'd told me the whole story. He needed to know what I was up to."

"But if they grabbed you, why didn't they get the diary?"

I gave him a twisted smile. "I botched a lot of things on this deal, Charlie, but I didn't botch the diary. I knew the minute I read those pages I had to get it out of my hands. So I mailed it to my banker here in town with instructions for him to hold it in the vault for me. I didn't think even Milam Walsh would be crazy enough to tamper with the United States mail. Of course I didn't tell them that, but they wanted it badly enough to take me out in the woods to beat it out of me, after which they intended to kill me. I managed to get away from them, but I broke my foot in the process. And that's the story."

"You should have called me about this the minute you got your hands on it," he said.

I sighed and nodded. "I know, Charlie. That's what I intended to do. I was going to come back home, wait for the diary to arrive, then hunt you up after I had it safe in my hands. But that kidnapping scared the hell out of me, and I decided it was safer to try to cut a deal with Walsh for the book in exchange for his agreeing to leave me and Tía Carmen alone. After all, the problems of Jefferson County really aren't my concern. But I never got a chance to make that deal because he vanished."

He gazed unblinking at my face for the longest time, then he actually smiled and said, "Virgil Tucker, you are full of shit. Even if Walsh had agreed to leave you alone, you wouldn't have believed him. You ain't stupid, boy."

I smiled right back at him. "I can be, believe me. And there was a point there where I would gladly have traded the journal for his assurance that our business was finished."

"You're not telling me the whole story, though. And we both know it."

I laughed a little and shook my head and gazed out into the yard for a while, unwilling to meet his wise old eyes. Finally I turned to face him. "Think what you want, Charlie. But I'll tell you one thing we *can* agree on. Any sorry bastard that invades a man's home with the intention of harming him and his family deserves whatever he gets."

That hit him where he lived. He leaned back once again in his chair and rubbed his face thoughtfully for a few moments, saying nothing. Finally he nodded and asked, "Who murdered the girl?"

"My guess is that it was Nolan Dunning," I said. "But that's another of those things we'll never know for certain."

"Virgil, do you feel sure, and I mean dead sure, deep down in your gut, that they've both gone far enough away that none of this is ever going to come back to haunt us?"

"Charlie, I think they've gone about as far as they could possibly go."

He'd heard all he wanted to hear. We dropped the subject and let the conversation drift back to things that didn't matter while we sat and rocked and drank more coffee. Finally he rose to his feet. "You don't mind if I take this with me, do you?" he asked, holding up DeMour's diary.

"I'd be grateful for you to get it out of my sight. I wish I'd never seen the damn thing."

We shook hands and he started toward his car. When he was halfway across the yard, I called out, "What's your official report going to say, Charlie?"

He turned and pulled off his Stetson and wiped his brow with his shirt sleeve. After he'd squared his hat back on his head, he said, "I plan to dump your story and this book right in the governor's lap and let him make that decision himself. And if I know

Coke Stevenson as well as I think I do, we've both heard the last of Milam Walsh."

CHAPTER THIRTY-ONE

I resigned my Special Ranger commission by mail the week after Grist's visit and began devoting all my attention to the ranch. I never recovered my car, but it was a fair trade for my life, so I didn't complain. Pablo's nephew found me a metallic gray '39 Mercury coupe with low mileage. I trusted the kid's judgment enough that I bought it sight-unseen. I wasn't disappointed.

One fine, sunny Monday in April I'd been to the doctor in San Antonio. When I pulled up in front of the house in the middle of the afternoon, I found my aunt having coffee on the front gallery with a young Mexican woman who appeared to be in her middle twenties. As I hobbled up on the porch I could see that she was tall and slim, with long, coal black hair pulled in a bun at the back of her head. She had almond eyes and creamy skin and wore a well-tailored dress of dark blue, polka-dotted linen with a white lace collar.

"Come say hello to Miss Perez, Virgil," I heard my aunt say.

I limped over to where the two of them sat beside the little iron table that resided permanently on the porch, then pulled off my hat and reached out to shake hands. The girl's fingers were cool, and she seemed utterly poised, with a distance about her that was just as cool and remote as her hand.

"I'm pleased to meet you," I said.

My aunt sprang to her feet. "I'll go get you a cup of coffee, Virgil," she said and disappeared through the front door before I could refuse.

I eased myself into the third rocker and asked, "What brings you to La Rosa, señorita?" I asked.

"I have applied for a job at the elementary school in town, and the principal sent me out here to meet your aunt."

"Ahhh . . . I bet you'll get it."

"I hope so," she replied. "Your aunt said she would recommend me."

"That's all it takes."

"Really? How so?"

"Let's just say that the superintendent of schools values her opinion quite highly. Don't worry. You're as good as hired."

In a few moments Tía Carmen was back with my coffee. "You two go ahead and visit without me for a while," she said as she set the cup on the table. "There's something I must tend to in the kitchen."

"Sure, there is," I said softly as I followed her retreating back with my eyes.

The girl raised her eyebrows inquiringly.

"There's never anything in that kitchen that has to be tended to in the middle of the afternoon."

"No?"

"Definitely not."

"Then why? —"

"To leave us out here alone together. She's matchmaking. Or trying to, I should say."

"Oh, I see," she said, and then smiled a sly little smile.

I watched her face while I sipped at my coffee. The smile remained and her eyes boldly met mine. "Why do you look like the cat that ate the canary all of a sudden?" I asked.

"Because I know something you don't."

"Oh yeah? What?"

"We are cousins."

"Who?" I asked in amazement. "You and me?"

"*Sí,*" she said with a little laugh. "I am descended from Rosa Veramendi's older brother, Arturo."

"That's wonderful," I exclaimed, quickly taken with the idea. "That makes us what? Fifth cousins?"

"I think that's right. Fifth or sixth."

"Why haven't we met before?"

"Don Arturo died in the typhoid epidemic in the early 1870s, and his wife took the family back to Mexico City, where we lived for two generations. During that time our families lost contact with each other. Then my father brought us to Laredo shortly before I was born. It is only in the last year that we learned that Rosa had descendants still living here in Texas."

"Fascinating," I said, thoroughly entranced.

We chatted on for the better part of an hour, both enjoying it immensely. I learned about her family and that she'd gotten her master's degree at Peabody College up in Memphis the year before. She also told me that she loved to read and dance, and we talked about our favorite books. Tía Carmen reappeared twice and then vanished each time just as quickly as she'd come. I found the girl alluring, and she knew it. She found me interesting, too, and I knew it as well. When at last she rose to leave I walked her to her car. "Where are you staying?" I asked.

"I've rented a room from old Mrs. Niebling in town. Why do you ask?"

"Oh, I thought we might take Aunt Carmen up on her matchmaking."

"Ahh. I see. Exactly what are you proposing?" The sly smile was back on her face and her eyes were mocking.

"Maybe dinner and a movie in San Antonio this coming Saturday. I would be happy to take you dancing, but my foot . . ."

She didn't even pause to think about it. "Yes, I believe I would like that. But you must promise to be a gentleman."

"Of course," I said, opening the door of the car. "I'm always a gentleman."

"I think we both know better than that, Virgil," she said, using my name for the first time. I closed the door and stood and watched as her little Plymouth dwindled down the lane.

By the time I regained the porch my aunt had returned. "A fine girl, isn't she?" she asked.

"Indeed she is."

She smiled knowingly. "Now, that one would make a good rancher's wife."

"Tía Carmen?" I said, looking her squarely in the eyes.

"*Sí?*"

"Mind your own damn business."

This bought nothing more than a self-satisfied smile.

Two nights later the moon was full. After the blood had been drunk and the fire built, the old men and I sat around passing the bottle among us. Once the tequila had warmed my innards a little, I tried thanking them for standing by Aunt Carmen and me the day Walsh and his thugs came to kill us. But they would have none of it. "Such is our destiny," Alonzo said mockingly.

"*Sí,*" Pablo agreed. "Our fate."

"What are you fools talking about?" I asked.

"Are we not secretly known as Los Caballeros de La Rosa?" Alonzo asked.

"*Sí,*" Pablo agreed. "We only tend the cattle by day so no one will suspect."

"Suspect what?" I asked irritably.

"That we ride out by night like the great Zorro to rescue young *patróns* who have gotten themselves into difficulties with evil men from the outside world."

"*Sí,*" Alonzo agreed sagely. "As I said, it is our destiny."

"After all, are we not young and dashing?" asked Juan, he of the bent back and scarred face and missing fingers.

"To say nothing of handsome," said Pablo, his one eye gleaming in the firelight, his snaggle-toothed smile like a jack-o-lantern cut by a child's unskilled hand.

"Make light of it all you want," I said, "but I will never forget what you did."

We fell silent while the moon climbed higher in the sky. Alonzo threw more wood on the fire, and the bottle went round once again. At last Pablo began speaking of me as though I were not there. "It is good that Señor Virgil has come home to stay."

"*Sí*," another agreed. "But now it is time for him to take a wife."

"And he must have children."

"*Sí*," Pablo agreed. "Mischievous little *niños* like he once was who will liven things up around here."

"And who will pay him back all the pranks he pulled when he was young."

"You are right, my friend," Pablo said. "That would be justice indeed."

"But who will he marry?" Juan asked.

"Perhaps the pretty young señorita," Pablo said. "The one who came to see Tía Carmen earlier this week."

"Was she truly lovely?" Juan asked.

"Aeeee!" Pablo exclaimed. "Such beauty as to take a man's breath away. Tall and slim, the very image of Tía Rosa as she appears in the painting that hangs in the great room at the main house."

"Tía Rosa?" Juan asked.

"*Sí,*" Alonzo answered. "The young señorita and Señor Virgil are cousins."

"Damn!" I said. "Do you old buzzards know everything?"

"*Sí!*" Pablo said and cackled wickedly.

"But very distant cousins," Alonzo added. "Far enough removed that even the priests would not object to such a union."

"How could the priests object?" asked Juan. "If the law does not care, then why should the priests?"

"Because the Holy Mother Church cannot be conformed to the world," Pablo explained patiently. "It must have higher standards."

"No," countered Juan. "The Church must be subject to the law like everyone else."

"This is not the case," Pablo said. "The Church has a very special mission —"

"No, you are wrong, my friend. The law . . ."

I let my mind drift away and left them to their theological wrangling, these old men who never darkened the doorway of a church except at Christmas and Easter, when their wives' nagging made it impossible for them not to do so. The evenings were still cool in April, and that night not even a hint of a breeze was blowing. I leaned back against a mesquite stump and watched as the fire flickered and its smoke spiraled upward through the motionless air into the darkness of the night. Down toward the river coyotes began to call out, and somewhere nearby I heard the eerie cry of a screech owl. Yes indeed, I thought — perhaps I would marry the pretty señorita. Perhaps we would have many little *niños* and the old house would once again echo with the cries of children at play. And perhaps — just perhaps — there was such a thing as destiny. But for the moment, mildly and happily drunk, I neither knew nor cared. For the moment I was content to simply *be,* safe and secure out under the moonlit sky where the harsh, limitless land stretched far away.

ABOUT THE AUTHOR

Milton T. Burton was born in Jacksonville, Texas, and is a lifelong resident of the area. He has been variously a cattleman, a political consultant, and a college history teacher. He lives in Tyler, Texas.

The employees of Thorndike Press hope you have enjoyed this Large Print book. All our Thorndike, Wheeler, and Kennebec Large Print titles are designed for easy reading, and all our books are made to last. Other Thorndike Press Large Print books are available at your library, through selected bookstores, or directly from us.

For information about titles, please call:
  (800) 223-1244

or visit our Web site at:
  http://gale.cengage.com/thorndike

To share your comments, please write:
  Publisher
  Thorndike Press
  10 Water St., Suite 310
  Waterville, ME 04901